Tracey Jane Jackson
New York Times Bestselling Author

A Nun Walks Into a Bar...
A Nun-Fiction Novel

Sale of this book without a front cover may be unauthorized. If this book is coverless, it may have been reported to the publisher as "unsold or destroyed" and neither the author nor the publisher may have received payment for it.

A Nun Walks into a Bar is a work of fiction. Names, characters, places, and incidents are the products of the author's imagination and are used fictitiously. Any resemblance to actual events, locales, or persons, living or dead, is entirely coincidental.

Cover Art
Jackson Jackson
&
Tracey Jane Jackson

2016 Tracey Jane Jackson
Copyright © 2016 by Tracey Jane Jackson
All rights reserved.

ISBN-13: 978-1530220915
ISBN-10: 1530220912

Published in the United States

Acknowledgements

Thanks to Ellen for the amazing edits.
Amanda and Roslyn, thanks for the critiques…you guys are amazing!

Booklist

Cauld Ane Series

Bound by Blood
Cauld Ane #1

Bound by Fire
Cauld Ane #2

Bound by Secrets
Cauld Ane #3

Bound by Song
Cauld Ane #4

Bound by Dreams
Cauld Ane #5

Bound by Tears
Cauld Ane #6

Bound by Light
Cauld Ane #7

Bound by Joy
A Cauld Ane Christmas Novella

Civil War Brides Series

The Bride Price
Civil War Brides Series, Book #1

The Bride Found
Civil War Brides Series, Book #2

The Bride Spy
Civil War Brides Series, Book #3

The Bride Ransom
Civil War Brides Series, Book #4

The Rebel Bride
Civil War Brides Series, Book #5

The Bride Star
Civil War Brides Series, Book #6

The Bride Pursued
Civil War Brides Series, Book #7

The Bride Accused
Civil War Brides Series, Book #8

The Brides United
Civil War Brides Series, Book #9

Dedication

*This is all about Robin and her crazy suggestion:
"You know what you need to write about? Nuns!"*

*I thought she was nuts until Jackson came up with the title,
so this is also for him!*

ONE

Sister Abigail Eunice

I HAVE BEEN told I look like Mila Kunis, and you'd think that was a good thing, but in my line of work, it's more of a hindrance. You see, I'm a nun. Admittedly, I'm not a very good one, but nonetheless, I am, in fact, a nun.

Which (in a very roundabout way) led me to a tiny, hole-in-the wall bar at the edge of the Pearl District in Portland, Oregon, on a quiet Wednesday night.

I was supposed to be meeting my friend, Laura, for dinner, but as I stepped off the MAX, I realized I'd gotten off at the wrong stop and, as was my luck, the small wet sprinkle coming from the sky quickly turned into a downpour.

"Well, crap!" I snapped, then slapped a hand over my mouth. "Sorry, Lord."

Seriously, I was the worst nun *ever*.

I took shelter under an awning next to a building with a frog motif, but no other information, unsure of which street I was on. Frustrated, I fished my phone out of my purse and tried to figure out where I was. I had a missed call from Laura, and a new voicemail, which I could only guess meant she wouldn't be able to make it.

"Hey, lady. I'm so sorry, I'm stuck at work and I can't get down to the Pearl for another hour. Do you still want me to try or do you want to resched?" Yes, she said, "resched." "Anyhoo, text me and let me know what you want to do. Love ya, 'bye."

Laura Chan was my oldest friend. In fact, she was the only one who knew me before the nunnery, and therefore knew me as Sadie Ross, not Sister Abigail Eunice. Laura's parents had moved from China, and into the house next door, the summer before second grade. She'd spoken very little English, but we still managed to communicate and we roamed the neighborhood, inseparable until my parents' death. I adored her, even though she wasn't always reliable. Ever hopeful, however, I always gave people the benefit of the doubt, so here I stood, only slightly protected from the pouring rain. And it was *pouring*. I fired off a quick text to Laura, pressing send...just as my phone died.

"Oh, holy mother of—" I pulled my sweater closer around me and stepped toward the building entrance so I could warm up and perhaps borrow a phone, but just as I moved away from the wall, something came loose from above, dropping a bucket's worth of collected water on my head. I let out a quiet squeak and pulled off my now soaked veil, yanking open the heavy wooden door of the bar and slipping inside.

"ID," a gruff voice demanded.

I nodded even though I couldn't see anything in the dark space, reaching into my purse and pulling out my Oregon ID.

A large hand swiped it from me then handed it back. "Sister Abigail, you look lost."

I let out a snort. "You have no idea. I'm stranded and my phone died."

"Ryder can call you a cab."

"Ryder?"

"Owner." He nodded toward the back of the building. "He's at the bar."

"Do I really need to go to the bar?" I asked.

"Lady, he's got the number for the only cab company he trusts and if I let you leave in one from a company he doesn't trust, he'll be pissed."

I gave him a look of mock concern. "That sounds serious."

Bouncer dude chuckled. "Yeah, he's got this weird thing about sweet women being protected."

"What about women who aren't sweet?" I challenged.

"Those too." The bouncer laughed. "But the sweet ones always seem to get special treatment."

I smiled. "Okay, I'll head to the bar."

"Good plan."

I walked past the pool tables, dartboards, and a jukebox playing something with a heavy drumbeat next to the bar, the counter of which ran the length of the building. There weren't a whole lot of patrons, just a few who looked as though they paid weekly rent for their stools. However, I was surprised by the heart motifs hanging and taped up in a few key places. I guess it made sense... Valentine's Day was tomorrow, so the bar was probably getting ready.

A tall man with his back to me turned and I felt sucker punched. Like, as in, the breath left my body.

His light-blue eyes met mine and seemed to peer into my soul. I froze, unable to take one more step under the weight of his scrutiny. He crossed his arms, keeping eye contact, and I was drawn into his tractor beam-like pull. I inched forward, one baby step at a time, taking in his light-blond hair, a full beard—not quite Portland hipster full, but still sexy-as-heck full. When my gaze landed on his lips he gave me this incredibly delicious sideways smirk, and Lord help me, I wanted him to kiss me.

See? Worst nun ever.

"You lost, Sister?"

"How did you know I'm a nun?" Without my veil, most people just threw pitiful glances at my clothes as though I didn't know how to dress in anything fashionable. I wore a sturdy black wool

dress, black tights, and a gray button-up cardigan.

He chuckled. "Couple years of Catholic school. 'Course, I never saw a nun who looked like you, but it's your shoes that give you away. It's always the shoes."

"Oh." I bit my lip, glancing at my feet. "Well, you got that right. They call them sensible...I call them ugly."

"Not touchin' that one." Ryder smiled. "You need directions?"

I shook my head. "I'm that tale of woe, I'm afraid. My friend couldn't make our dinner date and my phone died."

"You need a cab?"

"Yes, but do you mind if I just warm up for a minute?"

"You want some tea?"

I couldn't stop a huge smile of relief as I sat on one of the stools. "I would *love* some tea."

"Give me your phone and I'll charge it for you."

"No, that's okay." I waved my hand dismissively. "I doubt you'll have a charger that works."

He chuckled. "You'd be surprised."

I pulled out my six-year-old flip phone and slid it to him.

"Right," he said.

"Solve that one," I retorted with a giggle.

"Oh, you don't think I can?" He pulled open a drawer next to the cash register. After testing several cords against my phone, he let out a, "Gotcha!" and faced me again, plugging my phone into the wall. "Found one."

"How is that even possible?"

He laughed. "We never throw anything away and people leave shi—ah, stuff here all the time."

I raised my hands and gave him quiet applause. "Well done, sir. Well done."

He grinned and handed me a cup of hot water and a couple of tea bags. I was pleasantly surprised to see he had my favorite licorice flavor and steeped it in the water while Ryder went about his business.

"You look like you're gearing up for Valentine's Day," I said, and sipped my tea.

Ryder shook his head. "Not my choice."

"Aren't you the owner?"

He chuckled. "Doesn't mean I'm not ruled by my patrons."

"Ah, so not a romantic, then."

"Just think men should show their women they love 'em every day...not wait for one day out of the year. The whole holiday is a farce, in my opinion."

I smiled. Maybe he *was* a romantic.

As he freshened my hot water, I wondered what my fellow sisters would think about the predicament I'd gotten myself into. Granted, they rarely left the abbey, but they also didn't have jobs like I did.

Being a fourth-grade teacher and working for the Catholic school next to our living quarters was a perfect setup for me. Lately, however, I'd been feeling restless and I know Reverend Mother noticed. In fact, I had a meeting with her in the morning and it sounded serious, so being late or tired would not be an option. Perhaps my ill-fated evening was cut short for a very good reason. Mother always says God works in mysterious ways.

"You ready for that cab?"

Ryder's question pulled me from my thoughts and I smiled, shaking my head. "Is it okay if I stick around for a little bit?"

"Knock yourself out." He glanced at his watch. "But you're outta here within the hour. It gets a little rowdy at night."

"Your bouncer warned me about you."

"Yeah?"

I wrapped my hands around the cup, warming them. "He said you're very protective of women."

He glanced behind me and then met my eyes again. "Bennie talks too much."

"Maybe so." I shrugged and then sipped my tea again.

"What do people call you other than 'Sister'?"

"Nothing. I'm Sister Abigail Eunice. Although my parents named me Sadie."

Now why did I share that? I hadn't used my real name in years.

He leaned against the bar. "Pretty."

My breath caught. "My parents thought so," I said once I could speak again.

"But not you?"

"No, I like it fine. I guess I don't really think about my name much." I shrugged. "My students call me Sister and I don't have many friends outside of...well, outside." I shook my head. "Gosh, that sounds so narrow."

Ryder grinned. "Sheltered perhaps."

"That's very gracious, Ryder."

He chuckled. "Never been called gracious before."

Elbow on the bar, I settled my chin in my palm. "That surprises me."

"Of course it does. You're a nun."

"Meaning?"

"You're gracious to everyone, so you assume others will be gracious as well."

"I'm not gracious to *everyone*. I'm a nun, not perfect."

Ryder laughed. "Fair enough."

"I should go."

"Probably a good idea." He grabbed his cell phone and put it to his ear. "Hey. Got time to drop someone home?" He faced me. "Where do you live?"

"Beaverton."

"Beaverton. Great. Yeah, five minutes works. Thanks." Ryder hung up and slid his phone back in his pocket.

"You're pretty friendly with the cab company, huh?" I took the last swig of tea and set the cup down.

"One of my guys is taking you home."

"I thought you were calling me a cab."

"Can't let a nun pay the cab fare all the way to Beaverton."

I frowned. "You don't think I can pay for cab fare?"

"Not what I said, Sister."

"Wow, you really take this whole I-am-man-hear-me-roar stuff, to a whole nother level, huh?"

His gaze went to something (or someone) behind me and he nodded. "Ride's here."

I decided not to argue; probably because it would do absolutely no good, and slid off my stool. "Thanks for the tea."

"Anytime, Sister."

Somehow, him calling me "Sister" felt lacking. I took a deep breath. Lordy, I was ridiculous...and I probably needed to confess, but I knew I wouldn't.

Again, worst nun award goes to...

Ryder grabbed my phone and stepped out from behind the bar. "My number's in there if you need anything."

"What would I need?" I asked, and took the phone from him.

He shrugged. "You never know, Sister. It's a resource. Feel free to use it."

What a strange thing to say.

"Thanks for everything, Ryder," I said, leaving my internal thoughts in my head.

"No problem." He nodded toward his friend. "This is Reese. He's gonna take you home."

Reese was tall, dark, and handsome as they say, but he had an edge about him that made me a little nervous. His hair was longer than Ryder's and kind of shaggy, and he was quite muscular. I was fairly confident he wouldn't hurt me, but had I met him under different circumstances, I might have declined a ride.

A warm hand settled on my back and I felt a shiver steal down my spine. I didn't notice Ryder had walked from behind the bar.

"You okay, Sister?" he asked.

"Yes, fine."

"You're safe with him, yeah? You have any issues, you call me."

"Okay." I stepped away from his touch and forced a smile. "Reese, it's lovely to meet you. Thank you for the ride."

"No problem." He waved his hand toward the door. "This way."

With a backward glance and smile to Ryder, I followed Reese out to the car, grateful he wasn't a big talker. Our conversation consisted of him asking me for my address and me giving it to him. The rest of the ride strictly featured me gripping the door handle (as was my habit). I hated cars and avoided them whenever I could.

It didn't take long to arrive at the rectory and I thanked Reese and climbed out of the car, a little taken aback when he followed. "I'm fine from here."

"Ryder'd kick my a—rear if I didn't make sure you made it inside safely."

"Right, his protection fetish."

Reese chuckled but didn't comment.

I led him up the brick walkway and to the back of the building where I unlocked the door and stepped inside. "Thanks again for the ride."

"My pleasure, Sister. Have a good night."

He walked away, and I closed and locked the door.

TWO

QUICK, UNEVEN FOOTSTEPS sounded on the hardwood floors and I smiled as I peeked around the corner. Reverend Mother had had a limp since childhood, and although it didn't slow her down, it did mean I knew when she was coming. "Hi, Mother."
    She smiled. "You're home early."
    I rolled my eyes. "Laura couldn't make it, so I found myself a little stranded in the Pearl."
    Mother's hand flew to her chest. "Oh my word, dear, I don't really like the idea of you riding the bus home in the dark."
    "I didn't. A very nice gentleman dropped me home."
    "Sister Abigail," she admonished. "Who is this man?"
    I filled her in; however, I left the part out about Ryder being gorgeous, and his friend almost equally so, and she relaxed...sort of.
    "Well, it sounds like you met a nice person. However, I would

caution you to avoid bars in the future."

I giggled. "I have no problem with that."

"Since you're home so soon, how about we sit down and have a chat."

"Ah, sure." I followed her into her office and sat across from her. I was a little nervous, which was silly. She'd been the only mother I'd known since I was eight, and she was always kind, but she seemed really tense tonight.

"I won't bore you with the suspense," she said. "I will get right to the point. I think it's time you went out on your own."

"I'm sorry?"

She smiled. "You are not cut out to be a nun, Sister—and I don't say that as a criticism. I truly don't believe you're called to this life."

"But—"

She raised a hand, cutting me off. "This life isn't meant for everyone, dear. There are sacrifices and requirements that I don't think you'll ever be ready for."

"Am I not committed enough? I can do better."

"Sweetheart," she breathed out, standing and making her way to me. She sat down in the chair beside mine and took my hand. "No one, least of all me, could or would ever question your commitment to God and your students. You are a gifted teacher and you're a beautiful soul...but you still cannot tell me why you chose to commit to this life."

I felt my back stiffen. She and I had spoken about this several times, but my answer never seemed to appease her. Deciding to take one more stab at it, I said, "Because I love it here and this is where I want to be."

"But have you prayed about it? Do you honestly feel you've been called to this life? When was the last time you went to confession?"

Each one of her questions felt like a dagger to my heart, because I knew she was right.

She sighed. "Oh, dear girl, you're so busy traveling down this road you didn't even stop and ask for directions." Reverend Mother ran her palm across the top of my hand. "Have you ever felt the

calling on your life?"

Did I? I didn't know anymore. Maybe I never knew. I blinked back tears. "I don't know how to live outside of these walls, Mother. I have a little money saved, but I doubt it's enough to live on for very long."

"You have your trust fund."

I shook my head. "I gave that to the church."

"The church didn't take it."

"What?" I gasped. "Why not?"

"Because you were eighteen years old. You'd spent ten years learning how to live without your parents and you fell into the role you currently serve. But you didn't really choose it...you settled for it. It was the balm that soothed the wound of your parents' death, but it's not really living, sweetheart. I knew that one day we'd have this conversation, so I kept the money in your name."

Mother Superior was in fact my great aunt on my mother's side. Only ten years older than my own mom and barely hitting her sixties, she looked much, much younger. As my only living relative, she'd taken me in (and loved me) when my parents had been killed in a car accident. At only eight years old I'd survived the accident, although I'd been in a coma for a few days and required several months of physical therapy. She'd been at my side the entire time.

I sank further into the chair. "Wow."

"None of this is going to happen immediately," she assured me. "You'll finish out the term, and in the meantime, you can take some time to look for a place to live and a new job."

"I have to find a new job?" I rasped.

"We only employ nuns to teach, dear."

"But I'm happy being a nun."

Mother gave a sad chuckle. "You're *comfortable* being a nun, but you're restless and you forget I knew your mother." She reached out and cupped my cheek. "You are just like her, Sadie, and I want you to be as happy as she was. You're never going to be truly happy confined by these walls."

I leaned my face into her hand, raising an eyebrow. "You're not asking me to be the nanny to seven kids in Austria, are you?"

Mother dropped her head back and laughed. "You don't play guitar, which I believe is one of the requirements."

"Well, just don't start singing about solving a problem like Sadie and it'll be all good."

"I'm already solving the problem of Sadie, sweetheart. I'm pushing you out of the nest. You need to fly."

"Touché," I grumbled.

She patted my hand. "Go and process all of this and we can talk more if you need to. We'll slowly transition you into your new life, okay?"

I nodded. I didn't really have a choice. "What about our dinners?"

"Honey, I'm still your auntie. We're family. Nothing about that will change. Plus, now you can call me Auntie instead of Mother. I kind of like that idea. I'm here if you need me, we'll still have our dinners, and I hope you'll give me lots and lots of great-great nieces and nephews."

Ryder floated into my mind and I shivered.

"Are you cold?"

"No." I forced a smile. "It's just that in order to give you those nieces and nephews I'll have to meet a man, and I don't know the first thing about dating."

Mother chuckled. "Let's get the job and home sorted first."

I grimaced. "Probably a good plan."

I rose to my feet, hugged my aunt, and headed to my room. Sparse though it was, it was home, and I now had to come to terms with leaving it.

My phone buzzed as I set it on my dresser, and I smiled. "Hello, Father," I answered.

"Hey. Sorry, is it too late?"

"Nope. Just got home from my canceled dinner with Laura."

Father Michael Denton was one of our priests. He was new by our church's standards—he'd been placed there two years ago, and honestly, he shouldn't be a priest. I mean, maybe he should, that was between him and God, but I heard a lot of women in our church lament the fact he was too pretty to be a priest and that it was a waste to the female population. They weren't wrong. He was

tall with dark hair and chocolate-brown eyes, broad shoulders, and an easy way about him. He was one of my closest friends, but totally off limits for obvious reasons.

"She canceled?" he asked.

"Well, sort of. She got stuck at work so I had the choice to wait for her or reschedule." I sat on the edge of my bed. "What are you doing up?"

"Going over a few things from the Bishop."

"Sounds serious."

Michael chuckled. "Nothing I can't handle."

"Did you know what my aunt was going to do?"

"Yes."

"You didn't think to warn me?"

"I'm sorry, Sister," he said. "It was confidential. If I could have told you, I would have."

I sighed. "I know. It's fine. Just sucks."

"Let's meet for coffee tomorrow and we can talk."

"That would be great, Father. Thanks."

"Better get back to it. I'll see you tomorrow."

"Okay, have fun."

"Oh, I plan to."

I giggled. "'Night."

"'Night, Sister."

I hung up and dragged myself to bed, prepared for a restless night.

* * *

Ryder

Ryder flopped onto the sofa in his office and dragged his hands through his hair. He was screwed. Totally and completely. The second the beautiful nun walked into his bar, he'd been knocked on his ass, and he wanted to find a way to see her again.

Damn it! A nun.

In what world did fallin' for a nun make sense? Sure as hell wasn't his.

Lifting a glass of whiskey, he took a swig just as his phone buzzed in his pocket. He answered it without checking the screen. "Ryder."

"Hey man, it's Cam."

Cameron Shane was a good friend, a private investigator, and happened to be an expert in all things kidnap and recovery related. He was perfect for it, particularly because you never saw him coming. He was an ex-FBI agent turned pastor, but because of his special abilities, occasionally took on cases where he knew he could help. Like now. Ryder had asked him to look into a family situation and they'd spent almost a month spinning their wheels until a lead popped up a week ago.

"Hey." Ryder sat up, his body on alert. "You got anything?"

"Followed her boyfriend to Savannah. All roads point to her being with him."

"*Georgia?*" Ryder snapped. "What the *hell* are they doin' in Georgia?"

"No clue."

"Damn it!"

"I need to do a little more digging and I may have to do it at home, but we'll find her, buddy. I promise."

Ryder sighed. "Yeah."

"One way or another. I've got a guy here who's going to keep an eye on things and we'll go from there."

Ryder squeezed his eyes shut, forcing the panic away.

"Ryder?"

"Yeah, I'm here."

"Okay. I'll be home day after tomorrow and we'll talk," Cameron said.

"Thanks, man."

"No problem."

Cameron hung up and Ryder dropped his face into his hands. If he didn't find her soon, he never would, and he didn't know if he'd ever be able to live with himself. He was the reason she was gone. Staring down at his phone, he tried to call Scottie one more time, but it went straight to voicemail. "Scottie, you need to call me, okay? I know I screwed up. I know you're mad, but I'm worried. Please, baby girl, call me soon, yeah? 'Bye."

Downing the rest of his whiskey, he forced his thoughts away from his wayward sister and back to the beautiful woman he'd met

tonight.

It was just too damn bad she was a nun.

Before he could get too wrapped up in what would never be, he was dragged back out front to deal with a customer service issue. A good ass-kicking always helped to tire him enough to sleep the panic away and if that didn't work, he had more than enough Jack Daniels at his disposal.

THREE

Sadie

Four months later...

I GRABBED A bottled water from my fridge and handed it to Laura. "Laura, thank you so much for helping me with all of this."

"Holy crap, are you kidding me? It's Nun Makeover 101. My specialty."

"Oh really?" I challenged. "Is this a new business venture?"

"Yes," she quipped. "I do need to work on how to market it though..."

"This is true."

"Plus, now I can call you Sadie again. Can I tell you now how much I hated Sister Abigail Eunice?" She shuddered. "*So* not you."

I laughed as I stood in the middle of my new apartment, a modest one bedroom, one bathroom in Vancouver, Washington,

just over the bridge from Portland. It was safe, you had to have a code to even get in through the gates on the property, and I had three very serious locks on my front door. "My aunt apparently couldn't wrap her mind around it either."

Even though I knew Auntie was right, being basically ejected from my old life still stung. I would start my new job at a lovely elementary school in Salmon Creek in a little over two months, but for now, I had some time to get used to my new life.

Which started now. Admittedly, I had no idea how it all worked, so when Laura offered to help me, I readily accepted. The vivacious, twenty-two-year-old woman standing before me was still exactly the same as she had been in school and, despite her penchant for not showing up for dinner on occasion, she was always there when it counted. Like now.

"Ready?" she asked.

"For?"

"Um, *hello*, shopping." She grinned. "You need clothes. *Real* clothes."

She had a point, but I had no idea where to start.

"And you need makeup."

"I've never worn makeup," I admitted.

"That's why we're going to the mall," Laura said, grabbing her purse. "My bestie's working the Clinique counter...she can give you some tips. Let's go."

I followed her from the apartment and into her car. I buckled my seat belt and gripped the handle, grateful she drove a little slower than she normally would (her words) to accomodate my lingering fear of automobiles.

"You know, you should learn how to drive," Laura mused as she pulled into a parking spot. "It would probably help you get over your fear. People who are afraid to fly often take flying lessons. I bet it's the same principle."

I pried my shaking hand from the door handle and nodded. "Ah, nope, that's okay."

Laura giggled. "You might change your mind now that you're living in the 'Couve. Fewer options for public transportation."

"The bus is just fine."

"For now." Laura smiled. "Come on, lady, let's get you looking like a normal person."

I followed her into the mall and we headed to the Macy's counter where a really pretty brunette turned and silently clapped. "You brought me a new victim," she said with a weird kind of glee.

Laura laughed. "Bethany Corona, meet Sadie Ross. Sadie, this is Bethany."

"It's so nice to meet you." Bethany shook my hand and then moved from behind the counter. "Now, let's see what we have here."

Laura's "bestie" was funny, bossy, beautiful, and a genius with makeup. By the time she was finished with me, I looked like someone totally different. Someone confident and pretty...someone who was most definitely *not* a nun.

"Wow," I breathed out.

"Right? I'm a rock star," she quipped, jabbing a blush brush toward me. "Remember that."

"I will." I giggled. "I don't even look like myself."

"Of course you do," she said, taking the mirror from my hand. "You just look like a better version of you."

I slid off the stool. "I want everything you used on me."

"Oooh, I love you already. Girls' night out. Friday. Sound good?"

"What does that consist of generally?" I asked, despite feeling like an idiot.

Bethany grinned. "A little bar hopping, a little dancing, a lotta drinking and maybe some flirting."

"Works for me," Laura said distractedly as she stared at her phone.

"I don't know," I said, butterflies flooding my stomach. "I've never been to a bar on purpose."

"You're not a nun anymore, right?" Bethany asked.

"Right," I agreed.

"We won't do anything you don't feel comfortable with," Laura promised. "You'll love it."

I reminded myself it was time to try out my new life. "Okay. Sounds fun."

"Awesome," Bethany said. "We'll meet you at your place and I'll do your makeup."

"That sounds so fun." I handed my debit card to her and, when she'd rung up my purchases, I slid the bag over my hand. "Thanks for everything."

"No problem. See you Friday."

Laura pulled me out of Macy's and we shopped until I couldn't take anymore. In the end, I spent close to a thousand dollars on clothing, bedding, and household items. I also let Laura drag me into the twenty-first century and bought a smart phone (which was free if I signed a two-year contract...it blew my mind). Considering the fact I'd once taken a vow of poverty, chastity, and obedience, I'd never spent that much money before (outside of my furniture), so I felt a little sick. But nothing I'd purchased was frivolous, I reminded myself as we lugged the bags back to my apartment.

"Oh, crap, I'm supposed to be meeting my parents for dinner," Laura exclaimed as she set the last bag on my counter. "I hate to cut and run, Sadie, but I'm late."

"Don't worry about it," I assured. "I need to transfer my contacts and learn how to use my new phone anyway."

She hugged me and I walked her to the door, locking up after she left and turning on the TV. It was the first purchase I'd made when I moved in, sixty inches of flat-screen beauty (priorities and all). One of the many reasons I made a pretty bad nun (in my opinion) was that I was obsessed with television and movies. It could have been called unhealthy, but it was part of me, and Mother had informed me I got it from my father, and now I was free to embrace my addiction.

Feeling a little rebellious, I grabbed a carton of my Häagen-Dazs stash, turned on the television, and sat down on my gently-used sofa with my old and new phones.

I transferred over the few numbers I had saved and then opened the user manual. As I flipped through the book, my new phone rang. I couldn't imagine who would be calling, and the caller ID simply said "restricted number." "Hello?"

"Hey, you called?" a man's voice asked.

"I'm sorry, who is this?"

"You don't know who you called?" he asked, sounding distracted.

I suddenly recognized the voice. "Ryder?"

"Yeah, who's this?"

"Uh, I'm so sorry, I have a new phone. I must have dialed you by mistake."

"Sadie?"

My heart raced. "You remember me?"

"Yeah, Sadie, I remember you," he said. "I mean, Sister."

"I'm not actually a nun anymore."

"How does that work?"

"Long story." I bit my lip. "Anyway, I'm really sorry I called. I just got a new phone and forgot your number was in my old one."

"You wanna get dinner?"

"When?"

"Tonight," he said.

"Tonight? Really?"

"Yeah."

"I was thinking about making a sandwich," I said, although, I was a quarter-tub into the Häagen-Dazs.

"Thinking about it?"

I glanced at the ice cream. "Yes."

I really should get some protein in my body. Pralines are protein, right?

He chuckled. "What are you eatin' instead?"

"How do you know I'm eating anything?"

"Just a guess."

"Smarty pants." I smiled. "If you must know, I'm having dessert first."

"Well, finish dessert and I'll take you for some real food."

"Don't you have a bar to run?" I challenged.

He chuckled. "It's Tuesday. I've got people who can take over."

"Um, well..."

"Dyin' to hear why you're not a nun anymore, Sadie. Put me out of my misery."

I gave in. "You'll have to pick me up. I'm in Vancouver now."

"No problem. Seven work?"

Ugh, half an hour. I pressed my lips into a thin line then took a deep breath. "Actually, is seven thirty okay?"

"Yeah. Text me your address and I'll be there."

"Okay. See you then." I hung up, sent my address...and panicked.

Rushing for the Old Navy bags, I grabbed a pair of jeans and a modest T-shirt, along with the hoodie Laura insisted I buy. She'd threatened to burn my nun cardigans unless I bought it, and even though I knew she wouldn't really burn them (I hoped), I liked it too. It was a pretty light blue which matched my eyes (according to Laura) and it was warm.

My lipstick lingered, albeit much lighter than before, but rather than trying to fix it or recreate what Bethany did, I left it in the shopping bag. I was afraid if I made an attempt to reapply it, I'd end up looking like one of the prostitutes my aunt warned me to stay away from. I was trying to break away from my previous life, yes, but I wasn't quite ready to break away that far.

My hair on the other hand, that was something I *could* handle. I had a lot of it, and I used to practice braiding and styling it even though I had to hide it under my veil. It was kind of my rebellion, albeit a secret one.

Even though my hands were shaking, I managed a mermaid side-braid that looked pretty but was something I could throw together quickly. I couldn't believe how nervous I was and nearly canceled, but a phone call from Laura bolstered my confidence and I managed to calm myself before Ryder arrived.

FOUR

Sadie

MY DOORBELL RANG just as I finished brushing my teeth. I wiped my mouth, careful not to smudge my quickly fading makeup, and rushed for the door. Pulling it open, my breath left my body at the sight of Ryder standing on my porch. My word, he was gorgeous. "Hi."

"Damn it, Sadie, you should have looked through your peephole."

I was a little taken aback at his irritation. "Who says I didn't?"

"Did you?" he challenged with a frown.

"Well, no, but I knew it was you."

"No you didn't."

"Yes I did."

"You would have if you'd looked through the peephole, but you just admitted you didn't, so, again, I say, no you didn't," he

returned.

"Ryder, it's a safe neighborhood and I don't have a whole lot of visitors."

"Sadie, it doesn't matter. You're not at the abbey anymore."

I crossed my arms. "Um, Ryder?"

"Yeah, babe."

"Grown adult here. Wanna try that again?" I managed to speak, even though the way he'd called me 'babe' made me shiver.

He dragged his hands through his hair. "Will you promise me you'll be more careful in the future?"

I rolled my eyes. "Wow."

"Shit." He shook his head. "Ah. Sorry."

"Sorry because you cursed or sorry because you don't know me and you're being needlessly bossy?"

He gave me the sexiest little smile. "Both?"

I shook my head. "Maybe this wasn't a good idea."

"Wait. Sorry. Seriously. I'm wrapping my mind around you not bein' a nun anymore, not to mention the fact that you're sexy as hell." He shook his head. "Gotta admit, I'm kinda feelin' like I'm goin' to hell for lookin' at you that way."

Well, that was nice...in a weird way.

"You think I'm sexy?" I didn't mean for that to come out so breathy...*darn it*! "I mean..."

He smiled. "Can we start over?"

"Sure."

I moved to close the door and he laid his hand on it. "What are you doing?"

"Starting over," I said.

Ryder laughed and let me close the door. He knocked again; I looked through the peephole and then opened the door. "Hi."

"Hi," he said. "You look beautiful."

"Thank you." I took in his dark jeans, motorcycle boots, and a back-ribbed long-sleeved T-shirt, and forced myself not to sigh. "You look nice as well."

He grinned. "How hungry are you?"

"Starved...you made me stop eating my ice cream."

"Well, I better feed you then."

I chuckled and grabbed my purse, following him to his truck after locking my door. Ryder held the door open for me and waited while I got settled before heading to the driver's side. I clicked my seat belt and gripped the door handle.

"You okay?" Ryder asked as he started the truck.

"Yep."

"Yeah?" He nodded toward my hands. "You expecting me to crash?"

I sighed. "I'm not a fan of cars."

"You don't have to be scared, Sadie. I'm a good driver."

"It's not you," I rushed to say. "My parents were killed in a car crash when I was eight and I have some residual issues because of it."

"Shi—sorry."

"No, I think that's the accurate word." I sighed. "I appreciate that you're being sensitive to me being an ex-nun, Ryder, but don't feel like you have to change because of that. I can handle swearing, evidenced by the fact I love anything Quentin Tarantino."

"Even Pulp Fiction?"

I blushed and admitted in a whisper, "*Especially* Pulp Fiction."

"Are you this new breed of women who love all those detective and murder shows?"

"Like FBI files and stuff?"

"Yeah."

"Is this a new phenomenon?" I asked.

"Yeah, apparently so." He chuckled. "Women are the largest group watching."

"Guilty." I giggled. "Another thing I should go to confession for."

"I think as long as your love of murder and death stays in the fictional world, you're good."

"You could be right," I said. "Do you go to confession?"

"No. How often do you?" he countered.

"I'm guilty on that front too." I sighed. "I haven't been for a really long time. I think it's one reason why Mother said I wasn't cut out to be a nun."

He pulled to a stop at a stoplight and faced me for a second.

"How do you get away with not going to confession as a nun?"

"Well, I think when you've known your church priests since you were eight, the anonymity kind of disappears."

"How did you end up at the abbey to begin with?" he asked, driving toward the bridge to Portland.

"Divine intervention?" I joked...sort of.

"Yeah?"

"My mom's aunt is the reverend mother and she was...*is* my only living relative. Child services had no issue placing me in her care for obvious reasons, and she has been amazing. She has so many stories of my parents and helps keep them alive for me. Plus I never felt like I was a burden."

"I see why you settled into the nun life."

I raised an eyebrow. "Mother used 'settled' as well. I guess I just didn't really see it."

"What about now? Do you see it?"

"Yes, I think I do. I've never fully fit in the nun world. And although I feel a bit like a fish out of water in this world, I feel more like me." I smiled. "I can watch Tarantino and not feel like I have to apologize to anyone."

"Except me."

"You don't like Tarantino?"

He chuckled. "I'm more of a Notebook kinda guy."

"Seriously?" At his expression, I smacked his arm with a laugh. "You almost had me."

"Gotcha to stop grippin' that handle, though."

I gasped and reached for it again. "How did you do that?"

"If I told you that, I'd have to kill you."

"Nice."

Before I could remember I was afraid of cars again, Ryder pulled up to a restaurant in the Pearl. Serratto. "I've heard this place is amazing."

"It's a favorite." He turned off the truck and climbed out, jogging to my side to open the door.

"Thanks," I said, and took his hand to maneuver down from the height of the truck.

He laid his hand on my lower back and guided me through the

side door, where a young woman greeted us and led us to a table. Ryder held my chair and then took his seat before the hostess handed us our menus.

"What's good?" I asked.

"Everything." He chuckled. "The boar pasta is my favorite, but really, you can't go wrong with anything on the menu. Do you want some wine?"

"I've never tried wine," I whispered, feeling like I was talking about something taboo.

"Right." He smiled. "No problem."

"That doesn't mean I wouldn't like to," I admitted. "What would you suggest?"

"How about I order a glass of Merlot and see if you like it? If you don't, I'll drink it."

"Do you like wine?"

"Yeah." He shrugged. "I prefer beer, but wine's good in the right situation."

I set my menu down. "Like now?"

"Exactly like now," he confirmed.

"Perfect."

The server arrived and I took a mental inventory of my budget, deciding I had enough for the tenderloin, but not quite enough for the salad as well. I ordered the steak and the waiter walked away.

"I can hear you thinking," Ryder said.

I shook my head. "Sorry, just doing mental math."

"Why?"

"Because I don't start my new job for over two months, so I want to be careful."

"Sadie, you're not paying for this."

I frowned. "What?"

"Dinner."

"Why not?"

"Because it's a date. I'm payin'."

"It's a date?"

He chuckled. "Yeah, Sadie, it's a date."

My heart raced as I laid my shaking hands in my lap.

"Why do you look horrified?" he asked.

"I don't look horrified."

He raised an eyebrow. "You look a little horrified."

"I'm not." I sighed. "Really. I've just never been on a date before, so this is a bit of a learning experience for me."

"Stick with me, kid, I'll be your Obi Wan."

I couldn't help a quiet giggle. "But Obi Wan and Luke didn't date. In fact, didn't Obi Wan skip out early and pawn him off on Yoda?"

"Am I dating a secret nerd?"

I shrugged. "I don't know how secret it is."

"You realize you just confirmed we're dating."

"What?" I gasped. "No I didn't."

Ryder gave me a sexy smile. "You kind of did."

"Didn't."

"Did."

"Holy mother of..." I didn't really know why this banter was irritating me, but it was. "*No*, I didn't."

"Okay, Sadie. You didn't." He raised his hands. "I was kidding. Didn't mean to piss you off."

"You didn't." I sighed, feeling ashamed. "Ryder, I'm sorry. This is all really new and you kind of make me feel off-kilter."

"Yeah?"

I nodded. "Can we start over?"

He chuckled. "Need us to walk in again?"

"I think we're good." I forced myself to relax. "I really am sorry."

"Don't worry about it, Sadie. I get it."

I pressed my lips into a thin line and then sighed. "I don't know if you do."

He ran a finger over the tablecloth as he studied me. "Well, I've never been an ex-nun, but I do know what it's like when you're drawn to someone but you don't really know where you stand."

"You do?"

"Yeah, Sadie, I do. I'm feeling it right now."

A quiet snort escaped my lips. "Ryder, you can't be serious."

"Why not?"

I cocked my head. "Because you're you."

"What the hell is that supposed to mean?"

"You're a confident, good-looking man, who owns what I'm guessing is a successful business, which means you're used to dealing with people...reading them. At least, I assume you are." I shrugged. "I'm an ex-nun, used to dealing with fourth graders. We're not really on the same playing field."

"Babe, I'm used to dealing with the rough kind of people. Salt of the earth, but still a little rough. You, on the other hand, are this sweet, innocent, and wholly polished beauty of a woman. Believe me when I tell you, I couldn't be on the same field as you, because you are way the hell out of my league."

Well, that was unbelievably sweet.

"Ryder." I felt my blush all the way to my neck.

"I like you, Sadie, so let's just try to forget about the differences in our backgrounds and get to know each other, okay?"

I nodded. "Okay."

He grinned. The server arrived with a glass of red wine and he slid it toward me so I could try it. I did not like it.

While I did my best not to show him that, his laugh indicated I had failed...miserably. "That bad, huh?"

"Sorry," I whispered.

"It's no biggie." He sipped the wine and then leaned forward a bit. "So, tell me why you're not a nun anymore."

"I'm not sure I know, honestly. I mean, I think it was the right decision, but now I'm not sure what my life's going to hold." I wrinkled my nose. "That sounds dumb."

"No it doesn't. You're in a transition period. For most folks that's part of life."

I couldn't help but give him a sad smile. "I've been avoiding being part of the masses, I think."

"Yeah?"

I nodded. "My world stopped when my parents died, but not in the way it does for some, or at least I don't think so. I've always been pretty happy and even though I missed them, I've never felt the hatred I was warned about."

"The stages of grief, you mean?"

I shook my head. "No, I'm pretty sure I went through those, but maybe the way a kid does. My aunt sheltered me from a lot of it. I had a couple of interviews with some policemen, but then nothing, and when I turned eighteen, I became a nun and went to school, sure of what my future held. Well, until four months ago when my aunt said it was time to move on."

"Kind of harsh."

"It wasn't. Not at all," I countered. "Auntie was right pushing me out of her nest, as she says, so now I think I'm in a bit of a let's see stage. I start my new job at the beginning of September, which means I have at least a couple of months to settle in. I'm kind of excited and nervous at the same time."

"An eternal optimist."

I smiled. "I've been called that before, so it's probably true."

"Still, it's gotta feel like a different world. You got any plans to help you adjust?"

"Well, my friend Laura—the one who bailed on me that night when I showed up at your bar—invited me to a girls' night with her and her best friend on Friday. I've never had a girls' night out, unless you count praying with ten other nuns in the church at midnight mass, so that'll be a new experience."

Ryder chuckled. "Yeah, I'm thinkin' it's gonna be a little different."

"Oh my gosh, I hope so. I wasn't a very good mass prayer."

"No?"

"No. My mind wandered to things like dinner...or lunch...or breakfast. Or *The Walking Dead.* And believe me, it's not really a good idea to be thinking about zombies when you're praying, especially when you're hungry."

Ryder dropped his head back and laughed. "No, can't imagine it would be."

"What about you? What's your story?"

"Pretty typical one, really. Deadbeat parents, sister who OD'd, yada yada."

I gasped. "Truly?"

"Yeah, but it's all good now."

I felt like he wasn't telling me everything, but I also didn't feel

I could pry. It wasn't really any of my business, but I was dying to know more.

"Did your sister die?" Nosiness won out, despite my best of intentions.

He grimaced. "You know, let's drop this shitty subject. More about you. You buy a car yet?"

I studied him for a few seconds and then let him have his secret. I shook my head. "I don't need a car."

"Sadie, you live in the burbs now, you should really have a car."

"Nope, I'm good. Besides, I don't have a license, so there's no point."

"You don't know how to drive?"

"No." I smiled. "But I don't really need to know."

"I'll teach you."

"You'll teach me to drive."

He grinned. "Yeah. I'm a great teacher."

I shook my head. "No, it's fine. I'm happy to take the bus."

The food arrived and I was glad for the reprieve in our conversation. Dinner passed quickly and before I knew it, it was time to go. Ryder had to get back to the bar and I had...well, I had nothing to get back to, but I didn't tell him that.

He took my hand as we left the restaurant and headed to the car.

"Ryder!" a man called.

We turned at the sound of his name and a tall, dark-haired man (who looked a little familiar) jogged towards us. Did Ryder know *anyone* ugly?

"Cam?" He released my hand and chuckled. "Where the hell have you been? I've left a shit-ton of messages."

They did their man-hug thing and I stood on the sidewalk feeling like an idiot.

"Just got back from Savannah. Sorry, it was last minute and I didn't have signal."

"What did you find?" Ryder demanded. Cameron glanced my way and Ryder suddenly remembered I was there. "Right, sorry. Cameron Shane, Sadie Ross."

I reached out my hand and he took it, his head cocking slightly. "I know you."

"You do?" I asked.

"Yeah. Just not sure how."

"She used to be a nun," Ryder provided, taking my hand from Cameron's and linking his fingers with mine.

"Yeah?" he said, and gave Ryder a weird grin.

"Yeah."

"Oh, wait, do you sing?" I asked.

He nodded. "Yeah."

"I think we met when we did the Reach Portland weekend."

Cameron nodded. "Right. You're part of the Beaverton Abbey."

"Yes."

He grinned. "I never forget a face."

Cameron was a worship pastor for a local church and he was amazing. "You're very talented," I said.

"Thanks. I appreciate that."

"Right, so we should get going," Ryder rushed to say.

I frowned. "We should?"

"Yeah, I gotta get back to the bar."

He'd just said he was taking me home, which meant he wouldn't be back at the bar for close to two hours. I raised an eyebrow, but didn't argue.

"Swing by for a beer sometime," Ryder said to Cameron.

"Thanks, man, I will. An hour good?"

Ryder glanced at me. "Make it two."

Cameron nodded and then smiled at me. "Sadie, it was great to see you again."

"You too."

Ryder turned me away from the handsome man and back toward the car.

"Are we really in that much of a rush?" I asked.

"No."

"Wait, what?"

He squeezed my hand. "He thought you were hot."

"What? The man's a pastor," I argued.

"So pastors can't find women hot?" Ryder countered.

I tugged on his hand, pulling him to a stop. "For argument's sake, because I really think you're insane, what if he *did* think I was attractive, why would that matter?"

"Because it does."

"That's not really an answer, Ryder."

"It's gonna have to be for now."

I bit back a reply because I really had no idea if I could say what I thought, or if what I thought was even normal. He was acting possessive and (if I was being honest) I liked it, but it also put me on edge. I decided instead to stay silent and process everything when I was alone.

"What?" Ryder asked as he held the truck door open for me.

"Nothing."

"I don't play that game, Sadie."

"Huh-uh. You don't get to do that."

"Hold that thought." He shut the door and jogged to his side, climbing in next to me and starting the engine. "What don't I get to do?"

"You don't get to play the taciturn card and then demand answers from me. I don't play *that* game."

"Fair enough." He pulled away from the curb and we headed back over the bridge.

That's it?

I stared out the window and tried not to overthink things... unsuccessfully. I was sure he'd at least try to come to some form of common ground, but apparently taciturn was the word of the evening. I shook myself out of my melancholy because it truly wasn't any of my business and he owed me no explanations, so it was irrational for me to even be disappointed. I conceded (to myself...sort of) that all of my feelings when I was around him were pretty illogical because I really liked him. A lot. I'd never felt like that before. Don't get me wrong, I'd met gorgeous men before, but Ryder sent my world spinning off its axis. I didn't know if it was because I was finally free to feel romantical or if it was him.

"Sadie?"

"Hmm?"

"I can't talk to you about a few things, babe, but it's not personal, yeah?"

"Yep."

"Sadie," he said on a sigh.

"What?" I smiled. "It's fine. I'm not taking any of this personally. Really."

"Is this a moment where you're bein' all female and telling me what I want to hear, all the while planning how you're going to murder me in my sleep?"

"That's an exclusively female thing?"

"Pretty sure cats do it too, but they're typically just waiting until the woman kills you so they can eat your dead body."

"Wow. You have an imagination on you." I shook my head. "But no, neither I nor my cats are awaiting your death."

"Yeah?"

"Yeah," I mimicked.

"You're sure?"

"Oh, my word, Ryder," I admonished. "We've met once."

"Tonight's technically twice," he corrected.

"Fine. But tonight we spent less than two hours with each other. It's all good."

"True."

He became monosyllabic after our little conversation and it was weird. He seemed to be brooding rather than relieved that I'd essentially let him off the hook. My brain leaned on my psychology experience which helped me recognize that it was him and his process. And since I knew it was him, rather than me, I internally shrugged off his mood while giving myself the same pep talk (albeit, internally) I'd give my kids when conflicts arose.

My heart, though, was another story.

A part of me wanted to argue a little more. A part of me wanted to know his secrets and figure out a way to help. But I wasn't that person to him, and that kind of made me sad. I really liked him and had felt a connection the first time we'd met. Perhaps it was the sheltered part of me romanticizing things, but there was something here and I wanted to explore it.

We pulled into the parking lot of my apartment building and I

reached for the door handle.

"Huh-uh," Ryder said in a warning tone, and climbed out of the truck.

At least his gallantry didn't die with his ability to form complete sentences. He opened the door for me and helped me climb down and then followed me to my door.

"I had a really lovely time," I said as I unlocked my door.

"Me too, Sadie. I'll call you."

I faced him and forced a smile. "Sounds good."

He lingered for a second, studying me, and I watched as his face went through a few expressions. "Right. 'Night, Sadie."

"Goodnight." I let myself into the apartment and locked the door, leaning against it to catch my breath. Good lord, he was a strange one.

After removing my makeup and pulling on pajamas, I settled myself on the sofa and loaded up *Die Hard*. I needed a little action to take my mind off my sudden desire for violence. Maybe Ryder was right...maybe I *did* want to murder him in his sleep, just a little. I'd have to adopt some cats first though to make his prediction accurate. I shuddered. I hated cats, so that was out.

For the moment, I chose to engage in a little Bruce therapy and, as sleep overtook me, my thoughts of Ryder morphed with Bruce Willis's balding head and made me smile.

FIVE

Ryder

AN HOUR LATER, Ryder chucked his keys on his desk and slammed his office door. "Damn it!" He'd royally screwed things up with Sadie and didn't know how to fix them. Talk about worst timing ever. If he could just find his sister, he could go about his life and figure out how to put the pieces of his shattered family back together.

"Ryder!" Bennie called as he knocked on Ryder's door. "Cameron Shane's here."

"Send him back, would ya?"

"Sure thing, boss."

Another knock brought Cameron, and Ryder waved him in. "What did you find?"

"She was sold."

"Shit!" Ryder slammed his fist against the wall, hissing in pain

as his knuckles connected with brick. The pain felt right. It felt deserved.

"Damn it, Ryder," Cameron snapped, and then yelled out the door, "Someone grab ice!"

"Who?" Ryder rasped, before bellowing, "WHO?"

"Russian mob."

"No, no, no, no, no!" Ryder chanted. "Shit!"

"Hatch?"

Ryder shook his head. "I don't know. Maybe. There might be a loose connection. I wouldn't put it past dear old dad."

"Look, we know who they are, at least who has Scottie currently," Cameron said. "We brought down a trafficking ring a few years ago. The Azhishchenkov's were head of that, and it's highly likely they're part of this somehow. We've got people in place. Scottie's in Savannah, we're just not sure where. Dalton Moore's got connections there, so he's gonna check it out."

"Your FBI contact?"

"Yeah."

"What the hell happened?" Sandra cried out as she rushed into the office with ice. "Honey, what did you do?"

Sandra Walker had been Ryder's bookkeeper and office manager ever since he opened the bar six years ago. A woman in her midfifties, she had teased, platinum-blonde hair, and piercings in her nose and lip, along with full sleeves of tattoos (and others she offered to show him on more than one occasion...he declined). She was a rough-talking, pack-a-day smoking, swear-like-a-sailor kind of woman, and Ryder adored her. But she was also a bit like a mother hen and had the tendency to peck him to death.

"It's fine, Sandy. Thanks."

"It's not fine, Ryder. You may have broken your hand." She gently laid the ice pack over his knuckles. "Let me wrap it for you."

"It's fine," he pressed.

"Stubborn mule." She jabbed a finger at him. "One hour, mister. I'm comin' back and if your hand is bad, you're gettin' an Xray."

Ryder rolled his eyes. "Yes, Mom."

She huffed and pulled the door closed on the way out.

"You're an idiot," Cameron accused.

"Probably." Ryder grimaced. "I want to go to Savannah."

"Figured you'd say that. Got us flights tomorrow morning. First flight out."

"Thanks, man."

"But there's another problem."

Ryder scowled. "What?"

"Three girls have gone missing in the last three weeks."

"Associated with Scottie?"

"Sort of," Cameron hedged. "They were last seen here at the bar."

"What the hell?" He shook his head. "No trace after that?"

"No."

Ryder swore again and sat on the edge of his desk.

"FBI's gonna be asking questions," Cameron said. "I talked to Dalt and he's gonna run it."

"Well, that's somethin', I guess," Ryder said. "How did you find out she was sold?"

"Scottie's ex. We picked him up at a dive bar in Savannah, but he was of no help. He was so strung out, we could barely get his name out of him. From what we could make out, he sold her for a fix in Savannah, but that's all he knows."

Ryder swore again. "You still have that bastard locked up?"

"Yeah. We're throwing every charge we can at him, and we'll get him locked up, but I don't know how much he'll be able to help us with finding her."

Ryder dragged his hand through his hair. "I had her home! She was getting past all this shit and then she runs off with him again. I don't know what the hell I could have done differently!"

"We'll figure it out." Cameron crossed his arms. "Dalton's meeting us in Savannah."

"Priority is Scottie."

"Yeah, man. Dalton's got a sister. He gets it."

Ryder nodded.

"I'll talk to you tomorrow," Cameron said.

Ryder gave him a chin lift and Cameron left his office. Ryder

settled himself on the sofa and dropped his face into his hands. He was gutted. He had a slight idea what his sister might be going through and it was enough to drive him crazy. In the end, he had a few choice words with a God he wasn't sure he believed in before getting back to work.

* * *

Sadie

Friday night arrived and I was giddy with excitement as I opened the door to let Laura and Bethany in.

"Are you ready to get your groove on?" Laura asked, hugging me.

I shrugged. "Is that a thing?"

"Hells, yeah it is," Bethany said, hugging me as well. "And if there's no groove, there will be alcohol, so that'll *give* us groove."

I giggled. "If you say so."

"Your hair looks amazing," Laura said with a grin.

I had pulled the sides back and tucked them under a piece of hair I'd teased and layered over the back. It gave me a little height and it was very Jennifer Love Hewitt ala *Ghost Whisperer* days. "Thank you."

"Can you do mine?" she asked.

"Of course." I raised an eyebrow, taking in her silky smooth bob. "But yours looks perfect. I'm not sure what I could improve on."

"It's so freakin' flat right now. I hate the summer."

I giggled. "Oh, I can give you a little volume. Piece of cake."

"Makeup first," Bethany ordered. "Then if we have time, we'll fix your perfect hair. I hate you, Laura, you know that, right?"

She giggled. "I do. And since we're not driving tonight, let's drink. I brought wine."

"Would you hate me if I didn't?" I asked.

Laura cocked her head. "You know you're allowed to, right?"

"Yes, it's just I don't particularly like it."

"Oh, well, then our goal tonight is to find something you do like," Bethany said.

"Works for me," I said.

For the next hour, we did what I'd seen all girls do in the mov-

ies and on television while getting ready for a girls' night out. We laughed, we critiqued, we told each other how beautiful we were, and then quickly told each other how much we hated each other because of how beautiful we were. It was a blast and it was *perfect*.

We were still giggling as we climbed into the backseat of our cab and headed to our first club destination in the Pearl. Pulling up outside the venue, we were early enough to grab a table and some food before the crush of the crowd arrived, and the dancing began.

"What can I get ya?" our scantily clad server asked.

"I'm going to have a cosmo," Laura said. "And so will my friend."

"Cosmo?" I asked.

"You'll love it, trust me."

I rolled my eyes but managed to nod an affirmative to our waitress, and then Bethany ordered something called "Sex on the Beach," and Laura ordered my food since I blushed so hard I had to hide my face.

As the night progressed, I discovered cosmos weren't really my thing, but margaritas were. Holy moly, they were delicious, and I managed to finish two in less than an hour. Halfway through drink two, I looked up to find the room spinning, so Laura made me drink an entire glass of water, which helped settle me a little.

"Is this normal?" I asked.

Laura giggled. "At the rate you're drinking, yes."

"So you're saying I should drink them slower?" I asked, taking another sip. This one was better than the last.

"Probably a good idea."

"But they're so good."

"I know," Laura said. "But the "drunk" will hit you like a brick, so you might want to slow down."

"Better yet, lay off the booze for a bit, hon," Bethany suggested. "You don't want to puke."

No, I certainly did not. And I really didn't like the fact the room moved on its own.

"Ohmigod, I love this song," Laura squeaked. "Let's dance."

Okay, so this is where things got a little hairy for me (well, hairier, because I was still feeling tipsy). I had never danced. Ever.

Which was fine because I didn't feel like I needed to put on a routine or anything, but since I wasn't particularly knowledgeable about music, I couldn't tell you the name of the song, let alone how to dance to it. I was flying blind as we hit the dance floor and I couldn't "find the groove" as Laura suggested.

I was sure I looked like a total idiot, but then some guy grabbed my hips with a grin and yelled, "Just move with the music, beautiful."

I was so shocked by the fact he'd grabbed me, I didn't react immediately. When my brain finally kicked in that a stranger had his hands on me, I tried to pull away. He held me tighter and ground his pelvis against my bottom.

"It's all good, gorgeous."

"Please, let me go," I yelled.

"Dude, she said let her go," Bethany snapped.

"Shut the hell up."

"*You* shut the hell up," she bellowed, and shoved the guy.

"Bitch!"

"Hey, don't call her a bitch," Laura growled.

Before the man could react, he was dragged back by his collar and shoved to the ground. "The ladies don't want to dance with you, which means you leave 'em alone."

I frowned. "Reese?"

He grinned up at me. "Hey, Sadie."

"What are you doing here?" I demanded.

"Business. I'm just gonna take care of this guy," he said, and dragged him out of the club without answering my question.

"Holy crap," Bethany rasped. "Do you know him?"

"Sort of, I guess." I shrugged. "He's a friend of Ryder's...or associate or something."

"He's smokin' hot!" Laura said, as she took my arm and walked toward the table.

"I'm not sure what he's doing here," I said.

"Doesn't Ryder own a bar?" Bethany asked.

I nodded.

Laura smiled. "Maybe this Reese guy works at a bunch of different places."

"You could be right." That was actually a possibility, so I nodded again. "Kind of a small world though, huh?"

As Bethany and Laura talked around me, my thoughts turned to Ryder. He hadn't called me all week and, because I was feeling irritated by that, I didn't call him, which meant I was missing him. My friends (and the alcohol) were helping me take my mind off him, but the second I saw Reese, that all changed.

A pair of snapping fingers appeared in front of my eyes and Laura said in a sing-song voice, "Earth to Sadie."

"Huh? Sorry," I said. "What did I miss?"

"I think a better question is what did *we* miss?" Bethany countered.

I sighed. "Nothing."

Laura shook her head. "This has something to do with Ryder."

"Why would it have something to do with Ryder?" I sipped my water in an effort to appear neutral.

Bethany gasped. "You like him!"

"What?"

"I want details."

"There aren't any," I said.

"They went on a date on Tuesday and he hasn't called her," Laura said.

"Laura!" I snapped.

"What?" She shrugged. "We're here for support. It's why you have friends in the first place."

Well, that was nice. I smiled. "Thank you."

"You're welcome."

"Now, spill," Bethany demanded.

* * *

Ryder

Anxious and sleep-deprived, Ryder paced the floor of his office, wondering what to do next. Savannah had been a bust. Scottie's ex had been moved by some FBI hotshots who'd basically taken over the investigation and refused to tell Ryder anything. Cam had leaked him enough information to frustrate the hell out of him, but there was nothing else he could do. Ryder had returned to Portland

late last night and had barely slept a wink since.

As happened a lot of late, his gaze landed on the photo of him and Scottie sitting on his desk. She'd just had her braces off, but even at sixteen, she looked so young. Reese (begrudgingly) had taken the picture at Scottie's request and it was one of Ryder's favorites.

"I'm gonna find you, baby girl. I promise," he whispered, just as his phone rang. It was Reese. "Trouble?" Ryder asked.

Reese chuckled. "Define trouble."

"Damn it! How bad?"

"Some asshat grinding up on her, but it's cool. I dealt with him."

Ryder ran a hand through his hair. "Is she okay?"

"Yeah, man, she's cool. A little tipsy, but cool. She and her ladies went back to the table."

"How tipsy?"

"How stalkerish do you wanna be here, man, 'cause we're kind of passing the border."

Ryder pinched the bridge of his nose. "Did she see you?"

"Kinda hard not to when I'm draggin' some douchebag away from her, but she didn't see me until then, and won't see me again...well, unless somethin' like that happens again."

"Okay. Thanks, man."

"No problem."

Reese hung up and Ryder slipped his phone into his pocket.

"Ryder!" Jake bellowed down the hall. "Need you out front."

"Comin'."

Ryder headed back to the bar and focused on pouring drinks and delivering food, all the while attempting not to fall asleep on his feet and to keep a smile on his face. It was almost impossible.

SIX

Sadie

"READY?" LAURA ASKED, grabbing her purse.

I frowned. I was having fun and didn't want the night to end quite yet. "We're going home?"

"No, hon," Bethany said. "We're heading to the next place."

I slid from the booth and grinned. "Oh, right. Cool."

Bethany grabbed my arm as I teetered slightly once standing. "I'm good," I assured her.

"The walk will help sober you up a bit."

I giggled. "Are you saying I'm drunk?"

"Well, only you can answer that, but I suspect you're at least a little tipsy."

"Is that when the world starts tilting? Because, yeah. I'm there."

Laura led the way out, shivering in the cool night air. "Crap, I

should have brought a hoodie."

"And cover up your fabulous dress?" I countered.

"You do have a point," she murmured. "This dress *is* fab."

Bethany giggled. "You won't be cold for long. We're not far from the Brass Frog."

I stopped walking.

"Sadie? You okay?" Laura asked.

I bit my lip. "You didn't say we were going there."

"So?" Bethany faced me, confused.

"It's Ryder's bar," I clarified.

"Seriously? He owns the Brass Frog?"

I nodded.

"We don't have to go there," Laura said.

"Um, yeah we do. It's like *the* place to be on a Friday night," Bethany argued. "Who cares if it's Ryder's bar? Plus, if Sadie's with us, we'll for sure get in."

"Um..." I *really* didn't want to go inside. I wasn't ready to see Ryder...I didn't know why, I just wasn't.

"We can go somewhere else," Laura continued.

Bethany rolled her eyes. "Okay, I don't want to be a total biatch, but seriously, who cares? If Ryder sees you out having a good time, that's the best revenge."

"I don't want revenge, Bethany," I said. "He hasn't done anything to me. But if we go to his place, he might think I'm stalking him or something."

"Hmm, you may have a point."

"What about the bar that's around the corner?" Laura suggested. "It's good, right? And it won't be as crowded."

"That might work," Bethany agreed.

I relaxed with a grin. "Sounds great."

We headed toward our destination and I was a little taken aback as we approached Ryder's bar. There was a line almost around the corner. "Wow."

"Right?" Bethany sighed. "They must be at capacity. No one new can get in until someone leaves."

"Is it always like this?"

Bethany shrugged. "After around ten or eleven, most of the

time. On the weekends, forget it. If you're lucky enough to get in, you typically stay."

That's what he meant when he said it got rowdy at night.

"How come?" I asked, curious now.

"One, their staff is hot...like I'd sleep with all of them, hot," Bethany said. "Two, their food is some of the best in Portland. Three, the music is off the chain...the owner, or booking manager, or whoever, are picky about the bands they bring in. And, four, they're hot."

I giggled. "I'm seeing a theme."

"Bethany measures everything on hotness," Laura informed me. "So, uggos are typically ignored by her."

"I feel somewhat relieved," I admitted.

Bethany laughed. "Like you don't know you're gorgeous. Whatever."

As we walked and talked, I caught something out of the corner of my eye and craned my head to see Reese sneaking behind a group of patrons waiting to be let in. He worked there, so I brushed it off...until we got around the corner and I saw him again.

This time I was a little curious. "Can you give me a sec, please?" I pulled away from Bethany and Laura and headed straight for Reese, whose face contorted into irritation as I approached. "Are you following us?"

"Hey, Sadie." He gave me a chin lift, effectively ignoring my question. "How are you?"

I crossed my arms. "Just as fine as I was almost an hour ago when you saw me in the club."

His eyes widened with mirth. "Yeah?"

"Yes."

"Well, it was good seein' you, Sadie."

"Huh-uh," I said, and gently grabbed his arm. "What's going on here? Are you following us, Reese?"

He gave me an annoyingly patronizing smile. "Babe, I have a lot to do on Fridays. Following you isn't typically one of them, so I'm just gonna check in with Janet about a booze order, then head back to the Frog."

"Oh, right." I dropped my hand and blushed. "Sorry, Reese. It

just seemed a little weird."

"No problem, Sadie. You take care."

I nodded and joined my ladies, not realizing immediately that he didn't "check with Janet" like he said he was going to. Instead, he stood at the door head to head with one of the bouncers while I slid into the booth next to Laura, before walking out without so much as a look in my direction.

"Ohmigod, he's so hot," Bethany breathed out.

"Aren't you dating someone?" Laura said.

"He's gay."

I choked on a laugh and spent a few minutes coughing uncontrollably.

"Are you okay?" Laura asked.

"Yes. But why would you date a gay man?" I asked as we showed our IDs and then found a table.

"Okay, get this," Bethany said, taking a seat. "Met him online a month ago, he and I have gone out on like, six or seven dates, he's a phenomenal, and I mean phe*nom*enal kisser. Last night, we go to dinner and we're talking about something random, I don't even remember what, and he says, "Well, you know I'm bi-sexual right?""

Laura swore which, luckily, covered my gasp.

Bethany waved her hands. "Never mentioned anything about sexual orientation on his profile...he's actively seeking women, but he drops that bombshell? Oh, hell no. I have no time for liars. I'm done."

"He's obviously confused," Laura said.

"Well, he can be confused on his own time. Or just be honest up front, you know? He's a cool guy, I'd totally hang out with him, but liars need not apply."

"Amen, sista," Laura said with a nod.

"I'm sorry, Bethany," I said. What could I say? This subject was so far out of my purview I was at a loss.

She shrugged. "It is what it is."

A server came by and took our drink orders and then Bethany said, "Speaking of available men. Since you apparently know that hottie, if you don't want him, could you introduce him to me?"

I giggled. "I don't really know him. He just gave me a ride home one night."

"But you know Ryder and *he* knows Reese," Laura said.

I nodded. "This is true."

The server returned with our drinks and I sipped the margarita, humming in pleasure.

"Come on, Sadie, hook a sister up," Bethany demanded.

I sighed. "If Ryder ever calls me again...and that's a big if...then I'll see what I can do."

"What if you see him again?" Laura asked.

I took another sip of my drink and sighed. "He kind of needs to call me in order for me to see him."

"Um, yeah, that's not actually true," Laura said.

"Huh?" I wrinkled my nose, my mind fuzzy.

"Ladies."

My head whipped to the side of its own accord and my stomach flipped as Ryder smiled down at us. Good Lord, he was delicious. Dark jeans, motorcycle boots, and a tight-black V-neck T-shirt that hugged his very muscular chest.

Laura shoved her elbow into my side and I squeaked. "Sorry. Hi Ryder. This is Laura and Bethany."

He shook their hands. "Nice to meet you."

"What are you doing here?" I asked.

"Reese mentioned he saw you, so I thought I'd come say hi."

"So, your boy, Reese," Bethany said, somewhat breathily. "Is he single?"

"Bethany," I admonished.

"What? You don't get anywhere or anything in life if you don't ask."

"I agree." Ryder chuckled. "Yeah, he's single, but he's not really the dating type."

"I don't want to date him, I just want some fun."

I groaned and dropped my face into my hands.

"Bethany. Nun...directly in front of you," Laura snapped.

"Oh come on. She's no longer a nun and even if she was, it's not like she's never heard about sex." Bethany leaned forward. "You do know about sex, right? Boys have a penis and girls have

a—"

"Bethany," I hissed, cutting her off as I raised my hands in surrender. "Can we please stop this fascinating subject of conversation for the moment? We can continue it when we're alone."

"Give him my number okay?" Bethany grabbed a napkin and a pen, scribbling digits on the paper and handing it to Ryder.

"No problem," he said, and then focused on me. "Can I borrow you for a minute, Sadie?"

"Ah—"

"Go," Laura said. "We'll watch your purse."

Ryder held his hand out to me, but I didn't take it as I pushed away from the table. I didn't miss his amused look of challenge as we made our way outside. The ground was a little uneven and I stalled for a second just as Ryder's arm wrapped around me to steady me. "Okay, babe, you've had a little, huh?"

"I'm okay." I gasped seeing his hand bandaged. "What did you do to your hand?"

"Nothin'."

"Did someone else do that, then?" I frowned. "You look wrecked, Ryder. Are you okay?"

"It's nothin', Sadie. Drop it."

I let out a frustrated groan and shoved his arm away, steadying myself on the back of one the chairs on the sidewalk.

"Babe, you should probably sit down."

"I *was* sitting down and you demanded my presence out here, so what is it you need, Ryder, because I have friends to get back to. I have also discovered I like margaritas, which is...are...also waiting for me back inside." Apparently, alcohol made me bold.

"Whoa." He raised his hands in surrender. "I get it. I didn't call you. I'm sorry. That was a dick move, but will you talk to me?"

I shook my head. "We *are* talking. So, can we do this so I can go back inside?"

"I figure since you have an aversion to me touching you, you might still be pissed about this week."

"Wow," I breathed out. "First of all, you're putting a lot of words in my mouth, especially considering you don't know me. Second of all, you don't owe me anything, Ryder, so seriously, it's

okay."

"How about I take you out next week? Make it up to you."

I flopped into the chair so I wouldn't fall down. "You don't have anything to make up."

"Why don't I swing by tomorrow and I'll give you your first driving lesson, then? I'll take you to lunch afterwards?"

"What happened to your hand, Ryder?"

"Nothin', it's fine."

I gave him a sad smile. "I'm going back inside now."

"Come on, Sadie, let me take you to lunch tomorrow."

"What happened to your hand, Ryder?" I asked, staring up at him.

"I punched a wall."

I forced myself to stay calm. "Why did you punch a wall?"

He shook his head.

"Okay." I pushed out of the chair and headed toward the bar.

"Wait." He took my arm and turned me around. "I can't talk about this."

"Can't or won't?" I challenged.

"Same thing."

"Not really," I countered. "State secrets, attorney/client privilege, clergy confession, that you *can't* talk about. Something that causes you emotional distress, the kind that makes you punch a wall, that typically falls under won't."

"You're killin' me," he ground out.

"Then I'm going to back inside to join my friends." I glanced down at his hand still holding my arm. "I don't want to cause you any more distress, Ryder."

He studied me for a few seconds before closing his eyes. "My sister's missing."

I gasped. "What?"

"She's been...actually, we think she's still being...trafficked."

"Oh, Ryder, I'm so sorry," I said, stepping closer and laying my hand on his chest. "What can I do?"

"Nothin', babe. I don't wanna talk about it."

I nodded. "Okay, I get it. The pastor...the one we met after our...date..."

He grunted his affirmative as he slid his hand to my neck, stroking my pulse.

"Cameron, right?" I leaned into his touch, "Is he involved?"

"Babe, hand to God, I don't want to talk about it."

"Right." I bit my lip with a frown. "Are there any leads?"

"Holy shit, Sadie, you're like a dog with a bone."

"I know, I'm sorry, I'm just...I've just never known anyone who's dealt with anything like this. I want to help."

"You can't."

I raised an eyebrow. "I can pray."

"Which does nothing."

I patted his chest. "It does when I do it."

He chuckled. "Ya think?"

"Try me."

"Yeah?"

"Close your eyes," I directed.

"No."

I cocked my head. "Yes."

Ryder stiffened. "I'm not praying with you on the street, Sadie."

"Yes, you are."

"I am not."

I gripped his arm and closed my eyes, forcing back a cheeky smile. "Dear Lord, we pray for protection over..." I opened one eye and asked, "What's your sister's name?"

He glared down at me. "Scarlett...we call her Scottie."

"Oh my gosh, what an awesome name." As he grumbled a four-letter word, I closed my eyes again, squeezing his arm harder. "We pray that wherever Scottie is tonight that you protect her and give her peace and that you help Ryder find her. Amen." I couldn't help a little bit of a triumphant smile as I focused on him again. "You just prayed with me on the street."

"Damn it."

"Feel better?"

"Nope." Even though he denied it, his body relaxed.

"Well, I do." I squeezed his arm. "I truly am sorry, Ryder. I will continue to pray for her."

"Can I take you to lunch tomorrow?"

"I don't know."

"Please, Sadie. When I'm near you, the demons aren't so scary. You drive them away. God, I've missed you this week." He stroked my cheek. "I should have called you, but I was afraid you'd hate me."

"Why would I hate you?"

He shook his head. "Because I'm not a good man."

"Why do you say that?"

"I can't." His expression grew tortured. "Babe, sorry, but I can't do that to you."

"Okay," I whispered. "It's okay. I see you, Ryder. I see your heart. I could never hate you."

"Let me see you tomorrow." He dropped his forehead to mine. "Better yet, call me when you're ready to head home. I'll drive you."

"We're cabbing it home, it's fine."

"I'm taking you." His expression turned pleading. "Yeah?"

"All three of us?" I asked. "Laura's car's at my place."

"Yeah, babe. All three of you."

"Okay." I smiled. "I should get back to my friends."

He kissed my forehead. "I'll see you in a bit."

"'Bye." I headed back into the bar, but glanced over my shoulder to see him give me a gentle smile before walking away. His kiss lingered on my forehead and I took a deep breath. I wanted more. A lot more. His claim that he wasn't a good man didn't ring true for me, but I'd heed his warning until I got to know him better. I might have been sheltered, but I wasn't stupid. The fact was I trusted Ryder. As naive as that might be, it was true. I had always been a pretty decent reader of people, and I knew he wasn't as bad as he might think he is. I just had to test my theory first.

"What did Ryder want?" Laura asked as I arrived back at the table and took my seat.

"He wants to drive us home."

"Oooh, will Reese be with him?" Bethany asked.

I giggled. "I have no idea."

She jabbed a finger at me. "Text him and tell him to bring

Reese."

"Buy me a margarita and I'll think about it."

"Deal," Bethany said, and waved her hand toward our server.

SEVEN

Ryder

RYDER PULLED HIS phone out of his pocket as it buzzed. Sadie was ready to go. One a.m. He shook his head, chuckling as he wondered how she was holding up with the nightlife schedule. He didn't imagine she had a lot of experience (if any) when it came to partying.

Heading to the back of the bar, he cut across the parking lot to Janet's place, walking around the front and stalling when three guys shoved into Sadie's booth. She looked uncomfortable, Laura looked bored, but Bethany was lapping it up.

Ryder schooled his expression as best he could in an effort to hide his irritation that some asshat was all over Sadie and not picking up on the fact she clearly wasn't interested. She caught his eyes and relief covered her features, which pissed him off more.

"I'd suggest you get your hands off my woman," Ryder de-

manded.

He ignored Sadie's quiet gasp as asshat number one turned slowly to look at him. "And who's gonna make me?"

"You did *not* just say that," Bethany said incredulously. "You were born kinda special, weren't ya?"

"Bethany," Laura said with a groan.

"Well? Come on. 'Who's gonna make me?' What are we, like twelve? Dude, we've been trying to tell you she's not interested for the last twenty minutes, but you just keep comin' at her. Now her man's here and he's not one you want to challenge, so just walk away."

Sadie dropped her face in her hands and shook her head. Ryder couldn't stop a grin, considering Bethany had pretty much fought his battle for him and it was funny as hell. His grin faded when he saw Sadie shrink back. The guy had his hand in her hair and Ryder saw red. He reached out, grabbed him by the neck, and dragged him out of the booth. He was on the floor before Ryder broke a sweat. "I warned you not to touch her."

His friends rushed to help, but Janet's "muscle" made quick work of removing them from the bar. "You good, Ryder?" she asked.

"All good, Janet, thanks." Ryder pulled the first guy's arm up a little higher. "You done?"

"Yeah." He nodded. "Yeah man, sorry."

"Don't apologize to me," he snapped as he dragged him to his feet. "Apologize to her."

"Sorry, Sadie."

She nodded, but Ryder could tell she was still in shock. He handed the man off to one of the bouncers and held a hand out to Sadie. She took it and slid out of the booth. "You okay?"

She nodded again, but he couldn't get a read on her emotion.

He squeezed her hand. "Did I scare you?"

"Are you kidding me?" she whispered, and slid her arms around his waist. "That was awesome."

Ryder chuckled, pulling her close. "Yeah?"

She nodded into his chest. "He would *not* leave me alone. I was almost ready to pull out my pepper spray."

"You have pepper spray?"

She pulled away from him and frowned. "Of course I have pepper spray."

He grinned. "That's my girl."

"Do *you* have pepper spray?"

Ryder shook his head. "Don't need pepper spray."

"Oh, right, because you've got mad skills."

He gave her a gentle squeeze and whispered, "Because I have a gun."

She gasped. "On you?"

"Always." He set her away, taking her hand. "Ready, ladies?"

A collective "yes," came, and Ryder led them through the bar and out the back door.

"Do you really have a gun?" she asked in a whisper as he pulled open the truck door and helped her inside.

"Yeah, babe, I really have a gun." He squeezed her thigh. "Buckle."

She nodded and pulled her seat belt across her lap. Ryder headed to the driver's side and climbed in. Sadie didn't say much as he drove over the bridge to her place. She still gripped the door handle like it was a lifeline and he hated that for her. Bethany and Laura chatted away in the backseat, but Sadie stayed silent unless they asked her a direct question, and then she'd answer quickly and with as few words as possible.

"Sade?"

"Hmm?" She turned toward him.

"You okay?"

"Oh, yes. I'm fine." She smiled. "Just tired."

He tugged her arm away from the door handle and linked his fingers with hers, giving them a gentle squeeze. Sadie settled her head against the headrest and closed her eyes. He liked that once she took his hand, she didn't try to grip the "oh, shit" handle again, but he didn't like that she seemed withdrawn.

By the time Ryder pulled into Sadie's parking lot, she was out. He made sure Laura and Bethany got off okay (and that Laura was in fact sober), then he collected Sadie, who was still snoozing in the front seat. Opening the passenger door, he reached over her and

unbuckled her belt. She started a little and opened her eyes. "Hi."

"Hey, baby, you're home."

"Oh." She slid her foot to the running board, teetering precariously, but Ryder grabbed her before she slipped off it.

"Careful." He smiled, searching her face for some kind of emotion, particularly if she was angry with him.

"I'm okay. I'm just super sleepy."

"Those margaritas kicked in, huh? I got you, baby." He lifted her down and set her on her feet, making sure he had an arm around her tightly. "Grab your keys, Sadie, while we have light."

"Good idea," she said, and rummaged in her purse. "Got 'em." She waved them in the air.

Ryder chuckled, taking them from her and guiding her upstairs to her door. He unlocked the apartment and followed her inside, closing the door behind him.

"What do you mean, I'm your woman?" she asked, facing him, her face still somewhat void of emotion.

Here we go.

"What do you think it means?" he asked, keeping his voice as neutral as possible.

She crossed her arms. "I think it means you've made some arbitrary decision without talking to me about it."

Damn it, she sounds irked.

"You datin' anyone else?"

"Ah. Well, no," she conceded.

"Do you wanna date anyone else?" he challenged.

"I don't know. No one else has asked."

Wrong answer. He frowned. "Yeah?"

Sadie shrugged, but he didn't miss her blush as she headed into her kitchen.

"Sadie?"

"Do you want something to drink?"

"You got beer?"

"No." She grabbed a glass from the cupboard and filled it with tap water.

Ryder set his keys (and hers) on the counter and leaned against it with a smile. "Am I freakin' you out?"

"Yes. A little." She sipped her water and then studied him. "We've been out one time, Ryder. I hardly think that's dating."

"Oh, I don't know. I'm countin' tonight as well."

"Tonight is *not* a date."

"You don't think so?"

"*No*," she stressed. "Tonight was girls' night out, with you asserting your weird protection fetish upon us."

Ryder laughed. "It's a fetish?"

"You tell me."

"What's the disconnect here, Sadie?"

"What do you mean?"

"Are you really pissy because I'm concerned about your safety, or is it something else?"

She turned toward the sink. "I didn't realize I was being 'pissy.'"

"*Babe*." Sadie busied herself putting her glass in the dishwasher and Ryder watched her. Damn, she was cute. "Sadie, look at me."

She closed the dishwasher and faced him but didn't quite meet his eyes.

"Babe, what's going on?"

"I'm just trying to process what all this means. One second you're saying ignore our backgrounds and get to know each other, then you're saying you're not a good man. You say you're going to call, and then you don't—for good reason—but still. I'm not mad or upset; I'm just a little overwhelmed. I'm feeling things that are really confusing right now and I don't have anyone to talk to. I tried to talk to Laura, but she says every man has some form of alternative motive, and they all lead to getting a woman into bed, and Bethany thinks I should sleep with a few guys 'before I make my choice.' I don't really have any desire to do that, just so you know."

Ryder stamped down his rage at the thought. "Glad to hear it."

She met his eyes. "I don't know if you and I will ever work, and I can't figure out if it's worth it to even try."

"Why don't you think we'd work?"

"Seriously?"

"Yeah, babe, seriously."

She took a deep breath. "Our backgrounds couldn't be any more different. I also may not be a nun anymore, but it hasn't changed my commitment to God or His ideals. How long are you going to be good with us not having sex? Because I don't intend on doing that until I'm married."

He shrugged. "As long as it works."

"I'm sorry?"

"Baby, I can't promise things are gonna be perfect or that we're gonna last forever, but I *can* promise I won't make you change who you are or what you believe. You want to abstain, we'll abstain. It'll be hard, because you're fuc—freakin' sexy as hell, but it won't kill me."

He could see her smile even though she was trying not to. "According to Bethany it might."

"Stop listening to Bethany. She's pretty, Sadie, but she's obviously batshit crazy. And she's not you. She also doesn't know me. So, get to know me and then decide for yourself."

"I guess that's fair." She bit back a yawn.

"You should sleep. Drink a bunch of water before you go to bed and keep ibuprofen close, 'cause I have a feelin' you're gonna have a hell of a hangover in the morning."

"I never got drunk, Ryder," she challenged. "Plus I drank more water than alcohol."

"What tequila did you have in those margaritas?"

Sadie shrugged. "I have no idea."

"Did you pay less than ten bucks for each drink?"

She nodded.

"Trust me, honey, you're gonna have a hangover."

"You're saying if I'd paid more than ten bucks I wouldn't have one?" Sadie asked.

He smiled. "No, you probably would, but trust me; a Patron hangover is easier than a Cuervo Gold one."

She dropped her head back with a groan. "I have no idea what any of that means."

Done being separated from her, he closed the distance and pulled her into his arms. He backed up against the counter again,

so he could scoot down to her level. She was tiny, which was something he liked about her. "One day soon I'll show you."

"You'll teach me how to drink better?"

He chuckled. "Sure, something like that."

She wrapped her arms around him and settled her cheek to his chest. "I have to admit, I really like this."

He stroked her hair. "Me too."

"If you promise this will happen on a regular basis, we can negotiate the dating thing."

"If it means you'll agree to date me, I'll promise this will happen on a regular basis."

Sadie giggled. "You don't miss a beat."

"I'm hot for teacher; I can't miss a beat when you're smarter than me."

She dropped her head back and rolled her eyes. "Whatever."

"I'm gonna kiss you now," he warned, and before she could object, he covered her mouth with his. She sighed and sank into him and he slid his hand to her neck and deepened the kiss.

God, she was magnificent. Maybe not having her in his bed *would* kill him.

Reluctantly, he broke the kiss and dropped his forehead to hers. "Where the hell did you learn to kiss like that?"

"Nowhere." Sadie took a few deep breaths. "You're the first, Ryder. Was it okay?"

"Baby, it was amazing."

She licked her lips and widened her eyes. "Can we do that again?"

Ryder grinned. "We can do *that* whenever you want to."

"Okay, then I'm good with dating you."

He laughed. "Damn, babe, you're a hard sell."

"You agreed super quickly to my terms, so how hard of a sell could I be?"

"I think I might be a little afraid of you."

She giggled. "Kiss me again and I'll change that."

"Minx."

He kissed her until it was clear they could pass the point of no return with relative ease, and forced himself to break their connec-

tion.

"Wow," she said on a breath, and stepped away. "You are lethal."

"Back atya, baby."

"I like that *way* too much."

"Yeah?"

She nodded with a grimace. "I should really go to confession."

"You might get tired."

"Why?"

"Because I'm gonna make it so you have to go to confession every day."

Sadie dropped her head back with a groan. "Okay, I'll make sure I pray every night a little longer, then."

"Put in a good word for me."

"Always."

Ryder grinned. "I'm gonna go before I can't."

"Probably a good idea."

"I'll call you tomorrow and we'll do something."

"Not before eleven."

He chuckled. "I can do that."

He grabbed his keys and Sadie followed him to the door. "Text me when you get home."

"I will," he promised.

After one more extended kiss at her door, he forced himself away and headed home. He chose to call her instead of texting and they talked until she could no longer form coherent sentences. He let her go with the promise of something fun the next day and fell asleep dreaming of his beautiful girl.

The next morning Ryder was awakened by the buzzing of his phone. Hoping it was Sadie, he answered without checking the screen. "Ryder."

"Hi...um, Ryder?"

"Yeah? Who's this?"

"It's Taylor Watkins. I'm calling to see if there's been any word on Scottie?"

Taylor was Scottie's best friend, and he found it strange that she hadn't reached out to him until now. He'd called several times

and even dropped in at her home unannounced, but her parents always played referee and he was never able to see her. Even Cameron (who'd used his FBI credentials to gain access) had gotten nowhere.

"No. No word yet," Ryder said.

"I'm so sorry this happened."

"I'm gonna find her, Taylor," he said. "Has she reached out to you?"

"I wouldn't know," she admitted. "I'm actually borrowing a friend's phone right now. My parents wouldn't let me call and actually took my phone away. I'm only allowed to make monitored phone calls."

"Did they tell you I called a few times?"

"Yeah, but I really don't know anything."

He sighed. "Well, keep your head down, sweetheart. Stay safe. I'll find Scottie."

"Promise?" she whispered.

"Promise."

"Okay. Thanks, Ryder. I gotta go."

"Okay, babe." He hung up and ran his hands through his hair. God, he hoped he found his sister soon.

EIGHT

Sadie

ONE WEEK LATER, I opened the door and grinned. Ryder held a bouquet of lavender roses in front of his face and he lowered them with a wink. He'd had an emergency at work the Saturday before, so we weren't able to see each other, and we'd only managed a few stolen hours over the past few days, but today was a promise of quality time which I'd been looking forward to.

"Hey." He leaned down to kiss me as he stepped inside.

"Hi. What are those for?" I asked.

"You're getting your first driving lesson."

I frowned. "What?"

"Today's the day, baby. You're going to learn to drive."

"Oh, really?" I challenged. "So, you think you can butter me up with roses?"

"Somethin' like that. Is it working?"

"Not in the slightest," I lied, and pulled a vase down from the kitchen cabinet.

"You're gonna do great."

I shook my head as I filled the vase with water and set the roses inside. "We can't start lessons. I don't have my learner's permit."

"We're gonna stick to the parking lot of the school."

"Your truck's really big."

"Didn't bring my truck."

"You didn't? How are we going to drive?"

He chuckled. "I've got a car."

"You do?" I asked, surprised.

"Got a bike too, but we'll start with driving lessons first. My Harley might be a bit much for you right now."

"Oh, you're hilarious." I faced him and bit my lip. "We don't need to do this. I'm happy to take the bus."

Ryder crossed his arms. "Sadie, you really should know how to drive."

"Why?" I challenged. "Is it one of those laws where now that I'm no longer a nun I have to actually *function* in real society?"

He laughed. "Sure, we'll go with that."

"I don't want to ruin your..." I frowned. "What did you bring?"

"A very tame sedan."

"I don't want to ruin your very tame sedan."

"Babe, you can't. We'll stick to a big empty parking lot and it'll all be good."

"Is it red?" I asked as I arranged the roses. "I've heard a statistic where more red cars get pulled over than any other."

"It's silver, and we're unlikely to get pulled over in a parking lot."

I bit my lip again. "Okay, but if I'm really bad, can we give up?"

He grinned. "No way."

"I'm a really slow learner."

"I don't believe that for a second."

I wrinkled my nose with a sigh. "I'm blind?"

"Nope."

"I might have contacts, you don't know...and I might be out of

them. One Eight Hundred Contacts might have been closed."

He crossed his arms and cocked his head. "Do you have contacts, Sadie?"

"No," I grumbled.

Ryder stepped toward me, placing his hands on the counter, pinning me in. "Damn, you're cute."

"Bargaining is cute to you?"

"You're not getting out of this driving lesson. You know it, I know it, and yet, you're coming up with all these ludicrous excuses, that you *know* are ludicrous, and doin' it while standing in the middle of your kitchen staring at me with a goofy grin on your gorgeous face. So, yeah, you're cute."

My word, he was sexy.

He grinned and leaned closer. "I'm gonna kiss you now."

I licked my lips. "You are?"

Ryder nodded. "Yeah, baby, I am."

"Okay," I whispered, and his mouth covered mine. I gripped his shirt as he stroked my cheek, laying a thumb against my chin and pressing gently. I opened my mouth and his tongue swept inside, making my knees weak.

Wowzer. This was even better than the first time.

Ryder broke the kiss and rested his forehead against mine. "Damn," he breathed out.

I smiled. "I still really like that."

He chuckled. "Me too."

"Can we do it again?"

His answer was to pull me closer and kiss me again. This time I broke the kiss with a groan. "I see why women fall under the spell of men."

"Yeah?"

I nodded. "Yeah."

Ryder cupped my cheeks and grinned. "I see why men are fascinated with ex-nuns."

"Oh, really? That's a thing?"

"It's a thing *now*." He released me and stepped back. "Time to drive."

"Darn," I breathed out.

"We can make out a little more if you want," he offered.

"Yes, please."

"But then we're going to drive."

I wrinkled my nose even as I began to lean toward him. We made out for far less time than I would have liked and then he led me downstairs and to his "tame sedan." A beautiful silver BMW that probably cost as much as my annual paycheck.

"Direct me to your new school and we'll start there," he said after he'd closed me in.

I did as he asked and was relieved to find the lot was completely empty. He smiled at me from the driver's side and squeezed my hand. "Ready?"

"No."

"Come on, baby, you're gonna do great."

I swapped places with him and he gave me a tutorial on how to adjust the seats (I had to move them forward a *lot*, since he was six-one and I was five-four), and then he walked me through the basic information of what everything did.

"So the left pedal is the accelerator and the right is the brake?" I asked.

"*No*, the—"

"Kidding," I joked, interrupting him.

Ryder grinned as he shook his head. "Cute, baby."

I really loved it when he called me "baby."

Was that weird? That was probably weird.

"What?" he asked.

"What, what?"

"You have a funny look on your face."

"I thought I was cute," I challenged.

He laughed. "Always, but you looked a little weirded out."

"I really like it when you call me 'baby,' and I was thinking it was kind of weird that I liked it so much." Yep, I just spit it out like that...I really was weird.

"It's not weird."

"No?"

Ryder shook his head and kissed me gently. "Nope."

"Okay," I whispered.

"Okay," he mimicked, and sat back in his seat. "Start her up."

"Um, how?"

"Right. Insert the key here and just press the button."

I pressed the button and then pressed it again. Nothing.

"It's okay, Sadie, you don't have to press it twice. Once turns it on, twice turns it off."

I nodded and did as he instructed, the car humming quietly at his direction. "Oh, that was easy." I slid the car into drive and pressed the accelerator...and was not prepared for the car lurching forward. I slammed on the brake and squeezed my eyes shut at the sound of Ryder's expletive. "Sorry, sorry," I rushed to say.

Ryder laid his hand on one of mine, tugging gently. I released the death grip I had on the steering wheel and my hands lost their white pallor.

"This is never going to work," I complained.

"It's gonna take some time, baby. You'll get it."

"Before or after I ruin your car?"

"Hopefully before," he admitted.

"I'm so sorry."

"Don't be." He smiled. "Ready to try again?"

"Nope."

"After you put the car in drive, let your foot off the brake slowly. The car will move forward without the accelerator, then you can add speed as you need it. Got it?"

"Nope."

He chuckled and lifted my hand to his lips, kissing my palm. "You can do it."

I grumbled my disagreement as he released my hand and I tried again.

We spent close to two hours in the parking lot and I almost cried when Ryder said we were done with the lesson. I slid the car in park and faced him. "How bad?"

"Baby, you did great."

I bit my lip and shook my head. "You're being really gracious right now."

He stroked my cheek. "You hungry?"

"Starving."

"How about we hit a drive-through and head back to your place?"

"I love that idea." I raised an eyebrow. "But only if there's kissing later."

"Oh, there'll be kissing, baby. You can count on it."

"Okay. I vote Burgerville," I said, and climbed out of the car.

We swapped places, and before hitting the drive-through, Ryder wanted to go shopping so he could stock my place with beer and a few things he liked to eat. This both scared and excited me, because it meant he'd be at my apartment often enough to drink said beer and eat said food.

Errands run, we arrived back at my apartment and I couldn't have been happier to get out of the very tame sedan. We walked inside and I fell onto my sofa.

"You gonna help put this stuff away?" Ryder asked.

"Not if I can avoid it," I admitted, craning my head to look at him.

He grinned, closing the distance between us and leaning down to give me the sweetest upside-down kiss I'd ever had. Well, the first I'd had, but still no less sweet.

"Did I tire you out?"

"Little bit, yes," I said, reaching up to cup his face.

"Sorry, baby."

"Forgiven...if you feed me."

"I'll put the beer away and then feed you, yeah?"

"I see where your priorities lie," I retorted.

He chuckled and headed back into the kitchen. I reluctantly hauled my butt off the couch and joined him. Since he'd put most of the groceries away, I unpacked our dinner, grabbing plates and napkins and setting them on my small table.

"We're eatin' fancy."

I giggled. "*This* is fancy?"

"Yeah, baby, this is fancy."

"Stick with me, buddy. I'll pull you into the high-class world."

He sat in the chair next me and chuckled. "Lookin' forward to it, Sadie."

"May I try your beer?"

"You bet." He slid the can toward me.

I took a swig and sighed with pleasure. "Oh my word, that's delicious."

"Yeah?"

I took another sip. "Yes." I read the label and smiled. "Guinness, you might be my new favorite."

"You drink that, I'll grab another one."

"Thanks, honey."

He pushed away from the table, but before heading to the kitchen, he leaned down with a smile. "FYI, baby, I love it when you call me 'honey.'"

"I have never called you 'honey' before."

"Yeah, babe I know. Just makin' sure you know I love it."

I rolled my eyes. "You're ridiculous."

He kissed me quickly, then grabbed a beer and took his seat again.

"Do you date a lot?"

Ryder shook his head. "One woman man, baby. Always have been."

"*Did* you date a lot? Before me, I mean."

"Had a few women I spent time with over the years, but no one I could see goin' long-term with." He gave me a lopsided grin. "Till you."

"You see this going long-term?"

"Don't you?"

Did I? I hadn't really gotten that far yet, I was still trying to process all the emotions that flooded me every minute of every day.

"You don't have to answer that, Sadie."

"No, I want to. I'm just trying to figure it out." I leaned my chin in my palm and studied him. "I like you. A lot. I think you're gorgeous, you're easy to talk to, and I've never felt more comfortable with anyone than I do with you. I feel like I can be totally me and, since I don't really know myself all that well, it's helpful, you know?"

"Yeah, baby, I do."

"So, long-term? I kinda feel like we're in this and it's working

and I really like it, but I also wonder what's going to happen when we're tested. Do our spiritual, emotional, and physical core beliefs match up?" I sighed. "I don't know if I'm saying any of this right."

"I hear you, Sadie," he said, and took my hand. "And I think they do."

"Really?"

"Yep."

I raised an eyebrow. "Says the man who won't go to church. Do you even believe in God?"

"I used to believe in God. Not sure where I stand currently, but I'm workin' it out." He shrugged and went back to his food. "And you don't need to go to church to be spiritual."

"No, you're probably right." I took a bite of my burger and forced down my opinion.

"Spit it out, Sadie."

I swallowed. "My burger?"

"Babe, say what you were goin' to say."

"No."

"Why not?"

"Because I don't want to have an argument with you on a subject we'll have to end up agreeing to disagree on."

"You might be surprised," he countered.

"Pretty sure I won't be," I grumbled.

"Now who's putting words into whose mouth, babe?" he said, his voice low and irritated.

"Okay, fine." I jabbed a fry I at him. "I think it *is* important we go to church because God says we should. There's a verse in Hebrews that specifically says we shouldn't give up meeting together because it's important to encourage one another as the end times draw near."

"And I think organized religion, particularly in the western world, isn't quite what God had in mind. You're right, we should meet and encourage each other, but I'm not overly interested in sitting in a building with other sheeple, listening to some egomaniac priest, reverend, or clergyman, who may or may not be a child molester, tell me when to sit down or stand up. Pastors in this country, in my experience, tend to have a king-of-the-world men-

tality, touting the importance of whatever the hell they're speaking on that week, all the while sticking their dicks where they don't belong and stealing from the very people they're supposed to love and protect as Christ loves the church. So, no, Sadie, going to church isn't really my thing."

I felt sick. Partly because I knew he was right, but also because this was obviously going to be an area we'd never see eye-to-eye on. "Father Denton isn't a child molester. He's also not an egomaniac. He's actually a bit like you, but like I said, you and I are going to have to agree to disagree."

"Guess so."

"And by the way, I'm not a sheeple." I stood and gathered my trash. "Unlike a sheep, I have a mind that I use on a daily basis and I don't trust someone's word as law unless I test it against what the Bible says. The people I choose to have in my life are people who do protect me, and I include Michael Denton in that group. He might be a priest, but he's a really good guy and an even better friend."

"Sadie," he ground out as I walked into the kitchen. He followed me, setting his plate in the sink.

"Don't, Ryder. You don't have to explain yourself or try to backtrack—"

"Wasn't gonna do either, babe."

"Oh." I shrugged. "Well, good. You're entitled to your opinion."

He took the plate I was holding and dropped it in the sink, pulling me against him and pinning me to his chest. "I know you're not a sheep."

"Coulda fooled me."

"I'm sorry if I was a little passionate in the delivery of my opinion."

"A little?" I challenged.

"I love that you stand up to me and that I don't scare you. That's new for me."

I settled my cheek to his chest and closed my eyes. "I'm sorry that's new for you, Ryder, because I see your heart and I understand your passion. But I won't allow anyone to bully me, you

have to see that."

"I see it, baby. I just wonder where I fit if I can't protect you."

"Holy mother of..." I stared up at him. "Seriously? If you're looking for a damsel in distress, you're barking up the wrong tree."

He grinned and kissed my nose. "Woof."

"Dork." I giggled and settled back against him. "Did you or did you not take care of that guy in the bar?"

"I have a feeling Bethany would have taken him out eventually."

"You might be right about that."

"How old's this priest guy?"

"Wow, talk about a subject change," I said.

"Just answer the question."

"Michael? I don't know, maybe thirty."

"And just how close are you? How long have you known him?"

"We've known each other for about two years. That's when he was placed at our church." I cocked my head. "Why?"

"Keepin' a finger on the pulse of my competition, baby."

"What?" I pushed away from him with a frown. "He's a priest, Ryder. Not competition."

"He's still a man, Sadie, and you're you, so he is most definitely competition."

"What the heck is that supposed to mean...I'm me?"

"Gorgeous, confident, sexy as hell. No man can resist you."

"You're insane."

He pulled me back to him with a grin. "Doesn't mean I'm wrong."

"Michael is not competition, Ryder. Trust me."

Ryder stroked my hair as he held me. "I *do* trust you...it's him I'm gonna watch."

"I think you need psychiatric help," I said, wrapping my arms around his waist, trying not to sigh out loud at the blissful feeling his hands in my hair created.

"I think I need to stretch out on the sofa with my woman and make out while we pretend to watch a movie."

This time I did sigh out loud. "Perfect."

Ryder chuckled and released me so we could deal with our dishes and grab more beer. As promised, he delivered on the making out, but we also managed to stream and actually watch a movie as well. All in all, it was a perfect date, sans the driving lesson.

NINE

Sadie

TWO SUNDAYS FOLLOWING the driving lesson from Hades, I caught the bus down to Beaverton, guilt swarming since I'd been too tired to attend mass the weekend before. Admittedly, this was the first time ever I'd wished I'd had the thirty minutes a car would have saved me to sleep. I was exhausted. Ryder didn't leave until well past one (the same happened the previous Saturday which is why I skipped mass) and even then, it was tough letting him go. I was falling hard and fast for the man and didn't know how to stop it...not that I wanted to. We'd had another blissful week of togetherness and I loved every second. Well, every second that wasn't spent driving. He'd insisted on two more lessons, which had gone better, but still, ugh. I hated driving, *hated* it.

Arriving at the Abbey, I let myself in and headed to my aunt's office. I heard a man's voice mingled with hers so I knocked even

though the door was open. It sounded like Michael's but he was out of town, so I was intrigued.

"Good morning, Sadie," my aunt said, and rushed to hug me.

Father Michael stepped into my line of sight with a grin. "Hey stranger."

"Hi!" I said in surprise, and walked into his hug. "I thought you were still in Florida."

"Got back yesterday," he said, and released me. "How are you doing on the outside?"

"Not bad, I think. I start my new job in seven weeks, so ask me then."

"You'll have to give me your new number in order for me to do that."

"You've lost your power of telepathy?"

He chuckled. "It only works when you're wearing your habit."

"Dang it, I forgot that rule." I giggled as I pulled out my phone and sent him my number. "Just texted you, so now you have it."

"Thanks. I better go spend some time in prayer. It's a heavy sermon today."

"I'll try not to fall asleep."

Michael grinned. "Me too."

He left my aunt's office and I hugged her again. "I really hate not seeing you every day."

"I feel the same way, honey." She smiled and cupped my cheeks. "You look beautiful."

"I do?"

Auntie nodded. "Happy."

"I *am* happy. Ryder's amazing. I can't wait for you to meet him."

"Me too." She released me and grabbed her Bible. "Let's get inside. Mass waits for no one."

I followed my aunt from the abbey across the courtyard and through the side door of the church. She had a few things to tend to before the service started so I left my Bible on the pew and headed to the restroom. As I turned on the faucet, it attacked, and I bit back a curse as water splashed onto my shirt. Grabbing copious amounts of paper towels I did my best to blot myself dry, but then

the bells sounded, so I knew I had to get inside.

I continued to dab as I headed from the lobby toward the sanctuary, unprepared for strong arms to lock around me like a vice.

"Hey!" I squirmed but the arms held me tighter and I looked up to find Ryder grinning down at me like an idiot.

"Hey, baby."

I gasped and turned to hug him. "What are you doing here?"

"A really smart lady told me it was important to go to church, so I wanted to surprise you."

"Or size up the competition?"

Ryder chuckled. "I thought you said he wasn't competition."

I squeezed him harder. "Touché."

He chuckled, leaning down to kiss me chastely. "More of that later."

"Yes, please."

"Why are you wet?" he asked, glancing at my chest.

"Attack of the ladies' room faucet. I'll tell my aunt after service. We better get inside." I grabbed his hand. "Coming?"

"I'm following you."

I led him to the seats I'd saved and saw my aunt give me an enquiring eyebrow rise. "Auntie, this is Ryder. Ryder, my aunt, Mother—"

"Just call me Sister, Ryder," she interrupted. "It's lovely to meet you."

"You too."

Ryder took his seat to my right and, with my aunt on my left, I felt like all was right with the world. Ryder linked his fingers with mine and we stayed like that through most of the sermon, which as Michael warned, was a heavy one. He spoke on integrity and how most of us, Catholics and Christians particularly, were missing the mark in being honest. There was far too much financial and sexual immorality at the highest level of churches, and it needed to stop. I thought it was interesting considering the argument I'd had with Ryder the week before, but I chose not to give him a "told you so" look...at least not until later.

"Will you join us for lunch, Ryder?" my aunt asked as we filed out of the church.

"I don't want to intrude on your time with Sadie, sister."

"Don't be silly. You're more than welcome. It'll give me a chance to scrutinize you."

"Auntie," I admonished. "You're not supposed to tell him that's what you're doing. We observe and judge silently!"

"My word, sweetpea, you're right. I'm sorry, I forgot."

Ryder dropped his head back with a laugh. "I see where Sadie gets her sense of humor."

Auntie grinned. "I'm a very bad influence, I'm afraid."

"If you come to lunch, you can drive me home," I said, hopefully.

"Or I could let you drive." He grinned. "Want to take our lives in your hands?"

Before I could retort, we arrived outside and Michael called us over. Ryder grabbed my hand and held tight as we made our way to him. "You're ridiculous," I hissed quietly.

"Not even close," he said.

Michael would never show me affection publicly, so I knew Ryder wouldn't have anything to object to, but he still didn't release my hand as I introduced the two of them.

"It's nice to meet you, Ryder."

Ryder shook his hand. "Nice to meet you too, Michael."

"Father Denton," I corrected.

"Not my father, baby."

I glared up at him, but Michael chuckled. "It's fine, Sadie."

"Coffee this week?" I asked Michael.

I felt Ryder stiffen beside me, but ignored him. My irritation was growing and I was about to tell him to forget about lunch.

Michael nodded. "That'd be great. I'll call you."

"Perfect." Tugging on Ryder's hand, I led him away from the receiving line my aunt was still wading through, and faced him. "Stop it."

"What, baby?"

"Stop posturing. Michael is a friend." I leaned closer, adding in a whisper, "He's also a priest."

Ryder gave me a crooked grin and shook his head. "It's all good, Sadie. He and I are clear now."

"Holy mother of...," I threw my arms in the air. "You are an idiot."

"That's one thing I'm *not*, Sadie." He crossed his arms and raised an eyebrow. "He may be a priest, but he's also hot for teacher, so whether or not you see it, he and I are crystal clear now."

I stared up at him in disbelief. "I cannot believe you."

"Ask him."

"I'm not going to ask a priest if he's attracted to me," I hisspered, glancing around, cognizant of the parishioners milling around us.

"Then trust me, baby, he's into you."

"You're beyond wrong." I raised my hand when he opened his mouth to say something. "No, Ryder. I never want to have this argument with you again."

He chuckled. "Suit yourself."

"Are you two ready?" Auntie asked as she approached.

I forced a smile. "Yes."

"Why do you look like you want to kill Ryder?"

"Probably because I do," I grumbled.

Ryder laughed, wrapping an arm around my waist and pulling me close. "She'll get over it."

"Not any time soon, bub."

He kissed my temple and whispered, "Challenge accepted."

"You're a butt."

Ryder laughed again and led us to his car.

* * *

Lunch ended up being an eye-opening experience. One that I'm not sure I liked. My aunt...the *Reverend* Mother...was a flirt. Not to mention a hopeless romantic. Ryder had her in the palm of his hand and if I ever decided he was not the man for me, I had a feeling my aunt would object. *Strongly.*

I mulled this information over on our way home. Once we dropped Auntie off at the abbey, Ryder loaded me into the BMW (he didn't want my aunt to have to climb into his truck...indicating he knew all along he'd be invited to lunch), and we headed for my

apartment.

"You okay?" he asked as we crossed into Vancouver.

"Honestly? I don't know."

"Break it down for me, baby."

"I already did."

He smiled as he switched lanes. "Ask him."

"Excuse me?"

"Ask Michael if he's attracted to you, Sadie."

I huffed. "I'm not going to ask Michael if he's attracted to me."

"Then you need to get over this."

"What?"

"If he's any kind of man, babe, he'll tell you the truth and then you'll know I'm right," he said. "If you don't want to ask him, which is your right, then you can't be mad at me."

"He's a *priest*."

"He's a man first, Sadie."

"A man who took a vow."

"I'm not arguin' that. But just because he took a vow doesn't mean he turns off his base desires. He may not act on them, but it doesn't mean he doesn't have them."

I crossed my arms. "Why are you pushing this?"

"Baby, I'm not, you're the one stewin' in the corner."

"I'm not stewing, Ryder, I'm irritated." As soon as I said it out loud, I realized it was essentially the same thing.

He chuckled. "I get it, but I needed him to know where we stood and now he does, so it's done."

"Is this what it's like being in a relationship?"

"With me it is, yeah." He glanced at me and then back at the road. "I protect mine, baby."

I didn't entirely know how I felt about that. Mostly because it made me feel tingly, but the logical side of me cautioned that his possessiveness might be dangerous.

Arriving at my apartment, Ryder parked and then faced me. "You gonna invite me up?"

"Do I have a choice?"

"You don't now," he said, and climbed out of the car. Gone was his previous jovial countenance, replaced with the same

guardedness he'd had a few Friday nights ago.

We didn't speak as I unlocked my door and led him inside. He closed the door behind us and dropped his keys on the coffee table. "Have at it, Sadie."

"I don't want to fight, Ryder."

"We don't need to fight, but somethin's crawled up your ass--"

I gasped. "Nothing has crawled anywhere near my bottom, thank you very much."

He dragged his hands down his face and took a deep breath. "Break it down for me. All of it. Don't filter; just tell me how you feel."

I set my purse on the sofa and faced him. "I'm scared."

"Of me?"

"A little, maybe, but probably not as much as I should be." I shrugged. "Mostly I'm afraid of all these feelings I have for you, and then you and your possessiveness. Do you know how many women we've sheltered because their men were 'possessive'?"

"Okay, baby, I hear you, so let me clarify," he said. "I'm not possessive...I'm protective. There's a difference."

"Slippery slope, Ryder."

"Maybe so, but not with me. I've said my piece, baby, it's done."

"He and I have plans to meet for coffee this week."

"So, have coffee with him."

I leaned against the sofa and bit my lip. "You're okay with that?"

"I won't say it doesn't bother me, but you're a grown woman and I trust you, so yeah, I'm okay with it."

"Oh."

"We done?"

"For now I guess."

Ryder chuckled and closed the distance between us. "Damn, you're cute when you're losing an argument."

"And you're obnoxious when you're winning one."

He ran his knuckles down my cheek. "Don't shut me out, okay? I know all of this is new to you...it's not really old hat to me either, but you just need to talk to me."

"Hello pot, I'm kettle."

He sighed. "Point taken, babe. I'm not always good at that part."

"So we both have stuff to work on, I guess."

"I'll try if you will."

I leaned against him and closed my eyes. "Sure."

"Am I hangin' with you for the rest of the day?"

"Don't you have to work?"

"Closed on Sundays, baby."

"Oh, right. I forgot." I squeezed him gently. "I need a nap, but you can stay if you want to."

"I'll find a game and you can nap beside me."

I grinned up at him. "You know just what to say to a girl."

"Only one girl I care about." He leaned down and kissed me gently, then I changed into yoga pants and a T-shirt and curled up beside him on the sofa. I have no idea what "game" he found, as I fell asleep quickly and stayed that way for several hours.

TEN

Sadie

WEDNESDAY MORNING, I caught the bus into Portland and got off on Alberta. Michael was meeting me at Helser's and since I'd never eaten there, I was excited to try something new.

I walked the short distance to the restaurant, glad Michael arrived before me and snagged a table because it was packed.

"Hey," he said, pulling me in for a hug. He wore jeans and a black T-shirt, looking far less priest and much more model gorgeous, which was a little disconcerting.

"Hi. Thanks for meeting me," I said, and took my seat.

"I could have picked you up."

I grimaced. "I'm still in the habit of following the old rules, I think."

He smiled and sat across from me. "Probably smart."

Our church had a rule that persons of the opposite sex didn't

drive or meet together alone (particularly if they were on staff). It was a good one in my opinion, because both sides were protected from rumor and potential temptation. My ride home with Reese had been an exception for me because I didn't feel I was in much of a place to object at the time.

"How was Florida?" I asked.

"Good. It was a nice break. Time with the family and such."

A server arrived and I ordered coffee and eggs Benedict, which Helser's was known for.

"So, tell me about this guy," Michael said once the server left.

"Ryder? Um, not much to tell. He owns the Brass Frog downtown and we've been seeing each other for a little while. It's still really new, even if it feels like we've known each other forever."

"So it's not serious?"

"I don't know that I'd say that." I leaned back in my chair. "We're dating exclusively, but getting to know each other at the same time, so it's not like we're engaged or anything. But I really like him. Why?"

"I'm just looking out for you."

"I appreciate that, Michael. But he's a really good guy...even if he's a little intense and bossy at times."

He frowned. "What do you mean by bossy?"

"He owns a bar and is used to getting his way, so he and I butt heads on occasion."

"If he ever hurts you, Sadie, I'll take care of him."

I choked on my coffee and worked to get my cough under control. Michael stood and rubbed my back, handing me a napkin.

"What do you mean, you'll take care of him?" I asked once he'd taken his seat again.

"I think it's pretty self-explanatory."

I groaned, dropping my face into my hands.

"Hey," he said. "Are you alright?"

"Ryder said you were attracted to me and that he made his opinion about that known to you."

"He did."

"Seriously?"

"Yes." He smiled. "Look, if we were in another place and time, you and I might have worked, but we're not, so it's not an issue."

I relaxed. "So he's wrong?"

"Can't say he's wrong, Sadie, but it's a non-issue."

"Except now I feel like an idiot," I grumbled.

"Why?"

"Because Ryder was right. How did he know and I didn't?"

"You're not an idiot." Michael smiled gently. "And believe me when I say nothing has changed. I value our friendship, Sadie, so beyond that, you have nothing to worry about."

"I wasn't really worried," I retorted.

He chuckled. "Maybe not. But Ryder was, right?"

I sighed. "Not anymore, since you did your man thing." I waved my hand in a circle on the words "man thing," and Michael laughed.

"Well, you just be careful, okay? I'm here if you ever need to talk."

"I appreciate that. Thanks."

Breakfast continued without revisiting the Ryder subject and by the time Michael had to go, it was almost noon.

"Are you sure I can't give you a ride?"

I shook my head. "The bus comes in ten minutes. I'm good."

"I'll wait with you, then."

"You don't have to do that."

He smiled. "I know I don't."

Before I could thank him, my phone rang. It was Ryder. "Excuse me."

"Sure thing."

"Hey," I said.

"Hey, baby. You still at coffee?"

"Just leaving, actually. Michael's going to wait at the bus stop with me."

"You want me to pick you up?"

"I thought you had a meeting."

"It's done," Ryder said. "I don't need to be back here until six."

"Ah, sure, that'd be nice."

"What are you wearing?"
Heat covered my cheeks. "I'm sorry?"
"What are you wearing?" he repeated.
I glanced at Michael as I said, "Jeans and a T-shirt."
"Good. I'm on my bike, then. Where are you?"
"Helser's."
"Right. See you in fifteen, baby."
He hung up before I could object to riding on his bike. I'd never been on a motorcycle before and I was scared to death.
"Are you all right?" Michael asked, his hand squeezing my arm.
"Oh, yes. Sorry." I dropped my phone back in my purse and slid the strap over my shoulder. "Ryder's picking me up, so I'll just hang outside and wait for him."
"I'll wait with you, Sadie."
"I thought you had to go."
"I do, but there's a little wiggle room."
"Okay, thanks."
I led Michael outside and we found a shady spot to wait. True to form, Ryder was there in fifteen minutes, and my heart pounded as I watched him pull his bike up next to us.
"Harley Fat Boy," Michael said. "Nice."
"It is?"
Michael nodded. "Very."
Ryder put the kickstand down and cut the engine before throwing a leg over and removing his helmet. "Hey, baby. Michael."
"Ryder." Michael extended his hand. "Good to see you again. Nice bike."
"You too, thanks."
Michael hugged me. "You okay?"
"Yep," I lied.
"Take care of her," he said, and then headed to his car.
Ryder reached out and pulled me to him, kissing me gently. "Hey, beautiful."
"Hi."
"How was breakfast?" he asked.
"Illuminating."

He cocked his head. "How so?"

"I'm not ready to share that yet."

"Yeah?" He grinned. "How come?"

"Because I'm not ready to admit you're right."

"About the priest?"

I nodded.

Ryder growled. "He admitted it?"

"Sort of."

"Shit." He gave me a squeeze. "No more coffees."

"You trust me, remember?" I smacked his chest. "And he's a priest, so nothing will ever happen. He promised me that."

"Why do you sound disappointed?"

"Because it's weird now and I adore Michael." I pulled away from him. "I kind of wish you hadn't said anything."

"So this is my fault?"

"No. It's no one's fault. I just wish I didn't know that if he wasn't a priest, he'd pursue me."

"He *said* that?" he snapped.

"Not in so many words, but yes. He also said he got your message, so you need to calm down a little."

He scrubbed a hand over his beard. "I knew this was a bad idea."

"I should just go home," I said.

"No, we're gonna hang out at my place until I've gotta go to work."

I let out a frustrated squeak. "Why do you have to be so bossy?"

"Maybe because my woman can't see that she's beautiful and sexy, which means I have to watch out for the assholes who want to get into her pants."

I gasped. "Don't be disgusting. Michael does *not* want to do that."

"Bet you twenty bucks he's headed for the confession booth as we speak."

"You're an idiot," I snapped, and headed for the bus stop.

"Where the hell are you going?"

"Home."

He caught up to me and took my hand. "Sadie, don't be ridiculous."

"You're the one being ridiculous," I accused, ripping my hand from his, and blinking back tears. "Michael is a *friend*. A really good friend, and that's all he'll ever be. But you're reducing our friendship to nothing more than some dirty sexual fantasy on his part. It's not fair and it's a really low blow. Michael is an awesome guy, Ryder, and if you spent half as much time getting to know him as you do railing on about what a horn dog he is, you'd find that out."

"Babe," he whispered, reaching for me again.

"*Don't* touch me! Now"—I glanced at my watch—"the next bus is in twenty minutes, so I'm going to head to the bus stop."

"Shit, Sadie, I'm sorry," he rasped.

"Why do you do this?" I challenged.

"Because I'm a dick."

"Well, that's not really a legitimate reason, Ryder. So, try again or I'll head home."

"We're really doin' this on the sidewalk?"

"Would you rather pray?"

His mouth slid up in a slight smile before he covered it. "Damn it, you're cute."

"Bus is on its way," I warned.

"You're not getting on the bus, Sadie, so just put it out of your mind."

"I'm not sure I want to get on your bike, so perhaps we're at an impasse."

Ryder slid his hand to my neck and thumbed my pulse. "Sometimes you make me feel totally out of control."

"What do you mean?"

"You have no clue how gorgeous you are, inside and out, and I feel like I need to encase you in bubble wrap and keep all the bad shit away from you...or better yet, lock you away somewhere so you can't leave me."

"Oh, 'cause that's not creepy."

"Let me be clear." He grimaced. "If you want to leave me, obviously, you are free to leave me. But I really hope you don't, be-

cause now that I know you, I don't think I can live without you."

"Um, Ryder, that's also a little creepy, considering one of the biggest things abused women have said to us when they've sought shelter is that they stayed because their husbands threatened to kill themselves if they left."

"Rest assured, I'd never kill myself, Sadie. I just mean that I like you in my life. You make it better and now that you're here, I don't want to lose you."

Wow.

That was unbelievably...sweet.

"Ryder."

His mouth covered mine and I gripped his leather jacket as I fell against him. He broke the kiss, sliding his mouth to my forehead and kissing it gently. "Be patient with me, baby, yeah? Jealousy's new for me."

"I can be patient until the cows come home, but you need to get a handle on some of this, Ryder. I would never cheat on you; it's not in me to do that." I stared up at him. "Are you projecting?"

"Meaning?"

"Are you worried that I'll cheat, or that you will?"

"I won't *ever* cheat on you, Sadie. If it ever got that bad, we'd be over, but I'd still never cheat."

"It's the same for me." I smiled. "So how about you just chill out?"

He chuckled. "Chill out?"

"Yep. Take a big ol' chill pill."

"Never heard a nun put it quite like that before."

"Not a nun anymore, honey."

"You've still got a little nun in you, Sadie. It's something I like about you."

I raised an eyebrow. "Yeah?"

"Definitely." He kissed my nose, then took my hand again and led me back to his bike.

Well, he kind of dragged me back to his bike. Either he didn't notice or he ignored the fact that my entire body shook. Opening one of the side thingies attached to the back of the bike, he pulled out a leather jacket, much smaller than the one he wore, and anoth-

er helmet. "This is Scottie's, but she's about your size, so it should fit."

"It's so hot, Ryder. I don't know if I can stand a leather jacket."

"I get it, but it's safer than what you're wearin', so you're wearin' it."

I swallowed as I reluctantly nodded.

He slid my purse from my shoulder and set it where the jacket had been before, then closed and locked the side thing while I pulled on the jacket. The helmet came next and by the time I was fully covered, I was sweating like a pig.

"Ready?"

I shook my head.

"You're gonna do great, baby. Just slide close to me and lean when I lean, yeah?"

I shook my head again.

"If you need to stop, tap my chest, okay?"

I reached out and tapped his chest, unprepared for Ryder's laugh. It was deep and it was belly. "Warn me when you're gonna be funny, baby."

"Warn me when you're going to make me get on a bike, honey," I retorted.

"I promise, you're gonna do great." He climbed on then helped me slide on behind him. Guiding my hands around his waist, he reached back and slid my butt forward. The touch excited me as I pressed even closer to him. He pushed the kickstand up, started the bike, then backed it out before taking off to wherever we were going.

I couldn't help a squeak of fright as we lurched forward.

"Hold tight!" he yelled back to me, and I did as he ordered... gladly.

ELEVEN

Sadie

BY THE TIME Ryder pulled up a long driveway that led to a surprisingly large home overlooking Portland, I had no idea where we were or how we'd gotten there. I'd kept my eyes closed the entire time...you know, due to the terror of being on a fatal crash magnet. He inched into the garage which opened as we approached, and shut off the bike. I didn't let go.

He pulled off his helmet and looped it over one of the handlebars. "You can let go now, baby."

"Nope. I'm good."

He slid his hands to mine and pried them from his waist. "I've got you. Throw your leg over and I'll make sure you don't fall."

"I can't."

"Yeah, you can."

"My whole body is made of jelly."

He chuckled, gripping my thighs. "Take your helmet off, Sade. We'll start small."

"Don't let go."

"I won't."

I leaned harder against him, my front to his back, and pried the helmet off my head, handing it to him so he could loop it over the other handlebar. I internally shuddered at what my hair must look like right about now, but my hands were shaking so hard I doubted I could fix it if I wanted to. Didn't matter. If my hair was a mess, it was Ryder's fault, so he'd just have to deal with it.

"Put your hands on my shoulders and stand up on the pegs, then throw your leg over, okay?"

I nodded and followed his instructions as he wrapped an arm around my waist to make sure I didn't fall. My feet made it to the concrete floor without incident, but I kept an iron grip on his bicep as he climbed off the bike.

After helping me with my jacket and removing his, he wrapped his arms around me and pulled me close. "You okay?"

"No. I never want to get on that death machine again. You're obviously a great rider, but it scares the dickens out of me."

He chuckled. "Okay, baby, I'll drive you home in the Bimmer later."

"Don't you mean Beemer?"

"If I had a BMW motorcycle, then, yes, it would be Beemer," he informed me.

"Seriously?"

"Seriously," he said.

"Are you a car nerd?"

"Reese is," he admitted. "I gotta say, you're adorable with helmet head, baby."

My hands flew to my hair with a groan. "Show me the bathroom and a brush, please."

He grinned and led me through a door and into the house, hitting the garage door button on the way.

"Oh, my purse," I said.

"I'll get it. Bathroom's first door on the right down the hall," he said, pointing toward the back of the house. "Make yourself at

home."

I nodded and headed that way, finding a brush in the first drawer. After fixing what I could of my hair, I took a minute to look around. The bathroom was small, but looked recently updated. Bead-board decorated light-blue walls, except the one with the tile shower/tub combo. The room was big enough to accommodate double sinks. The counter had a unique blue and gray granite top, and the toilet looked new...if it wasn't, Ryder was really good at keeping it clean.

I washed my hands and then headed back the way I came, distracted by the huge picture window overlooking the city.

"Purse is on the counter," Ryder called.

"Thanks," I said distractedly. I couldn't help myself from stopping and staring.

"What do you think?" Ryder asked, slipping a hand around my waist.

"It's incredible." I leaned into him. "How long have you lived here?"

"I bought the place about six years ago and gutted it, so been fully in for two years."

"Did you do it yourself?"

"Some of it. Friends helped."

I faced him, running my hands up his chest and looping them behind his neck. "Nice friends."

"Yeah, they're more like brothers."

"Any word on your sister?"

He shook his head.

I stroked his neck. "I'm sorry, Ryder."

"We're close. I can feel it."

"Are you going to fill me in?"

He sighed, dropping his forehead to mine. "You sure you want me to?"

"I want to know everything about you. Good and bad. I can handle it."

"I need a beer for this."

I cupped his cheek. "Kiss first."

Ryder leaned down and kissed me, holding me for several pre-

cious seconds.

"You hungry?" he asked after breaking the kiss.

"I just ate several baby chickens and half a pig, I'm good for a little while."

He chuckled and led me into the kitchen. Natural hickory cabinets framed a huge kitchen with more granite covering countertops galore and a massive island that seated six. The island had a sink and dishwasher, but I noticed there was another sink by the window. A commercial stainless-steel stove with six gas burners sat proudly against one wall, with double ovens built in next to it. The fridge looked like it could not only power the space shuttle, but also hold enough food to feed a football team.

"Wow. Is there anything in this house that doesn't look like a showroom?" I asked.

"I like to cook, what can I say?"

I settled myself at the island and hummed in agreement. "Mmm, I like to cook too, and I'd give my left arm to cook in a place like this."

"You've got carte blanche, baby. I'll give you a key and the alarm code so anytime you want to surprise me, you can."

I grinned. "I'll check bus schedules."

He shook his head. "You'll cab it or call Reese."

"Oh, really?"

"Really."

"The bus is safe, Ryder."

"Sure. At commute time and during the day, but I don't like the idea of you riding it when it's virtually empty or dark outside. So, you cab it or you call Reese."

I waved a finger toward him. "This kind of bossy I can handle, FYI."

Ryder grabbed my hand and kissed my palm. "Good to know."

After retrieving himself a beer (and me a soda), he led me back into the great room and pulled me onto the sofa. I shifted and wrapped an arm around his waist, snuggling into him.

Ryder took a swig of his beer and settled it on his thigh, hugging me tighter with his free arm. "Scottie and me are tight. Well, we were, before." He took a deep breath, pausing for a moment. I

stayed as still as I could to give him a little space to think. "Scarlett's always been sensitive and a little strong-willed, and she butted heads with Mom, but she had Dad wrapped around her finger. Well, she thought she did. Only Dad's not a person to be manipulated, so even though she thought she could, she found out the hard way just what kind of man he is. She's almost ten years younger than me, and I got the hell out at seventeen, which meant Scottie was left behind." He let out a quiet breath. "Eight years old and she had to navigate that shit alone."

I kissed his chest, still saying nothing.

"Dad's an officer in a pretty nasty MC"

"MC?" I asked.

"Motorcycle Club. They're one-percenters, which means they believe they're above the law."

"Oh, like Sons of Anarchy."

"Not a television show, though, baby. Real people killing other people and selling girls to perverts for profit."

I gasped, sitting up with a frown. "Your dad sold girls?"

"The Club did...does. Originally, the sperm donor—my father—was the cleanup guy...the hatchet man, so to speak," Ryder said. "It's why they call him Hatch."

"How did you end up in a Catholic school?"

"My mother's hail Mary pass at an attempt to reform me. I was in for middle school, but then it was back to normal school for high school. Probably because they kicked me out."

"Why did they kick you out?"

"Some rich douche said I was cheatin'. I wasn't, but he kept accusin' me, so he and I had a conversation after school."

"Uh-oh."

"I think he saw my point of view lookin' up at me from the ground with a bloody lip."

I shook my head. "Ryder."

"I was young, baby, and since I was the kid of a biker, they wouldn't even listen to my side of the story, so they kicked me out."

"I'm sorry."

"Don't be. Between you and me, I hated it. Probably because

none of the nuns looked like you."

I rolled my eyes. "I can't imagine you as a student. You would have been trouble."

He grinned. "Only if you were lucky."

"So what happened with Hatch?"

"When he decided he didn't want to kill without purpose anymore, he ran drugs and prostitutes, but then some of his cronies mentioned Scottie, and Dad decided to go a different way."

I forced back bile. "He sold your sister?"

He scowled. "Not right away, you know, 'cause he's 'not a monster.' He was gonna give her a 'choice.'" He used air quotes to stress what his father said. "But yeah, he was gettin' ready to make a deal when Scottie ran. She didn't make the right choice, apparently. How she got loose from Hatch is still somewhat of a miracle, but she ran straight to me, and it's been the two of us against the world for the last five years or so."

"How old is she?"

"She just turned nineteen."

I couldn't believe it. "He was going to sell her at fourteen years old? I think that's the absolute definition of a monster."

With a nod, he tugged me back onto his chest, kissing my temple. "She had some pretty nasty people after her after she ran, but we took care of it."

"We?"

"Reese and a couple other guys you'll meet eventually."

"Do I want to know how you took care of it?"

"Probably not."

I'd give him that, because I wasn't ready to know, but also because I don't think he was ready to tell me. "So are they the ones that took her this time? The motorcycle gang?"

"No," he said. "She went off the rails about a year or so ago... met some douchebag who made her feel special, started doing drugs, and we fought constantly. I didn't handle it right. This is on me."

"What do you mean, you didn't handle it right?"

"Had an altercation with said douchebag, said douchebag resisted," he said with a sigh. "Landed him in the hospital for the

night."

I gasped. "Seriously?"

"Baby sister, Sadie. I protect mine."

"And how did that go?" I challenged.

"Didn't quite land the result I was looking for," he admitted.

"What result were you looking for?"

He stiffened, but I gave him a gentle squeeze and he relaxed. "I'd hoped she'd see him for what he was and calm the hell down for a while. She didn't. Well, I thought she did, because she played me for a few months, but they took off again about a month ago. Scottie's got this sweetheart of a best friend, Taylor. She's really into church, good family, and they were tight. Scottie was doin' great, but something happened and Taylor's parents said she couldn't hang out with Scottie anymore. Broke my sister's heart, but it also sent her straight back to the douchebag. What neither of us knew was he wasn't just a douchebag, he was a guy willing to sell her to pay off his drug debt, and get a bump to boot."

"So, she fell for a guy just like your dad."

"Yeah. Despite everything I did for her."

I sat up and turned his head to face me. "Maybe we don't start with that when you find her."

"Maybe not." He grimaced. "I had her back for two months. Right after I met you, Cam found her. I got her home, but now she's gone again. I screwed up, Sadie. Big time."

I smiled gently, running my thumb over his beard. "Then we'll fix it when we find her, okay?"

"Yeah."

I settled back against his chest. "Where are your parents now?"

"Mom's living her life at the bottom of some bottle. I don't see her if I can avoid it. Dad's doing twenty to life in Portland."

"Wow, that close?"

"Yeah. It's a pain in the ass, 'cause he still has reach."

"Reach?"

"His club's out of Gresham, so they're close enough to drive by the bar, drop in, check things out."

I craned my head to meet his eyes. "And do they?"

"Yep. Not often. Every couple months. You know, enough to

piss me off. We just keep our heads down and so long as they don't start shit, they move on without incident. He doesn't know where I live, so Scottie and I are safe here, but my business holdings aren't private."

"Does your dad know about Scottie being missing?"

"No clue. It's possible, I guess. Club's got people on the payroll everywhere, but Cameron's on *my* payroll and his contacts aren't dirty, so I trust Dad wouldn't know through them."

"Wow, Ryder, I'm sorry you're dealing with all of this."

"Thanks, baby."

"What can I do?"

"You're doin' it. You give me peace...well, until I have to sleep alone."

I smiled up at him. "Sorry, honey."

He leaned forward and kissed me quickly. "It's okay, Sadie. Just like having you close."

"Ditto."

Without letting me go, he set his beer aside and slid his phone from his pocket. "Ryder. Hey, Cam. Yeah? Shit, seriously? Ah, yeah, I'll call Reese. Tonight? Yep. Okay. Meet you there." He hung up and disengaged from me. "Cam found Scottie."

My eyes widened. "Really?"

Ryder nodded as he stood. "We're on the red-eye to Savannah, so I have some shit to do before I have to go."

"Right. Okay." I rose to my feet. "Can I do anything?"

"No." He walked toward the kitchen and I followed. "I'll have Reese swing by and check on you, but I need you home and safe for the moment."

My heart raced. "You don't think I'm safe?"

"That's not what I meant, sorry." Ryder faced me and pulled me close. "I didn't mean to scare you. I just mean that if you're at your place, I know where you are."

"Oh, okay." I smiled. "I hadn't planned on going anywhere except the grocery store tomorrow, so you're good."

"Reese'll drive you."

"Honey, the store's barely a block away. I can walk."

"Not up for discussion, Sadie." He released me and headed to

his desk area in the kitchen. "He'll be at your place whenever you want him to be."

I groaned. "I should have kept my mouth shut."

"I hate that you don't drive, babe," he said distractedly as he rummaged through papers on his desk.

"Well, that's not changing anytime soon, so you might as well get over it."

"Don't need to get over it. Reese'll drive you."

"This kind of protectiveness, I'm not a fan of, FYI," I retorted, leaning against the island.

"Well, that's not changing anytime soon, so you might as well get over it," he parroted.

"How does Reese feel about being forced to chauffer your girlfriend around?" I challenged as I followed him toward the back of the house.

"It's what he gets paid for, so I'd imagine he doesn't feel much one way or the other." He sighed. "Humor me, Sadie. At least until some of this shit is over, yeah?"

We walked into a large master bedroom and I couldn't stop the tiny breath of surprise as I caught sight of the view. Where the great room overlooked the city, the bedroom seemed shrouded in trees. I couldn't see another house anywhere near his.

Ryder grabbed a bag from the closet and started to throw clothes into it.

"How is your house so clean?" I asked, heading to the window.

"It's not typically. Cleaners come on Fridays and I haven't been home much."

The window overlooked a small backyard also surrounded by trees. I felt a bit like I was standing in a treehouse. "Your house is incredible."

Ryder emerged from the bathroom, a leather bag in his hand that he quickly shoved into his overnight luggage. "Thanks." He pulled out his phone again and put it to his ear. "Hey man, Cam found Scottie. Yeah. Yeah. You good with watching the bar for a couple days? Cool, thanks, man. I'm dropping Sadie home now, then heading to PDX. You got time to take her on some errands tomorrow? Yeah, I'll give it to her. Thanks. Yep. Okay. 'Bye." He

slid his phone into his pocket and glanced at me. "Reese'll be at your place at eleven tomorrow."

"What if that doesn't work for me?"

"Babe, don't be difficult right now, yeah? If it doesn't work, you can call him, but it's happening and he knows it, so don't dick around with his schedule just because you're pissed at me."

"I wouldn't say I'm *pissed* at you," I grumbled.

"Fine, irritated. Whatever." He swung his bag over his shoulder. "Reese has to pull bar duty as well as watch out for you."

"I'm perfectly capable of watching out for myself, Ryder. This is my point."

"Humor me."

He left the room and again I followed him back out to the kitchen. Once he grabbed his wallet and keys off the island, he handed me my purse and led me to the garage. After entering in a code, he locked the door between the house and car and threw his bag in the trunk.

"Here's a key to the house," he said, handing me a key ring with two keys on it. "The smaller one's for the mail, but I doubt you'll need it. The alarm code is 4122."

"4122, got it." I grabbed his arm as he unlocked the BMW doors. "I'll humor you, honey, okay? We can have a rip-roaring fight about it after you bring Scottie home."

"Appreciate that," he said, and finally cracked a smile...albeit, a small one. "I promise we'll talk more when I get home, yeah?"

I nodded.

"Okay, let's get you home."

I climbed into the car and, with my mind a jumble of thoughts and emotions, we headed to my place.

TWELVE

Sadie

MONDAY MORNING, I awoke to the shrill peal of my cell phone. I'd kept the sound on in case Ryder called and it would appear four a.m. was the earliest he could. Probably a good thing, considering I'd been awake until past midnight worrying. "Hello," I rasped, rubbing the sleep from my eyes.

"Hey, baby," Ryder said. "Just landed."

He sounded wrecked.

"Flight go okay?" I asked.

"Yeah. Can't talk, though. We're heading straight to Scottie."

"Okay, honey. I'll keep praying."

"Thanks. I'll call when I can."

"Okay."

"You okay?" he asked.

I smiled. Even when he needed to go, he was taking time to

make sure I was good. "Yep. Just sleepy."

"Go back to sleep. I'll call soon."

I nodded. "Okay. Stay safe."

"I will, baby."

He hung up and I took a few minutes to pray for him and Scottie before succumbing to sleep again.

* * *

Ryder

Ryder followed Cameron through the Savannah airport and into a taxi waiting at the curb. Cameron gave the driver the address and Ryder pulled a bottle of water out of his bag, taking a swig. "How far's the place?"

"Not far," Cameron said as he studied his phone. "Dalton's meeting us there."

"You're sure she's there."

"As sure as I can be."

Ryder didn't respond. There was nothing he could say. Cameron couldn't control whether or not Scottie had been, or might be moved between the time he'd found out her location up till now. He wiped his sweaty hands on his jeans, attempting to keep his worry buried.

The taxi pulled up to a nondescript building in a rundown area Ryder assumed was on the outskirts of Savannah, and after Cameron paid, they climbed out and headed inside. The cavernous room was dark and empty, and for all intents and purposes, appeared to be abandoned. Ryder followed Cameron toward the back where Cameron paused long enough to enter a code into a panel hidden behind a brick facade. A hidden door popped open and Cameron glanced at Ryder. "This way."

Ryder followed him down a long hallway where, after Cameron entered another code into another panel, they were admitted into a room that looked like an FBI war room.

A man about Ryder's age walked toward them. "Cam, you made it." His southern accent, along with his voice, was deep.

"Hey, Dalt." Cameron shook his hand. "Dalton Moore, Ryder Carsen."

Ryder shook the man's hand, forcing down the desire to demand to see his sister. He knew there were protocols. Knew he had to be patient...even if he didn't like it.

"So, we've got a lock on your sister, and we'll get her out, but we've hit a snag. There are about ten other young women with her, so we don't want to barge in guns blazing until we know we can get them out safely."

"Damn," Ryder breathed out. "You're sure she's in there?"

"Yeah, man. Visual confirmation."

Well, that was something at least. Ryder dropped his bag on the ground and paced the room while Dalton's team of six men and one woman did whatever the hell they did.

Cameron stood in the corner with Dalton and studied a computer screen as Ryder walked from one end of the room to the other like an idiot unable to help. He was completely impotent and it pissed him off. His phone buzzed and he glanced at the screen, his mood lifting to see a text from Sadie.

Hey, honey. Woke up suddenly. Hope you're okay. Remember, you got this. I believe in you, so does Scottie. Be at peace, sweetheart.

Ryder closed his eyes and took a deep breath, taking her words to heart. Beautiful didn't begin to describe her and he smiled inside at her sweetness.

"Ryder?" Cameron called.

"Yeah."

"Ready?" he asked.

Ryder nodded.

"We're driving, but getting out a block away," Cameron informed him.

"Okay."

"You'll stay in the car," Dalton ordered, before leading them around the corner then through a battered wooden door.

"Hell no."

"He'll hang back," Cameron argued. "Won't you, Ride?"

Ryder scowled, but gave a nod. He agreed somewhat loosely. If anyone came between him and getting his sister to safety, he would *not* hesitate to put them down. He fisted and unfisted his

hands as he followed the men into the black SUV. He desperately wanted to hit something...or someone, but he was stuck for the moment. They drove in tense silence for less than five minutes, pulling behind a brick building, the area around it vacant.

"Stay with the vehicle," Dalton ordered, as they climbed out of the SUV. Before Ryder could so much as argue, Dalton led his team around the corner, disappearing from view.

Gunfire came from within the building. Unarmed, Ryder wasn't sure what he could do, but he had to do something. Damn it! He needed to find Scottie. What if his sister became collateral damage? What if she was shot in the fray?

Screw it, he was goin' in. Hugging the house, he slid through the ratty screen door, nearly tripping over a body. Bending down, he checked for a pulse. Nothing. He was relieved that the dead man wasn't one of Cameron or Dalton's men, so that was at least one less threat. Lucky for him, the shithead had a gun. Ryder took it and crept toward the dark hallway. It was eerily quiet between rounds of gunfire coming from deeper within the house. He could hear creaking from above him, along with scuffling of feet and a din of men yelling between gunfire.

Ryder inched along the hallway, circumventing trash (including needles and food) on the ground. He stalled when he heard female voices on the other side of the wall. He stopped in front of a door that was slightly ajar and gripped his gun tighter. Taking a deep breath, he turned the doorknob, planted his feet, and aimed into the room.

"I can't move, Molly, I think my leg is broken. But as soon as you can, go."

"No, Scottie, I won't leave you," a young voice argued.

"You have to. You have to get help."

Glancing inside, he observed a window barred by iron allowed a little light into the room, but not much. A scream bounced off the walls and he stepped further into the room.

"Shhh," Scottie hissed. "Molly, quit screaming. *Please.*"

"Scottie, it's me," he said.

A whimper and another "shh" from Scottie.

"Scottie?" he said again, heading to what he assumed was a

closet door. "It's me."

"Ryder?"

"Yeah, honey. Come out." He reached for his phone, engaging the flashlight and sweeping it around the room before pulling open the closet door. The light fell on his sister, and he swore. Her face was so swollen, had he not heard her voice, he might not have known it was her.

With a groan of pain, his sister burst into tears and reached for him. He fell to his knees and pulled her into his arms. "You came for me," she sobbed.

He stroked her hair. "Baby girl, of course I came for you."

"I thought you hated me."

"Never. I could never hate you, honey."

"I'm so sorry," she whispered. "I was stupid. I should have listened to you."

"I forgive you, baby girl. I've got you."

She continued to sob, and Ryder pulled her close. "We need to get you out of here, sissy. I need you to pull yourself together for a minute. Can your friend walk?"

"Molly, her name's Molly."

Ryder nodded. "Molly, can you walk?"

"Yes," the little girl rasped.

"I can't, Ride," Scottie said.

He took a deep breath, shoving his rage deep inside. It wouldn't help them right now. He needed to get her out of there and to the hospital. "Your leg is broken?"

"Feels like it," she said.

"How many people are here?" Ryder asked. "Do you know?"

"Usually there are three or four," Scottie said.

"Okay, honey, I'm gonna lift you. Then we're getting the hell out of here. Molly, you need to keep up."

Ryder lifted Scottie easily in his arms, an indication she'd lost weight, which pissed him off even more as he moved as quietly as possible back the way he came. Molly's tiny hand gripped his jeans and he felt her hold on as he tugged her with them.

The gunfire had stopped for the moment and they made it out of the house without further incident. Walking quickly out to the

front of the house and to where the cars were waiting, he got the girls to safety.

"I'm going to be sick," Scottie warned, and Ryder set her down and held her hair back.

"Ryder!" Cameron bellowed.

"Here," he called back. "I've got Scottie and another girl."

As Cameron and Dalton approached, Ryder heard Dalton let out a series of curses and then give Cameron a blistering about his "buddy" and his issues with boundaries.

Cameron talked Dalton down and Ryder focused back on his sister. He held onto his anger as they loaded the girls (thirteen in total) into ambulances. He rode with Scottie and Molly (barely eleven years old) while Dalton and Cameron debriefed the local law enforcement. He held onto his anger while his sister whimpered in pain as she was poked and prodded by the doctors, and he held onto it when he was informed that not only was her leg broken, she had a fractured eye socket and three ribs that had been broken days ago and not treated.

Without warning, one of the nurses made an urgent call for a doctor while another stepped in front of him. "Sir, we need to take your sister into surgery."

"What's going on?"

"As soon as I know anything, I will come and find you. A nurse will bring you some forms to sign," she said, gently. "*Please.* Let us help your sister."

He was shoved out of the room and left to pace the hallway alone.

* * *

He'd been in the waiting room for almost an hour when his phone rang and he answered without looking at the screen. "Ryder."

"Hey," Sadie said. "I'm sorry, are you in the middle of stuff?"

Ryder let out a deep breath. "No, baby. It's over. We found her."

"Oh, honey, I'm so glad. Are you bringing her home?"

"Not right now. She's in surgery."

Sadie gasped. "What happened?"

"I don't know, they shoved me out of the room and took her in-

to surgery."

"What do the doctors say?"

"I don't *know*, Sadie. I'm waitin' for them to find me."

She sighed. "Sorry, honey."

"Mr. Carsen?"

Ryder glanced up to see a nurse standing at the edge of the waiting room. "Sadie, I need to go."

"Right. Of course. I'll check in with you later."

"Thanks, baby." He hung up and rose to his feet. "I'm Ryder Carsen."

The nurse smiled. "The doctor asked me to update you. Scarlett has hemorrhaged after a miscarriage, but surgery is going very well and the doctor is confident there won't be any permanent damage."

"She was pregnant?"

"Yes. About six weeks along."

He crossed his arms in an effort not to hit the wall. "Shit."

"We're going to take really good care of her." The nurse squeezed his arm. "I'll come and get you when she's in recovery."

She walked away and Ryder settled himself into a waiting room chair. It was gonna be a long wait.

* * *

Sadie

I hung up and flopped back onto my mattress, messing up the bed I'd just made, but I didn't care. I didn't like the way Ryder sounded. Defeated. Angry. Sad. I didn't have time to dwell on the phone call though, because my doorbell rang. I checked the peephole. Reese stood on the doorstep, waiting. I pulled the door open. "Hi, Reese."

"Hey, Sadie."

"I need to go to the airport."

"Come again?" he asked, walking inside.

"Ryder found Scottie, but she's in surgery, so I think it's bad. I think he's going to be stuck in Savannah for longer than expected."

"Babe, I don't know that that's a good idea."

I shrugged. "I don't care."

"When's the flight?" he asked.

"I haven't booked one yet."

"You're tellin' me you're goin' but you haven't booked a ticket."

"No, but I will."

"Sadie, you can't go to Savannah."

"I'm going, Reese. I'm a grown woman and you don't get to make that call." Reese swore, looking ready for a tirade, but I held my hand up. "You're not going to scare me off this road with your gruff facade, buddy."

"Damn it, Sadie, if I let you go to Savannah, Ryder'll lose his shit."

"No he won't." I crossed my arms. "He found Scottie, so the dangerous part is over. His sister's really hurt, Reese. He needs a friend."

"Cam's there."

"He needs *me*."

Reese dropped his head back and stared at the ceiling. I was pretty sure he muttered the F-word a few times to the sky, but I chose to ignore that fact and headed to my room to pack. I heard him talking on the phone as I grabbed a bag from my closet and threw it on the bed, then I stepped to my doorway and called, "Don't you dare tattle on me, Reese!"

He swore again and then my front door opened and closed and I was left to my own devices. Instead of packing, I opened my laptop and searched for a flight. No matter how big and frightening Reese was, if I had a ticket in hand, he couldn't object.

I started calling random airlines until I found one that had a flight.

Fifteen minutes later, I had the last seat (in first class which was going to put a dent in my savings but was worth it) on the redeye out of Portland.

My front door opened again and Reese's heavy footsteps clomped down the hallway. "You decent?" he called.

"Yes, of course I'm decent," I called back.

He stepped into the room and handed me his phone. "It's Ryder."

"Really, Reese? You tattled? Of course you tattled. What are you, like six?" I snapped.

Reese shook his head and left the room, but I didn't miss his slight smile.

"Hey, honey."

"What's this about wanting to come to Savannah?" Ryder asked.

"I don't *want* to come. I *am* coming. I arrive in the morning."

"You got a flight?" he asked, surprised.

"Yes. It was the last seat on the plane." I bit my lip. "I really want to be there with you, Ryder. If you don't want me, I'll cancel it, but it was really expensive, and I think I'm past the refund point, so…"

I heard him sigh. "Baby," he whispered.

I blinked back tears as my heart broke a little. He didn't need me. I was useless to him. "It's okay. I'll cancel the flight."

"No, don't," he rushed to say. "God, Sadie, you have no idea how much I need you right now, but I don't want you to feel pressured into coming. You sure you're okay with being here for this? It's not a good situation."

"Yes, of course I'm okay with coming." I forced myself not to do a happy dance. "I can see this might take some time for you to really *get*, but I'm here for you, honey. In the good times and especially in the bad."

"You're amazing."

In that moment, as I heard the relief in his voice, I knew I was in love with him. "I don't know about that, but I'm happy for you to think it."

He chuckled quietly. "Text me your flight info and I'll pick you up."

"No, I want you to focus on your sister. I'll grab a cab to the hospital."

"Not up for discussion, Sadie."

"Your sister needs you."

"And I need you, so I'm picking you up."

I sighed. "Okay. But if something happens and she needs you more, text me and I'll take a cab."

"Sure," he said, unconvincingly.

"I have a while until I have to be at the airport, so if you need anything, let me know, okay?"

"Yeah." I heard relief in his voice as he added, "Sadie?"

"Hmm?"

"Thanks, honey. You have no idea..."

I laid my hand on my chest to calm my heart. "I think I do."

"I hope so."

"Okay." I smiled. "I'll see you in the morning."

"'Bye, baby."

He hung up and I took a minute to revel in my brilliant plan.

"You done?" Reese asked.

I jumped at Reese's question. "Um, yes." I handed him his phone. "I'm not happy you went behind my back, just so you know."

"Don't much care," he retorted.

"I'm picking up on that," I grumbled.

"Look, Sadie, I'm not tryin' to be a dick, but Ryder and I are tight. You, I don't know, so if he wants you to stay put, you're gonna stay put."

"To clarify, you'd kidnap me?"

He swore again and the leveled me with a stare. "No, I would not kidnap you, Sadie, but I might hack into the airline's ticketing system and cancel your ticket."

I gasped. "You *wouldn't!*"

"If Ryder wanted you to stay put, I would."

"Well, FYI, he doesn't want me to stay put."

"Yeah, he told me."

"Right." I squared my shoulders in an attempt to brush off his coldness. "Well, I need to pack, then clean, then catch a cab, so for now, you're off duty."

He shook his head. "I'm taking you to the airport."

"You don't need to do that."

"Yeah, I actually do.

"You must have stuff to do between now and ten tonight."

"Yeah, I'm gonna grab some lunch."

My stomach rumbled and I covered it with my hand.

Reese raised an eyebrow. "You want me to pick you up something?"

"Where are you going?"

"Probably Chinese."

I swallowed. Wow, that sounded so good. "Would you mind?"

"Not a problem, Sadie. What do you want?"

I led him back out to the kitchen where I grabbed paper and a pen and jotted down my order. I tried to give him money, but he refused it and walked out the door.

Relief covered me when he left. I liked Reese, sort of, but he put me on edge. I knew he was wholly loyal to Ryder, so I didn't feel unsafe, but I also didn't like feeling as if I were being monitored. His whole "report back to Ryder" thing needed to stop. Better yet, Ryder's need to have him watch me needed to stop. As soon as Scottie was home safe, I planned to have a conversation with Ryder and sort it out.

Reese drove me to the airport two hours before my flight. I'd never been on a plane, and even though I watched a lot of movies and television, I still didn't really know what I was doing. I wanted all the time I could get to figure things out.

"You got your boarding pass?" Reese asked as he drove.

"I have it on my phone. I hope."

"You didn't check?"

"Yes, I checked, but since I've never done this before, I am leaving room for my ineptitude," I snapped, sarcastically. Good lord, he seemed to forget I was a relatively intellegent grown woman.

"Babe," Reese ground out and then grumbled something else under his breath and I was glad I didn't know exactly what he said. My stomach churned and I felt suddenly like an errant child at his disapproval. I had begun to despise "babe" when said by Reese (and Ryder, for that matter), because it was usually said with an irritating tone, and said to admonish rather than endear.

Reese drove into the short term parking and I frowned. "I thought you were dropping me at the curb."

"Sadie, you don't know what the hell you're doin'."

"I'm sure I can figure it out," I snapped.

He took a deep breath and I noticed his jaw lock briefly. "I'll walk you in, make sure you make it through security, then we'll be all good."

"I'm not a child, Reese!"

"I'm aware, Sadie, but you *are* Ryder's woman and he's asked me to make sure you're safe."

"Have you ever considered you don't get paid enough to babysit me this closely?"

"Every moment of every frickin' day."

(He didn't say 'frickin''...he used his standard F-bomb)

I crossed my arms and stared out the window as we maneuvered the parking lot.

After we parked, Reese held out his hand. "Phone."

"I'm sorry?"

"Give me your phone."

"Please let me see your phone, Sadie," I directed.

He scowled at me but didn't adjust his attitude, so I slapped my phone into his hand.

"Do you know what you're doin' with this?" he asked.

"I pull up the boarding pass, rub my phone under my arm...three swipes...sneeze on it, then hand it to the flight attendant."

His lips twitched slightly as he handed the phone back. "You don't hand it to the flight attendant, Sadie. You have it ready for the security people then hand it to the gate attendant."

"Got it."

"You sure?"

"Holy mother of God, Reese, I'm not an idiot!" I let out a frustrated squeak. "I will give Ryder some leeway when it comes to his protectiveness and occasional tendency to be a bully. I know he does it because he cares about me and he's seen the worst humanity can offer. But you don't get to do this with me. I will figure this out."

"Right," he said, and climbed out of the car, leaving me in my seat without so much as an acknowledgement he'd even heard me.

I stowed my anger, mostly because it was only affecting me at the moment and, after he grabbed my bag, I followed him inside

the building.

He walked with me to security. In fact, he walked as far as he could before he had to step out of the line. I chose to ignore him the rest of the way, but I knew he waited until he couldn't see me anymore...he probably did it just to irritate me. I might find him sweet if he wasn't such a jerk.

I made it onto the plane without incident and forced myself to forget about Reese and his overbearing nature.

THIRTEEN

Sadie

THE PLANE TOUCHED down in Savannah early the next morning, and I had to admit, flying first class didn't suck. I hadn't checked any bags, so I took a minute to stop in the ladies' room and freshen up a bit, texting Ryder as I left the bathroom.

I headed toward the end of the secure area, but instead of finding Ryder waiting outside baggage claim, he stood just beyond the security barriers, holding a bouquet of orange roses. His face lit up when he saw me, and I took a running leap at him, throwing myself into his arms.

He lifted me off my feet, kissing my neck and then my lips. "Hey, baby."

"Hi," I whispered, hugging him tight.

He lowered me to my feet and stroked my cheek. "I can't believe you're here."

"Ditto." I leaned into his touch. "How's your sister?"

"She's better. She came through surgery well, but she's going to be in the hospital for most of the week."

"That's great," I said, relieved. "Shall we go there first?"

"Visiting hours are over, but it's okay...she's asleep. They're gonna call me if she wakes up. She's also heavily guarded, so she's safe." He smiled. "How about we head to breakfast, then I'll take you to your hotel."

"Oh, shoot, I forgot to book a hotel room!"

Ryder chuckled. "I've got it covered, baby."

"You do?"

"I booked the room adjoining mine."

"You're amazing." I leaned against him with a smile. "Thanks, honey."

"Before you put on the hero worship, I debated on telling you the hotel was full so you'd be forced to sleep with me."

"You're ridiculous." I giggled. "Still amazing, but also ridiculous."

"I'm gonna want to keep the door between our rooms open as much as possible." He grabbed my bag, handed me the roses, and then wrapped an arm around my waist. "You've been warned."

"I can live with that."

"Good answer." He kissed my temple and led me to his rental car. "How was the flight? Did you navigate the airport okay?"

"You mean, did Reese hold my hand and lead me around like a child?" I retorted. "Yes."

"I didn't ask him to do that, Sadie."

"Well, he did it anyway," I said with a frown.

"I'll talk to him."

I sighed. "No, don't. You have enough on your plate. I'm just a little tired. I'm sure Reese was just trying to help."

"Yeah, baby, he would have been. Let's get you something to eat and maybe a nap."

"Probably a good plan."

After breakfast, Ryder drove me to the hotel. He'd checked in with the hospital three times while we were at the restaurant and Scottie was still sleeping on an off and barely lucid, so there was

time for me to unpack and maybe even shower.

He pushed open the door and I took in the space. A king-sized bed sat against the west wall, a sofa and coffee table next to it. Around the corner was a marble bathroom, and the window overlooked Savannah. It was beautiful to say the least.

"The room's really nice, honey," I said as he followed me inside. "A little fancy, don't you think?"

"I'm a fancy guy."

I smiled. "Right, I forgot about that."

He chuckled, taking a moment to kiss me thoroughly before opening the door between our rooms.

"Tell me what happened with Scottie," I said as I opened my bag and pulled out my bathroom supplies.

He filled me in, although I had a feeling he was leaving a few details out. What he told me was horrific enough, but I wanted him to feel like he could tell me everything if he needed to.

I bit my lip as I asked, "Eleven years old?"

"Yeah," he breathed out. "Just turned eleven and she'd been in the house about a week. The reason Scottie was so badly beaten was because she'd gotten between one of the men and Molly in an effort to protect her."

I gasped. "Oh, honey, that's awful."

He nodded, running his hands through his hair as he sat on the edge of the bed.

"How many girls were there all together?"

"Thirteen."

I made my way to him, sliding between his open legs and wrapping my arms around his neck. "I don't even want to think about what might have happened if the authorities hadn't found them."

He shook his head, settling his cheek to my chest, pulling me closer. "Me neither."

I ran my fingers through his hair and took a minute to pray. "You did good, Ryder."

"Not good enough to find her sooner."

"Honey, you helped to rescue twelve young girls *and* Scottie. You absolutely were good enough."

He dropped his head back to meet my eyes and studied me, sliding his hand to my neck and drawing me close, nose to nose.

"Do you know how beautiful you are?"

"Ryder."

"You calm me, you make me feel safe, as weird as that sounds. I don't feel out of control when I'm with you. You steady me. You make me want to be better...a man worthy of you. A man worthy of your world."

"Honey." I blinked back tears as I stroked his beard.

"Thank you for coming, baby. I seriously think I'd go off the rails if you weren't here."

"I'm happy to be the third rail so to speak...keep you electrified and on course."

He burst out laughing, pulling me to him. "Damn, you're funny."

"I needed to get off the heavy subject," I admitted.

"Okay, baby, I get it. Apparently, I'm the romantic in this relationship."

I slid my hands back in his hair. "I don't have a whole lot of experience in this department, but I think that's a good assumption to go with."

"I'll be your romance guide, baby."

"Thank you." I kissed him gently.

Ryder shifted and pulled his phone out of his front pocket, keeping me anchored to him. "Ryder Carsen. Yeah. Be there in five. Okay, thanks." He hung up and kissed me quickly. "Scottie's waking up. I want to get there before she's fully lucid."

"Of course." I smiled. "Do you want me to come with you?"

"Always."

"Ryder." I squeezed his shoulders. "It's okay if you want time alone with your sister. I don't mind."

He rose to his feet and lifted my hand to his lips, kissing my palm. "I'm gonna say this once, yeah? There will always be a place for you with me, Sadie. You never have to question whether or not it's the right thing. I like you. I like being close to you, so considering the fact I have to go and see my baby sister who's been beat to shit, I'd really like my train conductor there to make sure I don't

touch the third rail."

"No, honey, I *am* the third rail...I keep you electrified."

"Oh, right. Okay, third rail, electrify me."

I couldn't help but giggle. "Okay, Shakespeare. I'll come with you."

"Thanks, baby."

He kissed me one more time then led me out to the car and drove to the hospital.

* * *

Once inside, Ryder gripped my hand as we walked down the hallways and into ICU where his sister was recovering. I bit back a whimper at the sight of the tiny woman in the large bed. Her face was swollen, a bandage around her head, her leg elevated, also wrapped in copious amounts of bandage. I'd seen women broken and bruised from domestic violence before, but nothing as bad as this.

"You okay?" Ryder whispered, turning to face me.

"Yes. I'm okay." I blinked up at him and hoped I sounded convincing. We hadn't had time for a nap, so my exhaustion added to my general emotional-ness.

Ryder kissed my forehead then approached his sister's side. "Scottie?"

It took a few minutes, but Scottie finally opened the eye that wasn't swollen shut and burst into tears.

"Hey, baby girl. None of that," he crooned, and kissed her fingers (pretty much the only part of her body not bandaged).

"I'm sorry, Ride."

"Shhh. You're okay." He smiled. "I want to introduce you to someone."

"Ryder," I objected. "I'm not sure—"

"It's okay, Sadie," he interrupted.

I widened my eyes, then tried a glare, but he gave me nothing. The poor girl was not at her best and if I were her, the last thing I'd want, especially if I were in the hospital, would be to be introduced to a stranger. Ryder ignored my facial cues and waved me over.

"Ryder," I whispered.

"It's fine, Sadie."

I stepped to the bed and smiled down at Scottie. "I'm sorry, Scottie. I hope I'm not making you feel more uncomfortable."

"Scottie, this is Sadie." Ryder wrapped an arm around my waist. "Your future sister-in-law."

"What?" I said in shock. "He's joking."

"I'm not," he corrected, and an obnoxious smile covered his face.

"Ryd—"

"No point in arguing." Scottie reached her hand out to me. "If he said it, he means it," she rasped.

That freaked me out a little more than I expected, but I soldiered on.

"It's nice to meet you." I gave her hand a gentle squeeze. "I'm sorry I'm invading your space right now."

"It's okay." She yawned, shifting on the bed with a groan.

"You're in pain," Ryder deduced.

"I'll get a nurse," I offered.

"No. I got it," Scottie said, and pressed a red button next to her. Her body sank into the bed as she let out a sigh of relief.

I made my way to the chair by the window. Ryder sat on the bed beside her and held her hand. They chatted quietly as I tried not to listen.

"You must be Ryder," a soft, southern voice said, and I glanced up to see a pretty blonde nurse walking into the room.

"Yeah," he said.

"I'm Andi. I'm your sister's nurse for the next eight hours, so if you need anything, let me know. I'm just going to check her out real quick."

Ryder nodded and stepped away from the bed, sitting on the window seat next to my chair as Andi ran through vitals with Scottie.

I took Ryder's hand and gave it a squeeze. His face was pinched tight with worry, but he relaxed a bit and smiled gently.

"She's okay," I whispered.

He gave me a slight nod, but nothing more.

"Everything looks good, Scottie," Andi said. "When you're feeling up to it, Molly's been asking if she can visit."

Scottie sat up a little. "Is she okay?"

"She's doing great, hon."

"I'd like to see her."

"Maybe you should wait a bit," Ryder said.

"No, I want to see her," Scottie insisted.

Ryder stiffened. "You're still healing, Scottie. I think you should wait."

I squeezed his hand and got a scowl for my efforts, but I didn't back down. Scottie had been through trauma and she needed to make sure Molly was okay. "Honey," I whispered.

"I want to see her," Scottie insisted, ignoring her brother.

Andi smiled, patting her arm. "I'll bring her down in a little bit."

Scottie relaxed against the pillows again. "Thank you."

"I'm just going to borrow your brother for a minute," I said as I stood.

Ryder shook his head. "I don't want to leave her."

"We'll be right outside," I insisted, and tugged on his hand.

He reluctantly followed me into the hall, scowling as I faced him. "Wipe it," I demanded.

"What?"

"That churlish look off your face. Wipe it."

"Sadie," he snapped, dragging a hand over his beard.

"No. You're being a jerk. Stop it. Your sister has endured horrific trauma and—"

"One she brought on herself," he said, ungraciously.

I let out a quiet hiss. "Wow."

"Shit, babe, sorry. Saying it out loud makes me sound like a dick."

"Well, you're right about that."

"I don't know how to do this," he rasped. "I don't know how to watch her tiny, beaten, and bruised body lie in a bed two sizes too big while people poke and prod her. I don't know how to help her with the inevitable emotional pain that's gonna come because she lost a baby, especially when I'm happy about it. God, Sadie, she was raped repeatedly and got fuckin' pregnant! How the hell do you come back from that?"

"You love her."

He shook his head. "If she'd just listened to me—"

"Okay," I interrupted, laying my palms against his chest and dropping my head back to catch his eye. "You need to start by stopping the blame game. You both made mistakes, but you need to learn from yours and move forward. She'll have to do the same, but you have to *love* her now. Unconditionally. She needs you to support her, not judge her, and she will eventually need you to loosen the reins so she can be an adult, but for now, let's start small."

He slid his arms around my waist. "I'm sorry."

"Don't be," I said. "You get to be you whenever you're with me. That's the deal. I don't want the you that's holding back. I want all of you, so never feel like you have to filter. I might be small, but I have strong shoulders and if it means Scottie gets the filtered you for now, I'm all in."

Ryder grimaced. "I don't know if I can do this alone."

"Honey, you're *not* doing it alone." I patted his chest. "I'm here."

He relaxed, pulling me closer. "I forget that sometimes."

I hugged him tightly. "When you do, I'll remind you."

"Thank you."

"You're welcome." I smiled up at him. "Now, let's get back in there."

He kissed me gently and then led me back into the room.

FOURTEEN

Sadie

THREE DAYS LATER, Scottie was up and moving around. She was on crutches, but for the most part, she was able to hobble a few feet at a time, which was what the doctors wanted her to do.

I spent much of my time talking Ryder down off ledges, but as Scottie improved, he relaxed a bit more. As much as Ryder *could* relax, that is. Cameron had "men" posted outside Scottie's room twenty-four-seven, and the rest of the girls were on lockdown as well.

Molly was a bit of a worry. She had no family and had been in the foster care system for three years before she was taken from her bus stop. At least, that's what her foster family said happened. Cameron had done some investigation and suspected her foster father had something to do with her kidnapping, so she was now back in the care of the state and Scottie was not happy with that

fact...which instigated the current argument.

"You have to do something, Ryder," she said.

"What can I do?" Ryder asked. "She's not my kid."

"Figure it out. She can't go back into the system."

"She's already *in* the system," he'd snapped.

"Then find out how to get her out," she countered.

"Pain in the ass."

"Okay," I interjected. "This isn't getting us anywhere."

"I'm really tired," Scottie whispered. "I'm going to sleep for a while. A *long* while."

I squeezed her hand. "We'll get out of your hair for a bit, huh?"

"I think we should stay," Ryder countered. "Visiting hours aren't over."

"Sadie," Scottie begged. "Take him away, please. For at least four hours. Make him take a nap."

Ryder crossed his arms. "I don't nap."

"Yeah, he failed that part of kindergarten," Scottie droned.

I smiled. "Four hours...we'll be back at the beginning of the next visiting hour timeslot."

"Thank you," she whispered as she gave me a grateful smile.

I dragged Ryder out of her room and to the rental car.

"I don't know what she expects me to do," Ryder snapped as we drove to the hotel. "I'm supposed to be protecting her and she wants me gone. And then there's the Molly situation. What the hell am I supposed to do about her?"

"I have an idea." I pulled out my phone and called my aunt. Within minutes, Auntie had agreed to see if she could get permission to bring Molly across state lines. I hung up and grinned at Ryder as we sat in the parking lot of the hotel.

"What made you think of that?" he asked.

"She's a licensed foster parent. If they want to try to find Molly's relatives, Auntie could offer her a safe place to land for a while at least. Then Scottie would be close."

"You're a genius." He stroked my cheek, tugging me forward to kiss me.

I grinned against his lips. "You're easy to please."

He rolled his eyes. "You're the only one on the planet who

thinks so."

I couldn't stop a giggle. "Maybe so."

"You hungry or tired?"

"Honestly? Both."

"Food then nap."

"Food then swim then nap?" I countered.

"I can work with that."

"See?" I said. "Easy."

He chuckled and led me up to our rooms. Savannah was experiencing record temperatures and there were strict visiting hours at the hospital, leaving us pockets of time with nothing to do. Since the hotel had a great pool and hot tub, we bought swimsuits the day after we arrived.

Much to his objection, I'd chosen a tame, but very cute black one-piece. I tried on *one* bikini (because he'd picked it out and begged me to at least try it) and his eyes nearly bugged out of his head, so I figured that was just borrowing trouble. It's not that he didn't push me into the dressing room and kiss me senseless after showing him the one piece, but the bikini elicited a different expression from him and it not only turned me on, but made me a little nervous as well.

I wanted him with a desire I'd never experienced and I knew that if we didn't both exercise some self-control, it would be very easy one night to forget everything I believed in.

"You ready?" he asked, knocking on the connecting door of my room.

I pulled it open with a grin. "Yep."

I swallowed, taking in all of his beauty. He wore a pair of what he called board shorts. They were black with a cargo pocket on the right leg, and they sat low on his hips and skimmed his knees, but his bare chest was something remarkable to behold. Obviously, God took a little extra time when carving him out of stone.

"Babe?"

I blinked up at him...hard to do when I wanted to continue to stare at his body...and maybe lick him.

Holy mother of—yes, failed nun indeed.

"You keep staring at me like that and we're gonna skip the

pool," he warned.

"Sorry," I said with a groan. "I knew you'd be gorgeous, but I wasn't expecting perfect."

His mouth slammed against mine and I was guided back onto the bed and stretched out on the mattress. His lips never left mine as he pulled me close, the only material between us very thin lycra.

"Shit!" he hissed, breaking the kiss and falling onto his back. I bit my lip and slid off the bed, standing next to it as Ryder pulled himself together.

He sat up and ran his hands down his face. "I'm sorry, Sadie."

"Why?"

"Because I just accosted you, which I promised I wouldn't do."

"You didn't really accost me," I countered. "I was kind of a willing participant."

"Yeah, I picked up on that." He gave a defeated chuckle. "Let's get down to the pool. I obviously need to cool down."

"Not just you."

He climbed off the bed and kissed me again, this time a lot tamer than before. "You might kill me, you know."

"Please don't be mad."

"I'm not mad, baby." He ran his thumb along my lower lip. "Just want more and that's frustrating. But I'm not going anywhere, yeah?"

I nodded. "Me neither."

"Good."

"And, FYI, I want more too."

"I know, baby." He smiled, took my hand, and led me down to the pool.

* * *

One week later, Scottie was cleared to travel home. She, however, refused to leave without Molly, but Auntie hadn't gotten approval from the foster system to take her, so I was doing my best to keep Ryder from blowing his stack while Scottie dug her heels in.

"I'm going to kill her," Ryder said as he paced his hotel room. Visiting hours were over and we were back at the hotel packing and sorting out flights. "She is the most stubborn—"

"Okay, I think maybe you need to take a minute," I suggested.

"I don't have time for this shit."

"I get it, honey, but Scottie's worried about her friend. If the tables were turned, you'd do the same thing."

"I really don't need you to point out the similarities between myself and my sister right now, Sadie."

I stifled a smile and went back to my sorting.

"What did your aunt say?" he asked.

"She hasn't called back." I checked my phone. Still nothing. "It takes time, honey, you know this. It's the government, after all."

He swore, dragging his hands down his face. "I'm done. She's getting on the plane tomorrow, even if I have to drug her and drag her on unconscious."

I closed the distance between us, linking our fingers together (mostly to keep him from punching a wall), and smiled up at him. "I understand you're frustrated, and I totally get that this is because you love your sister and want her close so you can protect her, but—" He scoffed, but I wouldn't be deterred. "*But* she's been through a trauma...one that hasn't fully hit her yet, but it will, and when it does, you are going to have to be patient and sweet, and let her freak out without reacting...at least not in front of her. So until she can get into some intensive counseling, you need to speak your patience out loud. Fake it till you make it, if you have to."

"Sadie," he said with a groan.

"She's smart, Ryder. Like you. So she's picking up on your irritation, and she's pushing back because she needs to be in control of something. She's spent the last couple of months being raped--"

His hiss was almost as violent as a fist slamming into a wall.

"You need to hear the word, honey, because she needs you to wrap her in your big strong arms and hold her like a child...not threaten to drug her in order to get her to do your bidding."

"I wasn't going to let her hear it, Sadie."

"But she's picking up on it and whether she's willing to admit it or not, it's scaring her."

"I have to get back to the bar or I'll have nowhere to take her home to."

I rolled my eyes. "Business is so bad you can't take a week off without it crashing to the ground enough to lose your home and

everything else?"

"Damn it, Sadie, I'd rather you not be logical right now."

"Everything's going to work out the way it's supposed to work out, Ryder, so relax a bit, okay?" I rose up on my tiptoes and kissed him gently. "We'll be home before you know it and you can get to the business of getting Scottie happy and healthy."

"What about you?"

"What about me?"

"I want to make you happy too," he said.

"It's not your job to make me happy, but you do, almost without trying." I smiled. "Focus on your sister. I'm good."

He stroked his beard. "So, you're saying I don't have to try?"

I giggled. "That's what you took from that?"

"I may have inferred a bit."

"Hm-mmm, just a bit."

Ryder's phone sounded from his room and he left me to answer it. When he didn't come back for several minutes, I went looking for him. He sat on his bed his head dropped in one hand, his body rigid. "When? Yeah? Shit, Reese, you check the video? Damn it! Yeah, okay. We should be back tomorrow. I'll talk to Cameron and see if he can figure somethin' out. Yeah. Okay. I'll text you the flight number when I have it. 'Bye." He hung up and shook his head.

"You okay?" I asked, trying to giving him space, but concerned enough not to give him too much.

"No, baby, I'm not."

I stepped into his room and over to him, sliding between his legs. "Tell me."

He sighed and wrapped his arms around me. "Girls are goin' missin' from the club and FBI's pokin' around."

"Missing how?"

"Last seen at the Frog," he said. "Missing persons filed on almost all of them...a couple though...no one's lookin' for 'em. Reese checked the video footage and they were all there."

"How many?"

"Six so far."

I gasped. "All last seen at your bar?"

He nodded. "Another one disappeared Friday night. Also last seen at the Frog."

"That's awful."

"FBI thought I knew something. At least, they did until I came here, and two have gone missing since I left."

"Ryder," I said with a groan, stroking the back of his neck. "How could they possibly think you'd know anything?"

"They're coverin' all their bases, baby. I don't blame 'em for that. They have a job to do."

"I suppose I get it." I frowned. "I just can't imagine anyone looking at you, especially knowing what's going on with your sister."

He shrugged. "Well, they are."

"If you have to get back, I can stay here until we find out about Molly."

"No." He squeezed my hips.

"Why not?"

"Because you're with me. Period."

Before I could argue, my phone sounded and I pulled away to rush to my room. "Hello?"

"Hi, honey."

"Auntie. Hi. Do you have news?" I glanced up when Ryder walked into the room.

"Yes. Molly's approved to come."

I let out a sigh of relief. "I'm so glad. Thank you. For everything."

"It's no problem, sweetheart. Just let me know your flight information and we'll go from there."

"We'll get the next available flight out," I promised.

"Sounds good. I'll talk to you soon."

"Thank you." She hung up and I smiled at Ryder. "It's all set."

He finally relaxed (somewhat) and gave me what I thought was a valiant effort at a smile. "Thanks, baby."

"We'll get home and Scottie and Molly will both be safe."

He nodded.

"It's going to be okay," I promised.

"God, I hope so."

I chuckled. "Yeah, He's on it, honey."

"Smartass."

"Darn tootin'," I retorted.

He kissed me and we spent the rest of the day prepping to take everyone home. By the time I fell into bed, I knew four a.m. would come entirely too early.

FIFTEEN

Sadie

RYDER, SCOTTIE, AND I had been home for about a week before Ryder finally started to act like a human being again. Molly had settled in beautifully and my aunt was hoping she could make the situation permanent. I was dying to cook in Ryder's kitchen, so we planned a dinner party which would include my aunt, Molly, Scottie, Reese, and the two of us. I was learning quickly that whenever Ryder planned anything that didn't include just the two of us, Reese attended. I didn't know how I felt about it, but it wasn't like I could tell Ryder who to be friends with.

The Saturday of our planned banquet, Scottie napped while I cooked, the house alarm engaged and a "guy" posted outside. I wasn't entirely sure what that meant, but since I rarely saw him (his name was Marc, I think), I didn't feel like he was intruding.

I had discovered a kindred spirit in Scottie. She was sweet and

somewhat naive, despite her recent experiences, and she idolized her brother even when giving him grief. (Grief was my word; Ryder's was something far more dramatic and not repeatable).

I was staring out Ryder's large kitchen window, thinking about the events of late, when my phone rang, interrupting my task of peeling potatoes. It was Ryder. I answered and put it on speaker. "Hey, honey."

"Hey, how's the cooking coming?"

"Good. We'll be ready to eat around six."

"Room for one more?"

I glanced at the bag of potatoes. "Ah, sure."

"Thanks, baby."

I wiped the back of my hand over my forehead. "You *are* still going to be home in an hour, right?"

"About that..."

My heart sank as I swept my gaze around the disaster previously resembling a gourmet kitchen. "Oh my word, Ryder." I dropped a potato into the bucket. "You promised."

"I'm kidding, baby."

I let out a quiet groan. "You're a butt."

"I'm aware." He chuckled. "Love that you're in my kitchen and demanding I come home to help though."

I smiled. "I kind of love it too."

"Okay, baby, gotta go. I'll see you in an hour."

"Fifty-seven minutes," I corrected.

Ryder laughed. "You got it. 'Bye."

"'Bye honey."

I hung up and then heard a crash from the back of the house. "Scottie!" I called and moved quickly to her room. "Hey, sweetie, are you okay?"

She sat on the edge of the bed, her crutches at her feet. "I tried to reach them but only managed to knock them over."

I smiled and picked them up for her. "I know you want to be independent, Scottie, but let's not be a hero, okay?"

"I hate this."

"I know," I said gently. "You're a lot like your brother."

"Sorry."

"It's a good thing, sweetie," I assured. "He's my favorite person on earth, so if there are two of you, it's a bonus for me."

Scottie giggled and settled herself on her crutches. "How did my brother get you again?"

I led her out of the bedroom and into the great room. "His protection fetish."

"Ah, right. He's so weird."

I walked slowly as we moved toward the kitchen. "Just the perfect amount of weird for me."

"Can I help?"

"How do you feel about potato peeling?"

"It's my favorite thing in the world," she lied.

I grinned. "Thank the Lord. I need to prep the pies."

"You're baking too?"

"Just a couple of pies. Apple and pumpkin."

"'Just a couple of pies,' she says." Scottie cocked her head. "When are you moving in?"

I giggled. "When he puts a ring on it."

"So, soon," she retorted, and sat at the island.

"Let's not rush things, sweetie."

She picked up a potato and began to peel. "Have you *met* my brother?"

I smiled and washed my hands before grabbing apples to slice. "I doubt your brother's in any hurry."

"Then you're deluding yourself."

I glanced at her. "Don't put pressure on him, okay?"

"Sadie, he loves you. I don't need to pressure him, I'm pretty sure he's feeling it all on his own."

I bit my lip, setting the apple I was peeling on the counter. "You don't really think he feels pressure, do you?"

She shrugged. "Nah. He just hates it when he's not in your presence twenty-four hours a day."

I giggled. "He does not."

"He totally does." She focused on her peeling. "When you're not here at night, he paces the house for, like, *hours*."

"He does *not*."

"Sadie, he totally *does*."

I felt like this conversation wasn't going to make sense anytime soon, so I shut it down. "How are you feeling?" I checked my watch. "You're due for pain meds in about fifteen minutes."

"I'm actually good," she said. "But would you mind grabbing me a pop?"

"Not at all. What would you like?"

"Coke?"

"You got it." I opened the fridge, pulled out a soda, and handed it to her.

"Thanks."

We moved through our tasks silently for several minutes before Scottie paused, pressing her lips into a thin line.

"What, honey?" I prompted.

"Ryder told me you used to be a nun."

"I was."

"Did you like it?"

"Yes," I said. "But I like life now better."

"Because of Ryder?"

I smiled. "Partially, yes."

"Are you allowed to think that?"

I set a bowl in the dishwasher and faced her. "I think so. I think God knows what we truly desire and wants us to live our best life possible."

"Even if we...?"

"What, sweetie?" She shrugged and I leaned across the island and stopped her from peeling.

"Do you think God will remember me?"

"He never forgot you, Scottie."

"But I'm all messed up."

I moved to sit beside her and took her hands. "Honey, we're all messed up."

"But I'm a whore."

"You are not a whore!" I snapped, then realized I needed to be gentle. "Sorry."

"It's okay," she whispered.

"Look, we all have our demons, Scottie. God doesn't ever forsake us."

"Then why did He let this happen?"

Okay, Lord, here are the tough questions. I need some help.

"Sometimes bad things happen to good people, honey. I don't believe God wants it to happen, I think we're just stuck in a world of sin. And sometimes good things happen to bad people. In my very limited experience, it's important to look inside yourself and see where we can make some better choices—"

"Because of Dewy?"

"That's your boyfriend's name?"

I'm pretty sure I didn't succeed in keeping the judgment from my voice...granted, I didn't try very hard...but Dewy? Holy cow. Talk about natural selection just waiting to happen.

"He's not my boyfriend."

"Well, that's good. Particularly if he talked you into running away. It's a good choice to dump him."

Scottie frowned. "Sadie, he didn't talk me into running away."

"Ryder said you dated Dewy—"

She snorted in disgust. "I never dated Dewy. He's disgusting."

"I'm confused," I admitted.

"Taylor dated Dewy."

"Your best friend?"

She nodded.

"Honey, does Ryder know any of this?"

She shook her head.

"Scottie," I breathed out.

"Dewy threatened to hurt her, Sadie. It's the only reason I went with him in the first place."

"Ryder would have helped you."

"Dewy said if I told Ryder, he'd do horrible things to her. He told me in detail all the things he'd do...worse than what happened to me."

I couldn't imagine anything worse than what happened to her, so I felt a little sick.

Scottie grabbed my hand. "He knew her whole schedule, Sadie, and when we were at the mall, he made sure I saw him."

I gave what I hope was a bolstering smile. "Okay, sweetie. I think we should tell Ryder now."

"I can't handle him yelling at me, Sadie."

"He's not going to yell at you, honey."

"Have you met my brother?" she challenged.

"*I* will make sure he doesn't yell at you." I patted her hands. "Okay?"

She gave me a reluctant nod.

"Just focus on getting better, honey. We'll deal with the rest."

I slipped off the stool and went back to the pies while Sadie continued to peel potatoes. I'd just put the roast back in the oven and set the pies on the counter to await baking when I heard the garage door lift. I braced myself for an unpleasant conversation. Ryder walked in, glanced at both of us, and threw his keys in the dish on the desk.

"How's my girl?" he asked, and kissed Scottie's head.

"Good," she all but mumbled.

I wiped my hands and forced a smile. "Let's go have a chat."

Ryder raised his face to the ceiling, dropped the F-bomb, and then headed toward his bedroom without further comment. I squeezed Scottie's shoulder on my way past her and followed Ryder, closing the bedroom door behind me.

"If she's throwin' drama, I'll deal with it."

I crossed my arms. "Why do you assume she's throwing drama?"

"Because she's Scarlett Carsen."

"Ryder, I can handle teenage drama. This is something far more serious."

"What happened?"

I rolled my eyes. "I think you may want to sit down."

"Shit, baby, that bad?" he complained.

I filled him in on what Scottie had told me and bit my lip when I saw the vein on the side of his neck bulge out.

"You can't yell," I commanded.

"Why the hell can't I yell?" he bellowed.

I dragged my hands down my face with a groan. "Because I promised your sister I'd make sure you didn't."

He slid past me and pulled open the door. "Scarlett Fay Carsen, get your butt in here now."

"She's kind of on crutches, Ryder," I reminded him, more than a little ticked now.

"Damn it!" He stalked out of the bedroom (I followed) and into the kitchen where Scottie was trying to maneuver herself down from the island. She'd dropped one of her crutches and was trying to pick it up with the other.

"Wait, Scottie," I said, and rushed to her. "Just stay there. Ryder will come to you and he promises he won't yell." I glared at him. "*Right,* honey?"

He glared right back and leaned against the island, his arms crossed and looking as though he were about to kill someone. In a controlled (non-yelling, but just as scary) voice, he asked, "What's this about the douchebag being Taylor's boyfriend?"

Scottie shrugged. "Um, just that. Dewy and Taylor were dating...actually, they were hooking up more than dating, but yeah, they were together."

So much for the innocent, church-going girl Scottie was negatively influencing.

He took a deep breath. "So, you put your safety on the line for a bitch who lied and essentially threw you under the bus."

"She lied?" Scottie rasped.

"Yeah. Over and over again."

Tears slipped down her cheeks. "He said he'd kill her, Ryder."

"You were raped, Scarlett! Repeatedly, because she *lied*!" He'd kept his cool up until 'lied' which was delivered in a shout. I laid my hand on Scottie's back and gave Ryder a pointed look. "You were kidnapped," he continued, a little calmer, "and kept locked up in a shithole because she lied. I couldn't find you for *months*, little sister, because she *lied*. You lost a child, because she lied."

"I get that," she whispered./

"She's going to have to deal with this."

"Her parents will kill her!" Scottie argued.

"If I don't first, yeah."

"Don't, Ryder. It's done."

"It's not fuckin' done!" he bellowed again. "You were taken from me!"

"And you found me!" she shouted back. "If it had been Taylor,

no one would have looked the way you looked for me."

"Are you sayin' you offered yourself up so the douchebag wouldn't take Taylor?" Ryder's voice was lethal now, and I couldn't stop myself from stepping in front of his sister.

"I'm sure that's not what she's saying," I rushed to say.

"Sadie, stay out of this," he ordered.

I bristled, but didn't object. Now was not the time to read him the riot act. I wasn't stupid enough to poke the bear so I stayed silent.

"I didn't offer myself up, Ride," Scottie said. "It wasn't like that. Dewy threatened to kill her...well, worse than kill her if I didn't go with him. I didn't really take the time to think. It was spur of the moment. I thought we were just going to his house or something. I didn't know that he had other plans."

Ryder didn't get the chance to respond as the sound of a motorcycle roared outside.

"I'm canceling," Ryder announced, and I let out a squeak of frustration.

"I just cooked all this food," I mumbled to myself, even though it was probably a good idea to call the night off.

"Don't," Scottie said. "I want to see Reese. Please, Ryder."

"Reese *is* bringing Auntie and Molly," I pointed out. "I'd hate to make them turn around and go home. Molly, especially, has been looking forward to seeing Scottie."

He dragged his hands down his face. "This conversation isn't over. We're gonna revisit it once I talk to Reese and Cam."

"Can't wait," Scottie ground out, her countenance more irritated than worried.

I threw the pies into the oven just as the doorbell rang and stowed my irritation right along with them. Pasting a smile on my face, I followed Ryder to the door and greeted my aunt.

Dinner was pleasant, if somewhat strained, although I don't know that anyone picked up on any of that. Scottie and Molly were deep in conversation most of the night, while Reese was his normal aloof self and Oliver, one of the "extras", ate like my cooking was the first meal he'd had...well, ever...so I could be irked at Ryder without anyone noticing. When Auntie announced she should get

Molly home, I asked if Reese could take me as well. Scottie had long since crashed due to the pain meds Ryder forced her to take, so it wasn't like I needed to run interference.

"I'm takin' you, babe," Ryder said.

I put on the saccharin. "No need to go to all that trouble, *honey*. Reese can take me."

"Not happening," Ryder said.

Reese glanced at him and then me, then shook his head and muttered to himself.

"Oh, it's happening," I countered.

"I got Molly and your aunt in the car, babe," Reese said. "So, if you're coming, come now."

"She's not," Ryder said, stepping in front of me. "I'll call you later."

"Whatever, man." Reese jogged out to his truck and took off before I could object.

"What the hell, Sadie?" Ryder demanded, closing the door and facing me.

"Um, think back, Ryder."

"Considerin' I missed it the first time, how about you just fill me in on whatever the hell I did. It'll save time and I can get to apologizin'." He cocked his head. "Then we can get to make up kissing and I can show you how grateful I am at how much work you put into tonight."

I jabbed a finger at him. "Stop trying to distract me."

He grinned and pulled me to him. "What did I do?"

"Your biggest offense?"

"There were multiple?" he asked with mock surprise.

I wrinkled my nose. "When you and your sister make me the go-between, and then you tell me to stay out of it hurts my feelings, and honestly, irks me."

He sighed. "Yeah, I can see how that would." He took my hand and tugged me to the sofa, pulling me down on his lap. "I'm sorry, baby."

"Thank you."

Ryder smiled. "What about the rest?"

My irritation was gone in seconds since I knew he took what

I'd said to heart. "The rest isn't that big of a deal, especially since I'm leaving the cleanup for you."

He chuckled. "Fair enough."

"You need to go easy on Scottie, honey."

"I just can't believe she didn't tell me everything."

"Me neither," I conceded. "But she's like you on the protection front and I think she thought she could handle it."

"I'll deal with my sister later." He stroked my cheek. "Right now, I'd like to get to the making out part."

I giggled. "One track mind."

"No doubt." He grinned and kissed me. "Thanks for makin' dinner, baby. It was amazing."

"You're welcome. Cooking in your kitchen is heavenly."

"Wanna do it forever?"

"Huh?"

He kissed me again. "I love you, Sadie. I wanna make this permanent."

"Wow," I breathed out.

"Too soon?"

I shook my head. "I love you too, Ryder. I don't know about making things permanent yet, but I do love you."

He gave me a gentle squeeze. "How about we keep moving forward and I'll figure out something romantic when the time comes to propose."

"You're that sure about us, huh?"

"Hundred percent, Sadie. Told you I don't mess around."

"This is true." I looped my arms around his neck. "Nothing public, okay?"

"Baby, I know you. I'll make it perfect."

"Okay."

"For now, how about I grab you a pair of pajamas, we watch a movie and make out until we fall asleep." He smiled. "I could really use a night with you close."

"Okay, honey. I'd like that."

He kissed me again and then, after I changed into a pair of his pajama bottoms and a T-shirt two sizes too big, we snuggled on the sofa in front of the new Terminator movie until I fell asleep against

his chest. The last thing I thought as I drifted off to sleep was how comfortable he was as a pillow.

SIXTEEN

Sadie

THREE WEEKS LATER, I arrived home looking forward to the long weekend. I'd survived my first week at my new school, but I was tired and already needed a break. I'd seen Ryder the sum total of six hours over the past few days, my work schedule was taking all my energy, and the issues with Scottie taking all of his...not to mention the ongoing investigation for the six girls who had gone missing from the Frog. Ryder upped the club's security and had everyone on high alert, pulling overtime himself in an effort to keep anyone else from disappearing, and it was working. But his diligence meant our time together was limited, so I missed him horribly.

Unlocking my door, I stepped inside and switched on the light. An older man wearing motorcycle boots, jeans, and a leather vest sat on my sofa, his arm leaning against his knee, holding a gun

pointed right at me. I opened my mouth to scream, but a rough hand clamped over my mouth before I could get much sound out, and I was dragged to the chair next to my sofa.

"So you're the bitch who has my son turning over a new leaf," he said. "Never seen him go to church willingly before."

Hatch Carsen.

I didn't know who the other man was, but Hatch and Ryder looked scarily alike, and it made my skin crawl. My heart raced and I felt sick to my stomach. Were they here to kill me? Beat me? Rape me? The options of what might happen were way out of the realm of what my mind could handle.

"If Brick releases you, do you promise not to scream?"

I nodded, desperately wanting the filthy hand removed from my face. Ryder's father nodded to his crony, who stepped back and crossed his arms, blocking my only exit. I wiped my mouth and swallowed. "I thought you were in jail?"

"Witness recanted, which means they can't prove I did anything. Wasted a year of my life, but that's a story for another time."

I didn't know whether or not Ryder knew his father had been released, but now I was even more frightened. How did one get out of jail after being in for only a year? "How did you get into my apartment and what do you want?"

"B and E's a specialty of mine, and as far as what I want? Well, that's easy. I want to know where my girls are."

"What girls?" I asked, trying to figure out what B and E meant.

Hatch sat back, reclining as though he belonged on my sofa...in my living room. "The girls my son stole from me."

I frowned. "I don't know what you're talking about."

"See, darlin', I think you know exactly what I'm talking about, and it pisses me off that you're playin' dumb." He nodded to Brick. "Lucky for you, Brick here likes dumb bitches and bonus, you're pretty, so I'd imagine he's gonna have some fun with you."

I shot off my chair and made a run for my bedroom...I didn't get far. An arm clamped painfully around my waist and I was dragged against Brick's strong body. I screamed and kicked and did everything I could to break his hold, but he just held me tighter.

"Bring her here," Hatch ordered.

Brick threw me on the sofa and my head connected (hard) with the wall, dizzying me. I gasped at the pain. I tried to move again, but Brick slid his hand to my throat and squeezed, holding me to the pillows. I scratched at his arm, but it wouldn't budge.

"Loosen, brother. I don't want her dead...yet."

Brick did as he was ordered and I dragged in as many breaths as I could.

"Ryder currently has in his possession thirteen pieces of property that belong to me. You tell him that if they are not returned, there will be consequences that I'm pretty sure neither of you are willing to deal with."

"They are human beings!" I snapped. "They're not property."

He chuckled, glancing at Brick. "The girl's got spunk. I like that."

Brick grinned, his teeth rotting and yellow. He was terrifying.

"I also like that you've decided to come clean." Hatch leaned forward, his elbows on his knees. "Somethin' you may not know, darlin', is that my apple don't fall far from the tree, so to speak. He's been in the life long enough to know who the players are and how the game is played, and right now, he's playing a dangerous one."

I had no idea what he meant by Ryder being in the life. I probably didn't want to know.

"You are disgusting," I hissed.

"I think she'd fetch a high price, Brick," Hatch continued. "However, not enough to cover what I've already lost, so we'll save her for another time."

Brick licked my face and I tried not to scream again. I was afraid he might kill me if I did.

"The deal is, Sadie, I know where you work. I already have someone watching you, and I know you wouldn't want anything to happen to any of your students."

"What?" I squeaked.

"Isn't there a pretty little blonde girl there, Hayley? I've heard all about her. She's a foster kid who's a handful, from what I understand."

I forced back tears. Hayley Kennedy was actually one of my favorite students. Yes, she was a foster kid, yes she had guts and could come across as bossy sometimes, but she was also über smart and kind to her friends even when they weren't so kind to her. The first to help one of them if they were stuck on an assignment and the first to help me if I ever needed something. I adored her.

"She'd be the perfect addition to our harem, I'm thinking," Hatch said, and my blood ran cold. "No one would miss her."

"*I'd* miss her!" I snapped. "Don't you dare touch her!"

Hatch rose to his feet and walked to my door, turning when he reached it. "Tell Ryder I'm done with games. The girls are delivered to me in forty-eight hours...he'll know where...or he'll experience somethin' worse than hell." He sneered. "And so will you."

He and Brick walked out the door, closed it behind them, and I rushed to lock it, somehow feeling as though that would protect me.

* * *

Ryder

Ryder's phone rang and he smiled. "Hey, baby. Ready for the long weekend?"

"Ryder," he heard Sadie rasp.

He went rigid. "Sadie, what's wrong?" All he heard was sobbing. "Are you at home? Baby, where are you?"

"I'm at home," she hiccupped out.

"What's going on?"

"Can you come?"

"I'm on my way, honey. Don't move."

"I won't. But can you hurry?"

"What happened?"

"I need you," she said. "I won't move, just hurry."

"Okay, baby, I'm on my way." He called Reese as he climbed into the BMW.

"Hey," Reese said.

"Something's wrong with Sadie. Get Ollie and Axel, get to her place, and we'll go from there."

"You got it." Reese hung up and Ryder sped toward Sadie's,

practically daring a cop to pull him over.

Arriving at her apartment, he parked next to the fire lane and made a mad dash up her stairs. The door was locked, so he banged. "Sadie?"

"Ryder?"

"Yeah, honey it's me. Open the door."

"I..."

"Sadie, baby, open the door."

The door inched open and frightened eyes looked out at him, then Sadie pulled the door open fully and stepped back.

Ryder shoved down his panic as he walked inside, closed and locked the door. She paced the floor but moved away when he tried to get close to her. He forced a smile and reached out his hand. He wouldn't touch her until she was ready. Something happened to freak her out; he just couldn't imagine what.

She glanced at him and then his hand, before meeting his eyes again. She frowned, studying him like she was trying to work something out. "You look like him."

His heart stopped. "Who, baby?"

"Your dad."

"Baby, Hatch is in prison."

"No. He's not. He got out. The witness recanted."

Shit!

She raised a hand to her head and closed her eyes with a grimace. "It hurts."

"Your head?"

She nodded.

"He hurt you?" He tried to keep his rage in check, but he wasn't sure he'd succeeded.

Sadie wrinkled her nose in disgust as she rubbed her palm against her cheek. "I scrubbed and scrubbed, but it still feels so gross."

Ryder had no idea exactly what happened and he wasn't sure Sadie did either. Her sentences were scattered. "Okay, baby. It's okay."

"Ryder?"

"Yeah, honey."

"What's 'the life'?"

"I'm sorry?"

"The life. He said you've been in 'the life' long enough to know how the game is played."

Shit!

"I'm not in the life anymore, Sadie. I got out of it. It's one of the reasons my father hates me."

"But what is the life?" she asked again.

"Club life."

"You used to be in the motorcycle club?"

"Sort of. Not really. I left before I had to make a choice to be a recruit," he explained. "It's a really long story and I need to make sure you're okay. Can I hold you?"

She gave him a very slight nod and he didn't hesitate to pull her into his arms, stroking her back as she burst into tears. "He wants the girls, Ryder."

"Hatch?"

She nodded, closing her eyes. "Brick...he..."

"Brick was with him?" He leaned back to look for injuries. Brick was a mean son of a bitch and one of his favorite pastimes was beating women. Ryder noticed some redness around Sadie's neck, but she'd been grasping it, so he wasn't sure if the marks were made by her. "What did he do, Sadie? Did he hurt you?"

"He slammed me against the wall and squeezed my throat..." She whimpered when she touched the skin again. "He..." She shuddered. "He licked me."

"Let's get some ice on your throat," Ryder said, guiding her to the kitchen.

"He knows where I work, Ryder," she said as she took the ice from him and laid it over her throat. "He threatened to hurt Hayley if you didn't return the girls. He said he has someone watching me."

"Hayley is one of your students?"

She nodded. "The foster one I told you about."

"I remember."

"Hatch said he'd put her in his harem."

She shivered and Ryder pulled her to him. "I won't let that

happen, honey. Neither of you will be hurt."

The familiar sound of pipes elicited a feeling of relief for him, but frazzled Sadie.

"They're back," she squeaked, grabbing for Ryder.

He peered out the kitchen window and pulled her close. "No, baby, it's the crew."

"Hatch's crew?"

"No, Sadie. Mine. Reese and a few of my guys."

She sagged against him.

"Honey, Hatch won't touch you. You'll never see him again."

"You can't guarantee that."

He cupped her cheek. "You don't think?"

"Stop it!" Sadie shoved him away. "Your bravado's grating on me right now."

Ryder crossed his arms. "Sadie, this isn't bravado, it's a promise. He won't bother you again."

"We should call the police."

"And say what?"

"Oh, I don't know, maybe that your father broke into my *home* and threatened me?" she snapped.

"You don't understand how this works, baby. The police can't help you."

Before she could respond, a pounding at Sadie's door had her rushing to stand behind him again. He hated this for her. His father would pay dearly for doing it to her.

* * *

Sadie

I couldn't stop shaking. I'd never been so frightened in my life and it frustrated me. I should have called 9-1-1 before calling Ryder. I don't know why I didn't...I just felt I should call him first. I regretted my choice immediately, particularly when he stopped me from calling once he arrived. And now to find out he'd been in the same club Brick was in, it made me ill.

Someone pounded on my door and I lost my mind, grasping Ryder's shirt and burrowing against his back.

"Baby, I've got you." He took my hand, facing me. "It's just

Reese. No one will hurt you."

It took me a little while to fully hear and trust was he was saying, but he didn't move until I squared my shoulders and gave him a quick nod.

"I'm gonna answer the door now," he whispered.

I nodded again and he kissed my forehead before stepping away from me. I heard him talking to Reese at the front door. At least, I assumed it was Reese; I didn't want to leave the safety of the kitchen. I had a knife block directly to my left.

I'm not sure how long I stood next to the counter, out of view of the door, but Ryder came back in just as the sun set and darkness filled the room. "Baby?"

"Hmm?"

"I need you to pack a bag. You're coming home with me."

I shook my head.

He moved to stand in front of me, lifting my chin. "You're coming home with me. You're not goin' to argue."

"Yeah, I *am* going to argue."

"You can bow out of teaching for a little while—"

"I have to go back on Tuesday, Ryder."

"Or you can take a few days off."

I threw my hands in the air. "It's a *job*, not a hobby, Ryder! I have to be there on Tuesday."

"Baby, if you're at my place with Scottie and one of my crew constantly there, I'll know you're safe." He stroked my cheek. "*You'll* know you're safe."

"I can't move in with you," I argued.

"Sadie," he admonished. "You're not moving in, baby. You're coming to stay until I sort out this shit with the sperm donor."

I scowled up at him. "Please keep talking to me like I'm an idiot, Ryder, it helps."

He dragged his hands down his face. "Will you pack a bag, please?"

"Yes, but I'm going to stay with my aunt."

"No."

I didn't respond as I headed back to my bedroom, pulling my phone out as I went.

"Well, hello Sadie," my aunt said.

I heard Ryder's heavy footsteps as he followed me.

"Hi, Auntie. Would there be an issue with me staying with you for a few days?"

"Of course not," she said. "Are you all right?"

"Yes, but something happened. I'll fill you in when I get there," I promised.

"Okay, honey. I'll see you soon."

I hung up and grabbed a bag from my closet.

Ryder stood in the doorway. "You're not staying at the abbey, Sadie."

"You don't really have any say over it," I replied, pulling open a dresser drawer and gathering up some of the clothing I might need over the next few days. As I threw things into my luggage, Ryder gently grabbed my arm. His touch scorched me and I hissed as I pulled away from him. "Don't touch me."

"Sadie—"

"No! Your father broke into my home and threatened not only me, but one of my students!" I bit back tears.

"I know, baby, which is why I want you at my place."

I shook my head. "I think you and I need a break."

"Sadie."

"Just go, Ryder. Please. I can't deal with this right now."

"I'm not goin' anywhere, Sadie." He continued to stand next to my bed while I packed, his body stiffened, his arms crossed, watching me.

Within minutes my nerves were completely done in and I just needed...something. I didn't know what it was, but it wasn't him. "I really need you to go."

"Not happenin'."

I let out a frustrated groan. "You're just like him!"

"What the hell?" he snapped.

"I asked you to leave, Ryder, and you're standing in my bedroom refusing to."

With a scowl that didn't quite hide the hurt in his eyes, he turned and left my room, slammed my front door, and shook my apartment. I thought I'd feel relief. I didn't. I felt even more

lost...and a little mean...but I couldn't focus on that. I needed to get to the only place on earth I knew I'd be safe. I grabbed my bag, then my purse, and pulled open my front door.

Reese pushed away from the wall. "Hey, Sadie."

I noticed the parking lot was devoid of motorcycles; however Ryder's BMW sat in the red zone. I could only assume Ryder took Reese's bike and left the car. "Go home, Reese."

"Takin' you to your aunt's."

"I'm fine catching the bus."

He shook his head. "Don't do that, Sadie."

"Reese, seriously. I don't need a chauffeur."

"Don't need my brother's woman dead 'cause she decided to make a bad call, either," he responded.

"Pretty sure I'm not his woman anymore, Reese, so you're off the hook."

He dropped his head back and muttered his usual series of curses before studying me again. "Sadie, don't pull this shit, okay?" He tugged the bag from my shoulder and I locked my front door.

I wouldn't admit it, but Reese driving me to the abbey helped assuage the panic somewhat. In that moment, though, I wanted Ryder. I wanted to curl up in his arms and just cry, but I'd completely pushed him away, so I had to figure out what to do next. The only thing I knew for sure was that I couldn't return to my apartment. I had no idea how to get out of the lease, but the thought of going back there made me sick.

* * *

Ryder

As ill-advised as it may have been, particularly without Reese at his back, Ryder didn't head home as originally planned. He'd left Reese with his car and Sadie, then led his crew straight to the compound. It was time for a long overdue meeting with dear old Dad.

They pulled in, parked, and Ollie frowned as he dropped his helmet on the seat. "Looks shut down."

Bennie, Axel, and Blake hung back with the other guys, giving Ryder and Ollie space.

Ryder nodded. "Which means only one thing..."

They'd be meetin' with another club, their bikes somewhere out of sight so no one would know they're there.

"I don't think this is a good idea, Ride."

Ollie was the son of the club vice-president, and the latest one to distance himself from the illegal dealings of the club.

"He threatened Sadie, Ollie."

Ollie sighed. "Yeah, got it, brother. Just not sure it's a good idea to barge in when they've got a soiree goin' with another club. We're outnumbered, and I get that it's our parents in there, but not one of them have our back, especially now."

Ryder seethed with rage. Ollie was right, but that didn't mean he didn't want to wrap his hands around his father's neck and squeeze.

"I wanna know how the hell he got out without me bein' notified."

"I've got a call into our guy at the prison to find that out, Ride," Ollie said.

"Whatever you want, Ride," Blake said. "We got your back."

Before Ryder could respond, the storm door at the side of the building opened and Hatch and Brick walked out. Unfortunately for Ryder, there were more than a few men watching from inside.

"Well, lookie here, Brick. The prodigal son returns."

Ryder saw red, but before he could unleash his rage, Ollie laid a hand on his shoulder. "Steady, Ride."

"I see you got my message," Hatch said, crossing his arms and stopping a few feet from Ryder...Brick beside him.

"What do you want, Hatch?"

Hatch sneered. "I want my property."

"Sounds like a personal problem," Ryder retorted.

"It'll be your problem, you don't return 'em. I'll let you keep Scarlett. She's more trouble than she's worth. But the others? You got forty-eight hours, son."

"Not your son," Ryder hissed.

Hatch chuckled. "Forty-eight hours, Ride."

Ryder moved his hand, but Ollie squeezed his shoulder again. "Not worth it, brother. We're outgunned."

Hatch and Brick walked back into the building and Ryder pulled out his cell phone.

"Hey," Reese answered.

"You got Sadie?"

"Yeah, brother."

"You at the abbey yet?"

"Nope," Reese said.

"Meet you there," Ryder said.

"Okay."

Ryder hung up, swung onto Reese's bike, and led his crew away from his old home away from home. They split off at the entrance of the freeway and Ryder headed toward Sadie.

SEVENTEEN

Sadie

AS SOON AS Reese pulled the car into the parking lot, I jumped out. He swore and turned off the car, climbing out as well. "Sadie, calm down."

"Stick it, Reese. Oh!" Shocked a little by my outburst, I walked to the back of the car and tried to soften my attitude. "Sorry. I shouldn't have been so rude."

He chuckled.

I forced a smile. "You've delivered me to my aunt...you can go now."

Reese shook his head. "Walking you to your door. You know the drill, babe."

"Guess what, Reese? I'm a little over 'the drill.'"

"Yeah?" he retorted, opening the trunk. "Too bad I don't give a rat's ass, huh?"

"I'll carry my own bag, thank you very much," I snapped, grabbing it from the trunk and heading to the abbey door.

I knocked, and as soon as the door opened, I was pulled into the warm embrace of Michael. "Hey, Sadie. You okay?"

I shook my head and wrapped my arms around him. I heard Reese in the background mutter a few choice words, but I didn't care. I took comfort in my friend's arms...I didn't question why Michael was in the abbey that late at night (he shouldn't have been, no men past eight o'clock), or why he opened the door instead of my aunt, I just let him hug me.

"I've got it from here," Michael said, holding me close.

"No, man, I don't think you do," Reese argued.

I turned and faced Reese still standing on the doorstep. "He's got it from here, Reese. Thanks for the ride." I closed the door and dropped my bag to the floor just as my aunt shuffled into the foyer.

"How are you, sweetheart?" she asked, pulling me in for a hug.

"I'm good now." I smiled. "Where's Molly?"

"In bed."

"How about you fill us in?" Michael suggested.

I filled him in on what I knew, leaving out the parts about my fight with Ryder.

"Wow," he breathed out.

I nodded. "I just need a few days to figure a few things out."

"I'd like to help."

"I don't know how you can," I said. "But really, it's fine."

Before he could say anything else, someone pounded at the door. Michael pulled it open and Ryder shoved his way in.

"What are you doing here, Ryder?" I asked.

I was shocked when Michael grabbed hold of Ryder's shoulders. "If Sadie doesn't want you here, you're gone."

"Man. You need to get your hands off me," Ryder said, his voice low and lethal.

"Ryder, I told you I need space," I reminded him.

"We've got bigger issues than us right now."

I frowned.

"You seriously need to get your hands off me," Ryder said to Michael again.

"Michael, it's okay," I said, reaching for his arm.

"Some priest," Ryder said, a hint of sarcasm in his tone.

He glared at my hand touching Michael, but I squared my shoulders and asked, "What's going on? Why are you here, Ryder?"

"Let's take this into my office," my aunt suggested.

"I'm sorry, Sister. I'd hoped this wouldn't reach you," Ryder said.

"Well, let's see what we're up against before we worry about all of that," Auntie said.

It wasn't lost on me that Michael kept himself between me and Ryder as we walked down the hall to Auntie's office, but Ryder somehow maneuvered himself to be standing behind me when I sat in one the chairs facing my aunt's desk.

Auntie sat at her desk and smiled. "So let me know what's going on."

"Without going into too many details, the girls we liberated from Savannah were the "property" of a local motorcycle club and they want them back," Ryder said.

I shrugged away from his hand on my shoulder. My aunt raised an eyebrow but didn't press for details.

"I've contacted a buddy in the FBI," Ryder continued. "We're trying to keep the local cops out of it...the club has a few in their pocket."

"So that's why..." I let my sentence trail off. I recognized that I might not know everything that was going on right now and I trusted him enough to wait until we were alone to ask questions. Now, if I could just calm myself enough not to puke on Ryder's shoes, I'd feel a lot better.

"Where are the girls now?" Michael asked.

"They're safe for the moment, but that won't last for long." Ryder slid his hand to my neck. This time, I didn't shrug him off. "We're going to need to move them."

"What about their families?" Auntie asked.

"They don't have families," Ryder said. "That's what the club counts on when trafficking them."

"Scottie has you," Auntie pointed out.

"That was payback for her running."

"What about Hayley?" I asked.

Ryder squeezed my neck. "She's safe, honey."

"Just what is this 'club'?" Auntie asked.

"The Rockwood Spiders, out of Gresham," Ryder said. "They have a couple other chapters around the country, including Savannah, which is why the girls were there."

I shuddered and Ryder stroked the back of my neck. Much to my irritation, I couldn't stop myself from leaning into his touch. I was still mad at him and I didn't like it that he was anticipating my needs right now. Why couldn't he just be a jerk? It'd be easier to take.

"And why is Sadie sitting in my office, pale as a sheet?" Auntie demanded.

"Ryder's father broke into my apartment and threatened me."

"What?" Auntie cried.

Ryder's hand stilled and I heard Michael curse. I was so shocked by his use of language, my mouth dropped open as I stared at him.

"Sorry," Michael said to me, then added to Ryder, "I think you should leave."

I lost Ryder's hand on my neck.

"I'm okay," I rushed to say. "It was scary, but I'm okay."

"How long until they track her here?" Michael asked, his voice low and lethal.

"They won't," Ryder said.

"And how do you know that?"

"Because I do."

"Holy mother of—I mean...ah, sorry Auntie," I grumbled, and glared up at Ryder. "Will one of you please fill me in whatever it is you aren't saying?"

Before anyone could answer, Sister Maria walked in. "Sorry to interrupt, Reverend Mother, but there is an FBI agent here to see you. A Cameron Shane."

"Send them in, Sister."

"You called Cameron in now?" I asked, my stomach roiling. This must be way worse than I thought.

"I told you I called in the FBI."

The second Cameron walked in (with Reese, I might add), I stood. Partly in an attempt to put space between myself and Ryder, and partly because I felt less vulnerable standing.

"You said you called him for information...if Cameron's here, then..." I was going to be sick. "Is Hayley in trouble now? Real trouble?"

"No."

"I don't believe you."

"Sadie," Ryder whispered, reaching for me.

I raised my hands to ward off his touch. "Don't."

He frowned, but did as I asked. I leaned against the desk and waited for everyone to be introduced. As I watched Michael and Cameron shake hands, something about their introduction bothered me. I couldn't put my finger on it, so I chalked it up to being frazzled.

"Do you have the girls?" Ryder asked.

Cameron nodded. "They're secure, but we can't keep them there indefinitely."

"Why not?" I snapped.

"Because we can't guarantee their safety, even in the well-guarded safe house Cam has them in."

"What *will* guarantee their safety?" Auntie asked.

Ryder shook his head. "Honestly, I have no idea."

"Here would be safe," Michael said.

"How so?" I challenged. "Ryder's dad knows I'm an ex-nun—"

"He doesn't, actually," Cameron said.

"I don't understand."

"Electronically speaking, your time as a nun isn't recorded in any database," Ryder said.

"Because her name change and other information is filed here in paper form, rather than on any computers?" Auntie asked.

Ryder nodded. "Exactly. When I started dating Sadie, I knew there could be issues with her connection to me, so Cameron flooded the Internet with false information and job histories that wouldn't flag the school or the Spiders when they ran background

checks on her."

"Without asking me?" I snapped. Even though he had the decency to look somewhat contrite, I was livid. "Get out!"

"Baby—"

"Don't you *dare* call me baby!" I threw my arm out and pointed toward the door. "Get out!"

"Not goin' anywhere just yet, Sadie, so you need to wrap you head around it."

"Then *I'll* leave," I said.

"Babe—"

"Lose my number, Ryder." I rushed out of the office and toward the private nun quarters. I didn't even know where I was sleeping for the next two days, so I just kept walking until I hit the communal living area.

"Sadie?" Michael called.

I peeked into the hallway and saw him standing at the threshold. He wasn't allowed any further. The nun's area was off-limits to men, so I walked toward him.

"Hey."

He smiled, pulling me in for a hug. "I'm worried about you."

"I'm okay, Michael, I just need a minute."

"What can I do?"

"Honestly? Nothing." My stomach grumbled.

"How about we grab something to eat?"

I smiled. "I'm not really in the mood to go out. Rain check?"

"You've got to eat."

"I'll make something here. I'm good, Michael."

"I'm right next door if you need me."

"I know," I said.

"Anything, Sadie, okay?"

I nodded. "Thanks."

He studied me for a few seconds and then turned and walked away.

How the heck had my life come to this? Less than a year ago, I was living a sheltered but happy existence, and now I was in some weird romantic suspense novel I couldn't get out of. Admittedly, I didn't really want to, because I'd never felt so alive, but there was

no way I'd ever voice that out loud.

Right now I just needed a break.

My stomach rumbled again.

And food...I needed food.

As I headed into the kitchen, my phone rang and I glanced at the screen. Since I was apparently a glutton for punishment, I answered it. "I thought I told you to lose my number."

"Babe, I know you're pissed—"

"Thank you, Captain Obvious, but I don't think we need to rehash all of that."

"There are things you don't fully understand."

"You were part of a gang, Ryder."

"I wasn't part of it, Sadie, this is what I'm trying to tell you. I got out."

"Saying that kind of indicates you were in something that you had to get out of!" I snapped, frustrated with the back and forth.

"Look, recruits are chosen around eighteen. I was out before then. Most of us were. Bennie and Ollie were the only two who didn't get out early."

"I don't know what any of that means. And honestly, I don't really think I want to. This is all way too bad-movie plotline for me."

"Whatever, Sadie." I heard him take a deep breath. "I'm gonna say this once, and then you can have your space. You don't leave the abbey for the next three days."

"You don't really have any—"

"I swear to Christ—"

"Don't use the Lord's name in vain," I scolded.

I heard him bellow an expletive (away from the phone, luckily), and I couldn't help a devious little smile. Hopefully, I was making his life just a little more difficult...give him a small taste of his own medicine.

"Sadie," he started again, after another deep breath. "If you're not willing to stay with me, I need you to stay put until I can sort things out with the club. Do you hear me?"

"Oh, I hear you, Ryder. I'd imagine anyone within a three-mile radius can hear you."

"Woman, are you purposely trying to piss me off?" he snapped. "'Cause I will *not* be happy if I have to put a man on you. I will if you push me, but I'd like to keep all my resources working to figure all this shit out."

"Well, you do you, Ryder. I'm going to take the next few days to figure out what I want. Does that sound agreeable to you, sir bossy pants?" I walked through the kitchen and pushed open the double doors out onto the patio at the back of the property. The sun was low but hadn't yet set, and the day had been a mild one, so I drew in a deep breath and tried to relax.

"Stop being cute."

"I'm not trying to be cute, Ryder, but I won't be bullied into doing something I don't want to do. Do you hear me?" I mimicked.

"Right," he said with a sigh. "So I need to put a man on you."

"And draw a big red arrow pointing to the abbey for your father to find? Gosh, Ryder, that doesn't sound very smart at all," I droned. What Ryder didn't know was that there were tunnels under the church and outbuildings, which meant I could lose his "man" if I was so inclined. They were also a good hiding place should anyone find me here. "You need to focus on making sure those girls are safe. Including Hayley. They're what's important here. Not me."

"All of you are important, Sadie." I heard footsteps on the gravel and turned to find him walking towards me.

I frowned. "You shouldn't be here."

He dropped his phone into his pocket and crossed his arms. "Babe, you and I are gonna talk."

"I don't *want* to talk." I slid my phone into my pocket as well and forced myself not to wrap my arms around him. I loved the big fat jerk, but I didn't want him to know that.

"Pickin' up on that, but I'm not leavin' you here this weekend until we hash out a few things."

"Whatever." I slipped my hands into my jeans' pockets and shrugged. "Say what you need to say."

He smiled as he stared at me before uncrossing his arms and closing the distance between us. Before I could get my hands out of my pockets, I was pulled against his body and the top of my

head was kissed. "I love you, Sadie." I tried to wiggle away from him, but he just held me tighter. "Settle, baby."

"You're the most annoying man on the planet," I snapped.

He chuckled. "I know, but you love me."

"I can't believe you changed my official record without talking to me," I accused.

"Honey, we didn't change your official record. We just put a fake record in there in case the club went searching."

"Oh, 'cause that's different?" I glared up at him.

"It *is* different," he said. "I will do anything to keep you safe, you have to know that."

"I don't understand why you don't just talk to me about this stuff."

Ryder shrugged. "Honestly, I didn't think it would come up. I'm trying to shield you from some of this crap."

"Um, Ryder? Your dad broke into my home!" I cried. "You failed."

His expression darkened. "You don't think I don't know that?"

"Well, then why don't you admit that what you've been doing isn't working?"

"Why do you think I'm standing here right now?" he ground out.

"Don't you take that tone with me right now," I snapped, pushing away from him. "So far today, you've kept me in the dark, beat your chest like some ape-man while grunting half orders, and told me you flooded the Internet with false records about me without my permission. Not one time did you admit you did anything wrong or apologize for it. Not to mention, you're still giving me half-answers and evading some of my questions entirely."

He settled his hands on his head and dropped his head back, spouting expletives to the sky.

"You're a freakin' juvenile," I accused. "Not to mention a bully."

He shook his head, took a deep breath (he'd done that a lot today), and then said, "Sadie, I'm trying to protect all of you here. I get that you're used to sacrificing yourself, and I'm happy that there's a little part of you that's standing up for yourself here, but

understand that I want you safe too."

"Maybe if you didn't keep me in the dark, I could help," I ground out.

"Baby, there are things I *can't* share with anyone and that includes some bigger picture issues that you have, unfortunately, been dragged into. I'll share what I can, but Cameron and I, along with his team, are trying to keep twelve girls from being found and sold to bad men who want to use their bodies for some pretty damn disgusting reasons. This problem started before I met you, and I'd really hoped to keep you out of it, but the sperm donor made that impossible, so now I have to figure out how to keep twelve girls from being found and make sure the only woman I've ever loved stays *safe*!" His voice rose in volume steadily until he practically shouted "safe." "So adding to all of these issues with trying to save little girls from animals, is whatever has crawled up my beloved's ass so that now she won't listen to reason."

"You're the one who's crawled up my..." I pressed my lips into a thin line. I wouldn't say it. I wouldn't. I threw my arms up in the air. "Gah! You make me crazy!"

"Sadie, I'm sorry I didn't tell you everything that was going on. I love you. I'm gonna screw things up on occasion, but I need to know you're safe. Tell me what you need to hear so that I can go meet Cam and take care of this."

"Go, Ryder. I'm not stopping you."

He pulled me to him again, cupping my face. "Honey, you *are* stopping me. I can't be distracted. I need you to understand that."

"I'm really scared, Ryder," I whispered.

"I know, baby." He kissed me gently then wrapped his arms around me. I hugged his waist and settled my cheek on his chest. "I don't know how to make you feel safe until my father's dealt with, but I promise if you stay here you will be...at least I hope so. I'd feel better if you were with me, though."

"I have to go to work on Tuesday."

"Then come and stay with me and I can take you."

I shook my head.

"Will you at least come stay Monday night?" he asked.

"Will you promise not to make me crazy?"

"No."

I smiled against his chest. "You're a butt."

He gave me a gentle squeeze. "Do you know how much I love you?"

"Yes. Enough to make me crazy."

"Well, you're not wrong."

I leaned back to meet his eyes. "Why do you need me to stay with you?"

"Because it's going to be really crowded here."

"Um, why?"

"Because we're using the abbey as a hiding place."

"For?" I still wasn't getting what he was saying.

"The girls."

"Really?"

He nodded. "I doubt anyone will think to look here, and if they do, they can hide them quickly..."

"In the tunnels," I finished.

He nodded. "She filled me in on the secrets of the abbey."

"My aunt's getting way too into this cloak and dagger stuff." Suddenly cold, I rubbed my arms, fear setting in again.

"Hey," he said quietly, pulling me to him again. "I'm here, baby. I've got you."

I burrowed into his chest. "He said he'd do horrible things to me. Things worse than death."

"He won't."

"I'm not afraid to die, Ryder, but I *am* afraid of what Brick wanted to do to me. And the thought of him getting anywhere near those girls frightens me even more."

He stiffened as he held me tighter. "No one will touch you or the girls," he vowed.

"Promise?" I whispered.

"I promise, baby."

"Okay." I closed my eyes and relaxed against him. "I'll come stay with you."

Ryder slid his hand to the back of my neck. "Tonight?"

I rolled my eyes. "Ryder."

"Please, baby."

I sighed. "*Fine*."

"Thank you." He lifted my face and kissed every inch. I scrunched up my nose and tried to lean away but he just held me closer. "Settle."

When he puckered up for more, I laid my hand over his mouth and giggled. "You're insane."

He grew serious and smiled gently. "I thought I'd never hear that again."

"What?"

He stroked my cheek. "Your laugh."

"It's been a really bad day."

"In the definition of bad days, yeah, baby, it has been." He leaned down and kissed me gently. "I'm sorry I dragged you into all this shit."

"Technically, your father did, honey. I don't blame you." I waved my hand. "That doesn't get you off the hook for the other stuff, but this one isn't on you."

I was rewarded with a slight smile. "Let's get home. I'm gonna cook for you and then I have to meet with Cam."

I frowned. "I'm going to come to your place only to have you leave?"

He shook his head. "I'm gonna meet with him at my place."

"Oh."

"I told you I'm not gonna leave you, Sadie. I mean it."

"What if you have to deal with the girls?"

"I'm currently in the category of plausible deniability, so I'm staying away from the girls for the moment so no one sees my connection to them. Cam's handling everything from this point forward so that I can maintain it."

"Will you fill me in on your 'crew'?" I asked.

"Yeah, if you want me to."

"Yeah, I want you to," I droned sarcastically.

He wrapped an arm around me and pulled me close, kissing my temple. "Whatever you want, baby."

I relaxed against him, kissed him at the back doors, and then went inside to retrieve my bag.

EIGHTEEN

Sadie

I STARED OUT the windows of Ryder's family room, a glass of Guiness in my hand, finally left alone to my thoughts after arriving to chaos at his home. I'd showered and was blissfully lounging in a pair of yoga pants and a T-shirt, drinking beer. I could certainly get used to looking at this view every day. It rocked.

Apparently, today was the day to meet "the crew." Well, the majority of it, anyway. What I didn't realize (because Ryder didn't mention it...shocker) was that his basement was where the men congregated when something big needed to be dealt with. He didn't go into detail about what might constitute something big, and quite frankly, I didn't ask. I just didn't have the emotional capacity for answers at the moment. I had been shown the panic room, which nearly did me in, but it was secure, had a direct line to the cops, and had a way to escape through the backyard if need-be.

Good lord, I hope there'd never be a need.

Ryder said he'd chosen his house for a specific set of reasons, the biggest one being he could hide. His name wasn't on the deed...he technically owned it, but the house was held by a shell company he said he'd set up to hide certain assets from his father.

The house was also hidden from the road. You'd have to know it was there in order to find it, and then you'd have to be admitted through the gates or know the code to get in. You *could* find it by flying over it, but Ryder wasn't concerned about that, figuring the Spiders wouldn't go to that much trouble. I hoped he was right.

Before I'd been left to my thoughts, I'd met Axel and Blake (Ollie was also there and he was awesome). The one woman introduced in this ragtag band of men was Sandy. She'd worked for Ryder for a long time and she treated him like a son. I warmed to her instantly. She obviously loved him and looked out for him, and I liked her for it.

Axel was tall with dark hair and piercing blue eyes. He was a little more on the Portland hipster side for my liking, but he was certainly pretty. He also smiled a lot, but wasn't a big talker.

I don't think Blake was quite six feet tall, but he held himself like a much bigger man and had long silvery black hair he'd pulled back. The thing that stuck with me the most was that he had an Anson Mount look about him, complete with full beard and smirky smile. He made me a little nervous and it might have been because he appeared to be tattooed everywhere, including his neck, which was alien to me. I kept having to force my gaze away from his tattoos (Blake referred to it as "ink"). Ryder mentioned he was the oldest of the crew and I figured he had at least fifteen years on all of them.

Ollie, on the other hand, I liked. *Adored*. From the second he arrived, he treated me like a long-lost sister (as he did with Scottie), keeping me included in every conversation, asking questions so I wouldn't feel left out. He was the same when he'd come for dinner, but tonight he seemed a little more on alert. He was a little taller than Ryder and had dark-blond hair and hazel eyes. He was all lean muscle and had a few tattoos on his arms, but nothing like Blake.

Reese and the rest of the guys were handling business this weekend so Ryder could stick around home, but Ryder promised he'd introduce me to them another time, and I was grateful it was a small group for tonight's meeting.

Before the guys commenced their meeting, Ryder cooked. And, boy did he cook. Pork chops, garlic mashed potatoes, and cheesy asparagus were served without any assistance from me, and what I found most interesting is how normal this seemed. The men may not have been blood, but there was a brotherly bond there that was probably closer. They seemed to welcome me into the fold...and it was a fold I was really happy to be welcomed into.

Stories were flying around the table, everyone joking around since they'd pretty much known each other since birth, and I simply sat back and watched. It was awesome.

"Did you ever tell Sadie about when we were in those dirt biking trials?" Ollie asked.

"So, Scottie, how are you feeling?" Ryder asked in an obvious attempt to divert attention.

"What happened?" I asked, and then frowned. "Wait, don't tell me if he got hurt. I won't be able to handle it if there was blood or broken bones involved."

Ollie chuckled. "Only his pride was hurt."

"Ooh, do tell, then."

"Ollie, man, shut your mouth," Ryder ordered.

"We were fifteen, sixteen, something like that, and Ryder figured he'd do something 'dangerous' to impress some club princess—"

"What's a club princess?" I asked.

"Daughter of another club's prez," Scottie said.

"So, Ryder decided he was gonna wheelie by her." Ollie chuckled, and Ryder leaned over me to shove him on the side of the head.

I grabbed his arm and held onto it. "Continue," I said.

"We had a time to beat, but Ryder's problem wasn't speed, it was balance."

Ryder let out a rather rude expletive and I squeezed his arm as Ollie continued the story.

"So, he does his first lap, smokes everyone else's time, then he's coming up to the girls and rolls up into a wheelie...and flips his ass over, almost taking out the object of his affection at the same time. It was classic."

"She wasn't even that cute," Axel provided.

"She was smokin' hot!" Ollie said.

"You're a dumbass, Ollie," Blake snapped, nodding toward me.

I giggled. "I'm okay, Blake. But thanks for looking out for me."

Ryder's arm slid behind me and pulled me closer to him. "Ignore Ollie," he whispered.

"No way," I countered.

As the topic moved from childhood to talk about the bar and life in general, Ollie asked Scottie for the butter and she blushed so red, I thought she might be having some kind of allergic reaction. When she pulled herself together, she handed him what he'd asked for and dinner commenced, but I wondered how long that little crush had been going on.

I was staring out the living room window when arms wrapped around me from behind and I started a little. Ryder kissed the back of my neck. I leaned against him as he whispered, "How ya doin'?"

"I'm good, honey."

"Yeah?"

"Yes." I craned my neck to smile at him. "Is everyone gone?"

"Ollie's hangin' for a bit, but the rest have stuff to do." He turned me to face him. "Reese'll be here later."

I frowned.

"You don't like Reese, do you?" he asked.

"It's not that I don't like him, it's just..."

"Just, what?"

"He's kind of a jerk."

He chuckled. "*I'm* kind of a jerk."

"Well, I'm not kissing *him*."

Ryder sighed. "Break it down for me, baby. If he's said somethin' I'll talk to him."

"I already tried that."

"Yeah? You're brave."

I grimaced. "Not that it made any difference."

"Now who's being vague?" he accused.

So, I "broke it down" for him. I told him every offense Reese had ever committed from the airport conversation to the driving me to my aunt's even when I didn't want him to.

"He did all of those things because I asked him to."

"Yes, I heard you," I snapped. "But it's like he dismisses me when I talk to him."

"Like you're the little woman and he's the big man?" he asked, paraphrasing my words. "You've said the same about me."

"Okay, he's like you...sort of," I conceded. "But why would he need to call you if I want to go to Savannah? I'm an adult...if I want to fly to the moon, he doesn't have the right to stop me."

"No, but he *did* have to find out where I was at with everything so you weren't walking into a shit storm."

Well, crap, that was probably true.

"And he knew the club was watching us. We'd gone to great measures to hide much of the trip and movements around town, but we can never be sure who to trust. He didn't want you ending up in the wrong place at the wrong time."

"Oh."

Ryder slipped a lock of my hair behind my ear. "He and I were talking constantly, Sadie, and anything he did was to make sure you were safe. He made sure you and your girls were safe on your night out—"

"I'm sorry?"

"And it was a good thing, since you had issues."

"Ryder, back up. You had him follow us, didn't you?"

"Yeah."

"You didn't tell me about that! I knew it! He made me think I was nuts."

He rolled his eyes. "Well, him trying to keep my secret notwithstanding, he was looking out for you."

"I will concede it was nice he took care of the guy in the other club, but you should have told me," I said. "Actually, he should

have."

"Okay, baby. I'm not gonna rehash the stuff about lack of information with you, because I'm enjoyin' our peaceful interlude, but he isn't gonna share shit with you unless I say it's okay. You're my woman, not his, so it falls on me to do so."

I bit my lip. I hated it when he was logical. "Still don't like him being a bully."

"I will walk to him about that." He gripped my chin gently. "I can tell Reese not to come, honey, but he's family and he adores you, so it'd be great if you can deal."

I let out a quiet snort. "How could you possibly know he adores me, Ryder? The man only has twelve words in his vocabulary arsenal and the F-word seems to be his favorite. How he manages to use it as a noun, a verb, *and* an adverb is beyond me. Admittedly somewhat clever, but still a rather disappointing testament to the educational system of America."

Ryder dropped his head back and laughed. "This is exactly why he adores you."

"I don't get it."

"Baby, whether you know it or not...and, if I'm being honest, I think a part of you does know it...you're funny. But you're that wicked-smart kind of funny that makes people stop and wonder whether or not they were just insulted."

"I certainly don't mean to insult anyone."

"You don't think? Not even Reese?"

"Okay, well...maybe him a little."

"Exactly." Ryder smiled. "But Reese doesn't limit himself to one person. He wants to insult everyone. He's had it rough, baby, and that's all I'm gonna tell you because it's not my story to tell, but he likes you. Trust me. So if you could just ignore the tough outer shell and try to get—"

"To the ooey gooey center?"

"No, Reese doesn't have an ooey gooey anything," Ryder said. "But he does have a moral compass and it's the same as mine, so if you can get past my shortcomings, I really hope you can get past his. He's my brother, Sadie, but you come first, so if you want him gone, he'll be gone."

"Nuh-uh."

"Yeah, huh."

"Honey, I am *not* going to be the Yoko to your little band of misfits."

Reese roared with laughter as he pulled me against his chest. "John broke the Beatles up, Sadie, not Yoko. Poor Yoko just got dragged into shit."

"Oh. I don't really know that much about music." I set my glass on the coffee table and wrapped my arms around his waist. "I will try to like Reese."

"I'd appreciate that." He kissed me, then asked, "Scottie wants to watch a movie. You feel up to it?"

"Only if there's snuggling."

"Honey, I'm not a monster. Of course there will be snuggling. But if Ollie isn't feelin' it tonight, you and I can."

I couldn't stop a giggle. "You're insane."

"Crazy for you," he said, and kissed my nose.

Tugging me into the kitchen, we grabbed snacks, soda, and more beer and headed downstairs to watch some shoot 'em up movie. I couldn't tell you what it was because as soon as I was curled up next to Ryder, I fell asleep. I remember waking up at some point in the middle of the night, finding myself in Ryder's bed, his body curled around mine. I liked that. A *lot*, so I fell back asleep, a smile on my face.

* * *

A gentle kiss on my cheek, then my lips, awoke me and I blinked my eyes open to find Ryder standing by the bed grinning. "Good morning, Sleeping Beauty."

"Good morning. What time is it?" I asked as I stretched.

"Ten."

"And you're waking me before eleven on a non-school day...why?"

He leaned down and kissed me again. "I made breakfast, but if you want to sleep more, feel free."

I sat up. "Is there bacon?"

"Babe, is that even a question?"

"Hash browns?"

"Yeah, baby, I made all your favorites," he said.

"I'll be right out."

Ryder chuckled. "I'll pour the coffee."

I nodded and slid off the bed. My bag was in the guest room, so I grabbed a few things and headed to the guest bathroom. After changing and brushing my teeth and hair, I joined Ryder and Scarlett in the kitchen. "Morning, Scottie."

"Hey, Sadie," she said then shoved a bacon strip in her mouth.

I took the mug of coffee (and the kiss) Ryder offered and sat at the island. "How's your leg?" I asked Scottie.

She wrinkled her nose. "Itchy."

"Sorry, honey."

She shrugged. "It is what it is."

Ryder slid a plate piled high with food in front of me.

"Thanks," I said, rubbing my hands together.

He chuckled. "If you can't eat it all, I'll eat the rest."

"You don't think I can eat it all?" I challenged.

He raised his hands and shook his head. "Don't doubt you in the least."

"As it should be."

Ryder leaned against the counter, sipping his coffee, while I dug into the food.

"When do I get to get out of my cell?" Scottie asked.

"When this shit's dealt with."

She dropped her fork on her plate. "So never."

"Baby girl, I thought we talked about this," Ryder said.

"*You* talked."

He took a deep breath. "I want you safe, Scottie. So, I'm sorry you're stuck for the moment, but it won't be forever."

I continued to eat, impressed with Ryder's self-control. He hadn't yelled once...so far.

"Um, since Dad's always going to be a dick, I'm pretty sure it *will* be forever."

"Can't disagree with you there."

"What kinds of things do you like to do, honey?" I asked, pausing in my pig-like consumption of breakfast goodness (for the moment).

"Shopping," she said immediately.

"Wow, you needed to think about that, huh?"

She giggled. "You're funny, Sadie."

Ryder cocked his head, giving me his 'I-told-you-so' look and I smiled at Scottie. "So, besides shopping, what else?"

She shrugged. "I don't know. I miss my friends, but..."

"But?"

"Never mind, it's dumb."

I stroked her back. "What's dumb, honey?"

"I guess I just feel like we have nothing in common now."

"In what way?"

"Well, for one, none of them have been drugged, kidnapped, raped, and beaten to shit," she snapped.

"Scarlett," Ryder warned, but I held up a hand.

"No, they haven't," I agreed. "This has all been really horrible for you, sweetie."

She dropped her head in her hands and groaned. "I hate this. I hate that I can't get it out of my head. I want to go back...to when I didn't know better. Back to when I knew there were bad people out there, but didn't *know* there were, you know?"

I rubbed her back gently and nodded.

Ryder leaned across the island, tugging Scottie's hands away from her face. "Baby girl," he whispered.

"I'm sorry, Ride," she rasped. "You have bigger problems right now."

"You have nothing to be sorry for." He moved to our side of the island and gently pulled his sister off the stool and into his arms. "I love you, sissy. You can talk to us about anything anytime, and you're gonna see that counselor on Tuesday, okay?"

She nodded into his chest and he held her until she stopped crying. In that moment, I didn't think I could love him more.

"This isn't gonna take long, Scottie," Ryder promised.

"I really hope not."

"Do you want me to ask Ollie if he can pick Molly up? Maybe Sadie's aunt will let her stay over."

Scottie's face lit up. "Do you think she will?"

"I'll call her, honey," I offered.

"Thanks, Sadie," she said, and pulled away from Ryder. "I'll go get dressed."

I took one more bite of my hash browns, then grabbed my phone and called my aunt. Ryder called Ollie and we hung up almost at the same time.

"It's all set," I said.

"For me too," he said.

I grinned. "I'll text Auntie the details of who's picking Molly up *after* I finish breakfast."

"Sounds good." He grabbed my empty coffee mug. "Want more?"

"Is the Pope Catholic?"

"Well, you'd know better than me," he retorted, pouring me another cup.

I giggled. "You're wrong there, you know, considering you've corrupted me and all."

He set the coffee in front of me and then leaned down and kissed me. "I'm having fun corrupting you, FYI."

I licked my lips. "I kind of like it too."

He stroked my cheek. "Finish your breakfast."

I did as he ordered and enjoyed the heck out of it.

NINETEEN

Sadie

LATER THAT EVENING, I was curled up on the sofa upstairs attempting to read, but distracted by the view of the city lights. Scottie and Molly were downstairs watching a movie and Ryder was catching up on some work on his laptop. Reese had left an hour ago (I'd come to an internal truce with him, however, I still believed his life's goal was to push my buttons), and Ollie would be around shortly with frozen yogurt. I had an inkling Scottie might not be the only one with a crush, especially since Ollie had a similar lovesick look on his face around her, but kept my opinion to myself.

"Babe?"

I glanced up from my Kindle. "Hmm?"

"I've said your name three times." He smiled. "Must be a good book."

"The sentence I've reread four times is riveting."

He chuckled. "You okay?"

"Yep." I lowered my e-reader. "Sorry. Just distracted by the view. You can see all of Portland from here."

"Way better than the abbey, huh?"

"Yes, honey, it's way better." I shook my head. "How'd I end up in your bed last night, by the way?"

He walked over and leaned down to kiss me. "I didn't want you to wake up in the middle of the night...you know, if you had a nightmare or something...and be scared."

I reached up and stroked his cheeks. "So it was in case I woke up?"

He nodded.

"You're so giving, honey."

Ryder grinned. "I live to serve you, baby."

Still stroking his face, I cocked my head. "You know that's the first thing I noticed about you."

"Oh, yeah?" He kissed me again. "That I live to serve you?"

"Well, no, because here I sit and I don't have a Guiness in front of me."

He frowned. "That's awful. I should rectify that immediately."

I giggled. "Yes, you should. Once you do, you may have your "Sadie's servant" card back."

He clasped his hands at his chest. "Truly?"

"Yes, but there's a time limit, honey."

"Right." He bowed. "I apologize, Your Majesty."

I clapped my hands. "Chop chop, jester."

He laughed as he headed to the kitchen. Boy, he was pretty. I liked to watch him coming and going.

As he pulled open the fridge, his phone rang and he put it to his ear. "Ryder. Hey, man. Yeah." He stepped to the alarm panel and studied the screen. "I see you. Yep. I'll buzz you in." He pressed a button and then headed back to the kitchen. "See you in a sec." He slid his phone in his pocket. "Ollie's on his way up."

"I hope my beer goes with the yogurt." I waved my hand dismissively. "Aw, who am I kidding? I don't care." Ryder laughed and brought me a full glass of deliciousness and the can with the excess. "Thank you."

The doorbell rang and Ryder slid his gun from his holster, checked the camera feed again, and unbolted the door. Despite the fact his home was a fortress, my heart still raced a little as he opened the door.

I relaxed when Ollie arrived, paper bags filled with goodness in his hands. "I come bearing gifts."

Ryder locked up behind him and yelled down the basement stairs, "Scottie, Molly, Ollie's here."

"Crutches, honey," I reminded him, and reached for the bags.

"Hold up, Scottie," Ryder called again.

"I'll get her," Ollie offered. He handed me the yogurt and jogged downstairs, returning a few minutes later carrying a besotted (and giggling) Scottie. Molly followed, perfectly oblivious to what was going on.

That small observation gave me hope. As traumatic as being kidnapped and held in a horrible place was, Molly seemed to have been sheltered from the more horrific sides of it. Scottie had protected her from much of it. It proved to me (once again) how strong she was, and I had hope that she'd beat back her demons. If anyone could, Scottie could.

Ryder's hand slid to my neck and he gave it a gentle squeeze. "You okay?"

I stood on my tiptoes and kissed him quickly. "I'm good, honey."

"You sure?"

"Yep...and I'll be better when I get this chocolatey goodness in my belly."

He chuckled and kissed me again, then we all sat around the island and enjoyed our dessert.

***

Ryder

Ryder called Reese to check in and was reassured that everything at the bar was going well. He finally felt as though he could relax just a bit. At least until he heard Sadie scream. He hung up with Reese and made a run for the guest room, pushing the door open. "Sadie?" She screamed again and he stepped to the bed and turned

on the lamp. "Sadie? Honey, wake up."

She gasped and opened her eyes, staring up at him in confusion.

"Hey."

Sadie shook her head, reaching for him as she burst into tears. Ryder pulled her into his arms and held her as he stood beside the bed. "Bad dream, huh?"

"I'm okay," she whispered. "What time is it?"

"Just after midnight." He kissed her temple. "Wanna tell me about it?"

"Not yet." She was kneeling on the bed, her arms around his shoulders, and she buried her face into his neck.

"I've got you, baby." He slid his hand into her hair and forced himself not to focus on the short-shorts and tank top she wore. Damn, she was sexy.

"Hatch was in my room," she whispered.

Ryder stiffened.

"Not literally," she rushed to say, stroking his hair. "In my dream."

He relaxed and shifted so he was sitting on the bed and she was on his lap.

She gasped. "How did you do that?"

"Mad skills."

"Oh, right," she said with a giggle.

"That's better," he whispered, and stroked her cheek. "You have the best laugh."

"I do?"

"Yeah, baby, you do." He kissed her gently. "Do you want to tell me the rest of the dream?"

"There wasn't much else to it." She slid off his lap. "Just a rehashing of what happened on Friday, only it was here."

"Babe—"

"Nope, I'm over it," she said. "I don't want to talk it about it."

Ryder frowned.

"I'm good, Ryder."

"You gonna go back to sleep?"

She shook her head.

"Then you're not good, Sadie," he said.

With a shrug, she crossed her arms. "I'll warm up some milk."

Ryder cocked his head. "Yeah? Does that work for you?"

"I don't know." Sadie sighed. "I've never tried it."

"How about you come hang with me while I go through the video footage from the club."

"Are you sure?" Sadie bit her lip. "I won't be in the way?"

"Honey, you're never in the way." He stood and smiled. "But you need to put more clothes on or I won't be able to concentrate."

"Okay."

"I'll meet you in the family room."

Sadie nodded and Ryder kissed her before leaving the room.

After grabbing his laptop from his office, he pulled blankets from the chest in front of the sofa and then retrieved a couple of beers from the kitchen. Sadie walked into the room just as he set the drinks on the coffee table. Her clothing wasn't much better...yoga pants and fitted T-shirt...although, it covered more, she couldn't hide the sexy.

"What?" she asked, glancing down. "Do I have something on me?"

He chuckled. "Just sex appeal."

She snorted. "You're insane."

Ryder held his arm out and she slid into his embrace. "You're beautiful, Sadie."

"Thanks, honey." She gave him a squeeze. "You're pretty hot yourself."

"You okay?"

"Better now."

"You want a beer?"

"Actually, I kind of want tea," she said. "Do you have any?"

"Yeah." He smiled. "I grabbed some of that licorice shit you like."

"You mean the best tea on earth?"

"The most disgusting tea on earth?" he countered.

She giggled. "You really bought some?"

He nodded.

She grinned up at him. "I love you."

"Back atya. I'll make you some tea."

"I can do it." She headed toward the kitchen. "Do you want anything?"

"I'm good, baby." He sat on the sofa and pulled up the first feed from the club video surveillance.

Sadie returned, steaming cup in hand, and sat down beside him. "Anything?"

He shook his head. "It could take a while."

She pulled the blanket over her. "How do you deal with all those people?"

"I don't most of the time."

"You realize you own a meat market right?" she said, then sipped her tea.

"You know what a meat market is?"

"Television junkie, remember?"

Ryder chuckled. "Not by design, but yeah. The club's certainly turned into one."

"Who's that?" she asked, pointing to the screen.

"Bennie."

"No, behind him."

Ryder leaned closer to the screen. "I don't recognize him."

"Well, Bennie knows him."

"How do you figure?"

"Rewind a bit," Sadie said. "They're having a heated discussion."

He did as she suggested and he realized he'd missed that tidbit of information. "Yeah, they *are* having a heated discussion."

"But you don't know the other guy?"

Ryder shook his head. At least, he didn't think he did. He pulled out his phone. "Hey."

"You got somethin'?" Reese asked.

"Check Friday footage." Ryder checked the time stamp. "Sixteen twelve."

"What am I looking for?"

"Do you know the guy talkin' to Bennie?"

Ryder heard Reese click keys on the keyboard in the background. "Give me a few."

"Call me back," Ryder said.

"Okay, man."

Reese hung up and Ryder went back to the footage.

Sadie gasped. "There he is again."

"Yeah, I see that."

"Something's hinky," Sadie said.

Ryder glanced at her. "Ya think?"

She shoved his thigh with her foot, smiling over her mug. "Smarty pants."

His phone rang again and he answered. "What do you see?"

"That guy Bennie's talkin' to is a Spider," Reese said.

"What the fu—?" Sadie stiffened beside him and he laid a hand on her leg. "Do you know him?"

"I know of him," Reese said. "Flick, I think. He's a soldier...low on the totem pole."

Ryder didn't know Flick, but then again, he'd been out of the club longer than Reese. If a soldier was hanging around the Frog, Ryder had bigger issues. "Damn it."

"Yeah," Reese agreed. "I've sent what I know off to Cam."

"Okay, thanks. Watch for him tonight."

"Yeah, man. On it. Watchin' Bennie too."

"Good," Ryder breathed out.

"Any word on the girls?"

"No."

"Okay, I'm gonna get on this," Reese said.

"Thanks, brother." Ryder hung up, sat back, and let out a breath.

"Does Reese know him?" Sadie asked.

"Not really." Ryder rolled his head to look at her. "All he knows is that he's a soldier in the club."

Sadie shuddered. "Everything seems to end back with your dad, huh?"

He reached over and squeezed her knee. "I got you, baby."

"But who's got you?"

"What do you mean?"

She set her cup aside and sat up on her knees, moving his computer so she could straddle his lap. "I got you, baby," she parroted.

He smiled, laying his hands on her hips. "Yeah?"

Sadie nodded. "I can kick really hard."

Ryder laughed. "Really?"

She nodded again. "Yep. 'Course, the person has to be directly in front of me and someone has to be holding their arms behind them, because I'm useless at defending myself...as evidenced—"

"Shhh."

"I'm not saying that for sympathy, honey. I'm simply saying..." She sat back, defeated. "Dang it! I don't know what I'm trying to say. I was trying to be funny. I think you're wrong. I think I suck at it."

"Try again," he encouraged.

She bit her lip and he couldn't stop himself from tugging it from between her teeth and kissing her. He slid her to the sofa, stretching out beside her, then pulling her on top of him, continuing to kiss her. She tasted like licorice and it surprised the hell out of him that although he may have hated it in the past, on her it was an aphrodisiac. He needed to taste her...every part. Her quiet mews drove him insane, but it was when her hands slipped under his shirt and investigated his abs, he realized they needed to stop or he never would.

He dropped his forehead to hers and took several deep breaths. "Damn."

"Wow," she breathed out.

"You are so damn beautiful, Sadie."

She dropped her head to his chest and sighed. "So are you."

Ryder kissed her again and then held her close as they continued to catch their breath. Sadie's hair had come loose from her hair tie, and Ryder slid it away from her face and down her back. "Promise me something."

"What?"

He wove his fingers in her hair. "Never cut your hair."

"Never?" She craned her neck to look at him. "You want me to Crystal Gayle it?"

Ryder smiled. "Just not short. Your hair's incredible, Sadie."

"Okay, honey, I promise I'll never cut it short."

"Appreciate it." His phone rang, and he held Sadie steady

while he swiped it off the coffee table. "Ryder."

"Hey, it's Cam."

"Hey." Ryder frowned. "Problem with the girls?"

Sadie settled her chin on his chest, her body locked and alert.

"No, man. They're good," Cameron said.

Ryder gave Sadie an encouraging squeeze and she relaxed. "What's up?"

"How well do you know Bennie Pacciana?"

"Shit," he said. "That doesn't sound good."

"It all depends on how well you know him."

"He works for me, but he's not a brother."

"So I'm not gonna find anything?" Cameron asked.

Ryder shifted Sadie and sat up. "What the hell's goin' on, Cam?"

"He's dirty, Ryder, just gotta prove it."

"Damn it. Do you think he's got somethin' to do with the missing girls?"

"Yeah, man, I do."

Ryder scrubbed a hand over his forehead. "Okay. What do you need?"

"I have the surveillance Reese sent over, so for now, I need you to act natural. Act like nothing's out of the normal. I've got someone watching the girls and Sadie's aunt. They're safe, so just focus on business as usual," Cameron directed. "We've got a few things we have to do, but we're building a pretty strong case."

"Okay."

"I'll let you know when I have more."

"Thanks, brother."

Ryder hung up and dragged his hands through his hair.

"It's bad, huh?" Sadie asked.

"Yeah, baby."

"The girls?"

"They're safe. So's your aunt."

"And Hayley?"

"Got a couple guys on her, so she's good too."

She settled her hand on his back. "What can I do?"

"Take next week off?" he asked, hopefully.

Sadie sighed. "I can't, Ryder."

"Reese or I'll drive you and pick you up. Someone will be there all day."

She nodded. "Okay, honey. But they have to be inconspicuous. I don't want to bring unnecessary drama to the school. And I don't want the kids there in any kind of danger."

"Then call in sick," he demanded.

She took a deep, steadying breath. "I get that all of this is coming from a place of concern, but I also have a career that I don't want to jeopardize. So how about I make that call on Tuesday morning?"

He nodded. "As long as it's that you'll stay home, that'd be good."

She yawned. "Sorry."

"You should get to bed."

"Probably." She squeezed his arm. "What about you?"

He shook his head. "I'm gonna get a few things done."

"I'll wait up with you."

Ryder frowned. "You scared?"

"A little."

"I'll come lay down with you for a bit," he offered.

She relaxed. "You don't mind?"

"Stretch out beside my beautiful woman and hold her until she sleeps?" He rose to his feet and held his hand out to her. "No, baby, I don't mind."

Sadie smiled and took his hand, letting him pull her to her feet, then he led her down the hall to the guest bedroom and climbed into bed with her.

After she fell asleep, he didn't leave her. He couldn't. She felt too good in his arms. He stayed and let sleep take him as well.

TWENTY

Sadie

I AWOKE THE next morning sprawled across Ryder's body. Smiling, I kissed his chest and gave him a gentle squeeze.

"Mornin', baby." His voice was smoky and low and I pressed my lips into a thin line, wishing he was naked...I once again had the strong desire to lick him.

Yes, it was a really good thing I wasn't a nun anymore.

"Hi." I shifted so I could meet his eyes. "You stayed."

He gave me a sleepy smile. "Yeah, baby, I couldn't leave."

"I don't think I've ever slept so well."

"Same." He rolled me over so he could bury his face in my neck and kiss me in the sensitive spot behind my ear.

"Mmmm," I murmured. "I like that."

He chuckled. "I know."

"How about I get up and make breakfast?" I snuggled closer.

"You wake the girls."

"Deal."

He moved to leave the bed, but I held him tighter. "In a minute."

"Okay, baby." His hand snaked around me again and pulled me closer.

Ryder's phone rang, ending our cuddlefest, so we used the interruption to get up and face the day. I headed to the bathroom and then started breakfast.

"Hi, Sadie."

I looked up from the griddle and smiled at Molly. "Hey, sweetie. How'd you sleep?"

"Good." Her eyes widened. "Are you making pancakes?"

"I am. Do you like pancakes?"

She clapped as her head bobbed up and down. "I *love* pancakes."

"So do I," I confessed.

Scottie arrived a few minutes later and parked herself on a stool at the island while I slid plates with eggs, bacon, and pancakes toward them. "Where's your brother?"

"I think he's on the phone," Scottie said, and grabbed her fork.

I turned off the griddle and went in search of him. I found him sitting on the edge of the bed, his head in his hands.

"Ryder? Are you okay?"

He raised his head, his expression tortured.

"Honey? What's wrong?"

"A girl was found raped and strangled behind the Frog."

I gasped and knelt in front of him, taking his hands. "When?"

"About two hours ago."

"Wow," I whispered. "Who called you?"

"Cameron. He's there."

"Do you have to go?"

"No. I wouldn't leave you here alone in any case, but I've been ordered to stay put. Reese is on his way. Once he gets more information, he'll swing by."

I squeezed his hands. "I'm so sorry, honey."

"She was twenty-one, Sadie. Just turned," he rasped. "Her

birthday was yesterday, so they think she was celebrating at the club. Cameron's tracking down her family now."

"Does anyone know her?"

He shrugged. "I don't know anything other than her age. They're keeping everything confidential until they can find her family."

"Baby, I'm so sorry." I scooted forward so I could wrap my arms around him.

Ryder leaned into me, pulling me closer. "I couldn't deal with any of this without you, Sadie."

"I'm here, honey." I leaned back so I could give him a gentle smile. "I'm not going anywhere."

He slid his hands to my neck and stroked me under my jaw. "Thanks, baby."

"Are you hungry?"

"Yeah."

After he kissed me again, we headed back to the kitchen. Ryder pulled his sister close and hugged her.

"Hey, Ride."

"Hey, sissy. How'd you sleep?"

"Good." She tried to pull away but I watched him hold her tighter. "Ride? You okay?"

"Yeah, baby girl."

"Can I have my head back, then?"

Ryder loosened his grip but kissed her on the head and asked, "You know I love you, right?"

"Yes," she said, her expression growing concerned. "What's wrong?"

"Nothin'," he said. "Just want to make sure I say it more often."

Scottie gave me a "what's going on?" look and I nodded toward Molly. I was glad Scottie was a smart girl. She got that we'd tell her what we could later when Molly was gone.

"Do you want pancakes, honey?"

"That'd be great," Ryder said.

After greeting Molly, he joined me in the kitchen to make coffee. I turned the griddle back on and went about making him

breakfast.

* * *

Six hours later, Reese arrived, and we sat down and chatted idly for the benefit of Molly, who Ryder had decided would be staying until it was safe. Since it was a holiday weekend, we'd told the girls they could watch a movie and sleep downstairs. Molly was beside herself with excitement and I could have kissed Scottie as she played along so that Ryder, Reese, and I could talk alone.

"Okay, Moll, what are we watching first?" Scottie asked.

"Um, *Inside Out*?" Molly asked hopefully.

"Sure, I'd love to watch that one." Scottie rolled her eyes at me and Ryder. "*Again*."

"I'll help you down, baby girl," Ryder said, and picked Scottie up, heading downstairs.

I was left alone with Reese and we were still on tentative ground. "Can I get you a beer?"

"Beer'd be great, Sadie, thanks." I headed to the kitchen; Reese followed and sat at the island. "We good?"

"What do you mean?" I asked, all innocent-like.

He smiled, taking the beer from me and twisting off the top. "Babe."

"What?"

"Sadie, I know you were pissed at me. You don't seem pissed anymore, so I'm checkin' to make sure we're good." He took a swig of his beer.

I sighed. "I'm sorry, Reese."

"Don't gotta apologize, Sadie. Just tell me it's good now and we'll move on."

I smiled. "It's good now."

He tipped his beer toward me in a toasting gesture. "Good."

"But I'm still sorry."

"For what?"

"Not talking to you directly," I said. "I kind of forgot my own rule."

"Babe, I'm not a big talker, so I appreciate you took your issue to Ryder."

"Really?"

"Yeah."

"Are we becoming friends?" I asked.

"Don't have friends."

I giggled. "Well, that's a lie."

"Yeah?"

"Yeah," I retorted. "You've got me."

He grinned as he took another sip of his beer. "Works for me."

Ryder returned, glanced my way, and raised an eyebrow. I smiled and fetched another beer for him, raising my head for a kiss when he wrapped an arm around me.

"Thanks, baby," Ryder said.

"You're welcome."

Reese slid his iPad toward Ryder. "We've got a problem."

"Bigger than a dead girl dumped behind the bar?" Ryder challenged, and unlocked the screen. "Shit."

"Yep." Reese sipped his beer again. "*Way* bigger problem."

"What?" I asked.

"The dead girl is Taylor Watkins."

I gasped. "Scottie's best friend, Taylor Watkins?"

"One and the same. The also *not* twenty-one Taylor Watkins," he said.

I leaned forward and looked at the driver's license. "She had a fake ID?"

"Yep," Reese said.

"Who was workin' the door?" Ryder asked.

"Who do you think?"

"Bennie."

Reese nodded. "Yep."

"Would he have known?" I asked. "That she wasn't twenty-one? I mean, I wouldn't be able to spot a fake...not one as good as that one." I pointed to the screen.

"In our business, we know what to look for, but even if he didn't, he knew her."

"Wow," I whispered. "So he might have had something to do with it?"

Ryder pulled me against him and kissed my temple. "Yeah, honey. It's looking more and more like it."

"That poor girl." I forced back tears. "Her parents must be devastated."

"I'm gonna wait to tell Scottie," he said.

"You don't think she'll see it on the news?" I challenged.

"She's got a lotta shit on her plate, Sadie. I don't want to add to it."

"I get it, but wouldn't it be better coming from you?" I squeezed his arm. "Us?"

"Sadie's got a point, Ride," Reese said.

"I'm not talking to her with Molly here," Ryder said. "And I want to talk to Cameron first so I can get more information."

I frowned, but didn't comment. Scottie was his sister and, although I might feel like he was making a bad call, it wasn't my call to make.

"What if Cam doesn't call today?" Reese asked.

"Then I'll deal."

Reese shrugged. "Your funeral."

"Are you staying for dinner, Reese?" I asked in an attempt to diffuse the tension.

"What are you cooking?"

I slid out from Ryder's hold and headed to the refrigerator. "Beef stroganoff."

"Yeah?"

I smiled. "Yeah."

"Then, yeah, I'm stayin'."

Ryder chuckled. "Careful, baby, you feed a stray dog, they keep comin' back."

"Good thing you picked up enough to feed him, then." I pulled strip steak and the rest of the ingredients from the fridge.

"Ryder!" Scottie screamed up the stairs, and then the smack of her casted foot clunked on the carpeted stairs.

Ryder rushed for the stairs. "You okay?"

"Taylor's on the news."

"Media didn't waste any time," Reese muttered.

I noticed he continued to sip his beer rather than react. I intercepted Molly as she followed Scarlett up the stairs. "Why don't you take Scottie into your office, honey? Molly can help me with

dinner."

"I can?" Molly asked.

"Do you mind?"

"No!" she said, excitedly. "I've never done that before."

I smiled. "Well, get ready to learn how to make my famous beef stroganoff."

Molly grinned and followed me while Scottie went with Ryder. Reese stayed where he was, so I slid a chopping board and knife toward him. "Wash your hands and chop some mushrooms, would you?"

"I have to work for my supper, huh?"

"Darn tootin'," I said.

Molly giggled. "You talk funny, Sadie."

"You think so?" I asked as we washed our hands.

"I don't mind," she said. "You're always so nice. So is Mother."

"I'm glad to hear it, sweetie. Life's too short not to be nice," I declared.

She smiled. "That's what Mother says."

"You want to know a secret?" I asked.

Her head bobbed up and down.

"That's who I learned it from."

"I like her a lot."

I stroked her hair. "I do too, sweetie."

As we prepared dinner, Reese said virtually nothing, but he did a remarkable job on the mushrooms. I had just dumped the noodles in the colander to strain when Ryder walked back into the great room. "Everything okay?" I asked.

"Yeah. Scottie's taking a few." He kissed my cheek as he passed and opened the fridge for a beer. "What can I do?"

"If you and Reese could set the table, that would be great," I said.

I bit back a giggle as Reese grumbled about having to "drag his ass off a comfy stool to do domestic shit," while Molly and I put the finishing touches on dinner.

"I'll get Scottie," I offered after I set the stroganoff on the table.

"Okay, baby," Ryder said.

I made my way to Scottie's room and knocked on the door. "Come in."

"Hey, sweetie." I pushed the door open. She was lying on her back staring at the ceiling, her unbroken leg bended at the knee. "Dinner's ready."

She rolled her head to look at me and sighed. "I'm not really hungry."

"I know, honey, but you need to take some meds and you'll get sick if you don't eat."

Scottie sat up and nodded.

"Are you okay?" I asked. "About Taylor. I mean, I know you can't be *okay* okay, but are you okay?"

"I don't know what I am," she admitted with a grimace. "Ride said Tay had a fake ID. She didn't when she was with Dewy, so that was new to me."

"I can't even imagine where you'd get one."

"You'd be surprised how easy it is."

"Really?"

Scottie nodded as she grabbed her crutches.

"Did you tell Ryder?" I asked.

She smiled. "He knows, Sadie. Believe me. But, yes, I told him what I knew."

"It sounds like she got herself into a bad situation and couldn't get out."

"That's one way of putting it," Scottie agreed. "I know I did some pretty stupid things, but Tay was reckless."

"How so?"

"She was promiscuous. And I totally don't say that to slut-shame her, but she wanted to hurt her parents, so she slept with a lot of different guys."

"What about church?" I asked.

"Where do you think she met the guys?"

I frowned and shook my head. "Well, that's disappointing."

"Yep."

We arrived at the table and Ryder took Scottie's crutches and set them aside so she could sit down. I was preoccupied while we

ate, but everyone left me alone with my thoughts, which I wasn't sure was a good thing.

A few hours later, we were snuggled up on the sofa in the great room watching some football game Ryder had recorded earlier. I'd just gotten off the phone with my aunt and all was well at the abbey. Reese had left over an hour before, and Scottie and Molly were in bed.

"You're quiet, baby. You okay?" Ryder asked.

"I'm a little overwhelmed," I admitted.

"How come?"

"I'm just surprised that Taylor would go to church and then do something like get a fake ID."

"People live all kinds of lives while going to church, Sadie," he said, giving me a gentle squeeze.

"I get that. I'm not quite *that* naive, but having sex and getting a fake ID? That just seems so...I don't know, silly. I get that everyone is hypocritical on some level, but why go to church if it's not what you believe?"

"Don't Catholics just go to confession and have it all forgiven?"

"I suppose some do," I conceded. "But I'd hope that faith would be worth more than that."

"I don't really know why people do what they do, but the more I find out about Taylor, the more I see how screwed up her home life was."

"That's so sad." I sighed and cuddled closer. "Especially because they were so unkind to Scottie."

"No shit."

"It kind of makes me mad."

He tapped my bottom. "Yeah?"

"Yeah."

He chuckled. "Me too, baby."

"But then I think about her family and I'm still sad for them." I frowned. "We got Scottie back, you know?"

"I know."

"But they made Scottie out to be something she's not and she *still* tried to protect Taylor."

Ryder nodded, saying nothing.

"Her depth of character's pretty incredible, honey."

"She's a good girl," Ryder agreed.

"I think she got that from you."

"What?"

"Her character." I slid my hand to his neck. "You taught her that."

He leaned into my touch. "That's all her, baby."

I shook my head. "No. It's not. I love you, Ryder Carsen."

"Love you too, Sadie Ross."

He kissed me and pulled me onto his lap. I couldn't get close enough and found myself whimpering in frustration.

"Baby, don't do that."

I leaned back and frowned. "What?"

"Make those noises," he said. "I'm hangin' by a thread here..."

"I'm sorry," I whispered and buried my face in his neck. "This is really hard."

"Literally," he breathed out, holding me closer.

I giggled. "I'm impressed by your restraint, honey."

"That's what you're callin' it?"

"What do you call it?" I asked.

"Baseball stats."

"I'm sorry?"

"I run baseball stats through my head...it helps."

I leaned back. "While you're kissing me?"

He shook his head. "After."

"Oh, okay then."

He chuckled. "*That* works for you?"

"Well, it's better than *not* doing this."

"This is true." Ryder grinned. "But I'm warnin' you, we're not havin' a long engagement."

I rolled my eyes. "You're funny."

"You don't think I'm serious?"

"Ryder, we haven't known each other very long."

"Doesn't mean I'm not gonna marry you." He slid his hand through my hair. "I'm gonna make the proposal romantic, baby, don't worry about it."

"I'm not worried."

"It's good to know you'll say yes."

"Is that what you heard?" I challenged.

"I speak Sadie."

"That's a neat trick. *I* don't even speak Sadie."

Ryder laughed. "Stick with me, kid. I'll translate the world for you."

"Just figure me out and I'll be happy."

"You got it, baby." He pulled me closer and kissed me again. "You gonna sleep with me tonight?"

"In your bed, you mean?"

"Yeah." He patted my bottom. "'Course, you wanna do anything else, I'm open."

"Don't tempt me."

"Don't tell me what to do."

I giggled. "You don't like competition for your bossiness, huh?"

"Smartass."

"At your service," I retorted, then promptly yawned. "Sorry."

He chuckled and pulled me off the sofa. "Come on, baby, let's turn in."

"I don't think I should sleep with you."

"No?"

"I really want to be a good example for Scottie and Molly..." I shook my head. "Plus I think I'm way too attracted to you for me to be able to keep my hands off you."

"You *think* you are?" he challenged with a sexy grin.

"Stop it."

"Stop what, baby?" he asked innocently, sliding his hand to my waist.

"Looking at me like that." I shivered as his thumb stroked the skin at the top of my yoga pants. "And doing that thing with your thumb." I pressed my index finger into his chest. "You know it drives me nuts."

"Baby, what I can do with my thumb—"

"Stop." I laid my fingers over his lips as a shiver shot through me. He grinned and nibbled at my fingertips. "Don't."

Ryder chuckled. "Okay, baby, no more torture. We'll revisit that on our wedding night."

I stood on my tiptoes and kissed him. "You're kind of a butt."

"Yeah, baby, I know." He pulled me closer. "I love you."

"Love you too, honey."

"Go to bed." He patted my bottom. "I'll go take a cold shower."

"You naked two doors down doesn't really help," I grumbled, and headed for my room. I heard his quiet laugh as I walked away.

TWENTY-ONE

Sadie

I AWOKE WITH a gasp. Disoriented and frightened, I glanced around the room, not entirely sure what had scared me.

Sitting up, I climbed out of bed and tiptoed to the door. Nothing. The house was quiet, so I slipped out of my room and down to Ryder's. I pushed open the door and forced myself not to sigh. Ryder was on his back, one arm behind his head and the sheet and blankets at his waist. His ripped, bare chest exposed. Goodness, he was gorgeous.

He stirred and I whispered, "Ryder?"

I saw his head tilt and then, "You okay?"

"I think I had a bad dream."

He held his hand out to me. "Come here, sweetheart."

I didn't hesitate, running for the bed and jumping onto it, sliding against him. He pulled me close and kissed my forehead,

wrapping a blanket around me. "Do you remember the dream?"

"No. I just felt like someone was watching me."

"No one's watching you."

"Well, I know that now."

He chuckled. "I've got you, baby."

"I shoulda just slept in here."

"Probably," he agreed. "Never mind. You're here now. Sleep, baby."

"No. I want to snuggle more."

"Whatever you need, Sadie," he said, a slight hint of mirth in his voice. "I'm here to serve you, after all."

"Darn tootin'."

"You *do* talk funny."

"Whatever. Spoon," I demanded, and rolled over.

I heard him shift and then his chest was to my back and I wiggled closer.

"I love you, weirdo," he whispered, and kissed my shoulder.

I smiled. "Love you too."

Before he could wrap himself around me, his phone buzzed on the nightstand. I lost his heat as he rolled over to answer it. "Ryder. Hey." He sat up. "Shit. Okay, yeah. Okay. Yeah, Reese and Ollie are here."

"They are?" I asked.

He squeezed my arm. "No. Yeah. Okay, good. Thanks, Cam. We're ready." He hung up and stretched out beside me again.

"What's going on?" I asked.

"Four Spiders hit the Frog. Agents were waiting."

I sat up on my knees. "What do you mean, agents were waiting?"

"We're past the forty-eight hour mark, baby, so they're coming."

Holy crap! I hadn't even thought about that.

"What?" I squeaked, scrambling off the bed. "We need to go somewhere safe."

"Sadie." He sat up (totally calm and in control) and patted the mattress. "We are covered. Totally protected."

"What about my aunt and the girls?" I whispered. I'm not sure

why I whispered...because of potentially planted listening devices maybe? I was watching way too much crime TV.

"Totally covered, honey."

"How are they covered?" I challenged.

"One agent for every one and a half girls, plus one exclusively covering your aunt, plus an insider."

"An insider?"

"Someone Cam sent in. I don't know who. Better that I don't."

I crossed my arms, suddenly freezing. "When did Reese and Ollie get here?"

"About an hour ago. Reese is on the sofa in the family room, Ollie's downstairs."

"Why are you so calm?" I snapped, stomping my foot.

He sat up and held his arm out to me. "Come here, baby."

"I'm freaking out here, Ryder."

"I know, honey. Come here." He waved me over.

I inched toward the bed and he reached to grab my hand, pulling me down beside him. My breath left me with a grunt as he slid his hands under my arms and guided me up against his body. "Still freaked?"

"Um, *yes*."

He rolled me onto my back and kissed me. "How about now?"

"*Yes*, Ryder. You kissing me isn't going to change that."

"Since I can't do something more distracting, I was hopin' it would."

"Ryder." I frowned and pushed at his shoulders. "Are you going to tell me what's going on?"

He sighed, kissed me gently one more time, and flopped onto his back, pulling me against his chest. "Hatch said I had forty-eight hours. So I put things in motion during that forty-eight hours. Now we wait."

"Wait for what?" I whispered, my freak-outery rising with every second.

"For him to lay the rope he's going to hang himself with."

I let out a frustrated growl and sat up again. "What does that *mean*?"

"When he gave me that timeframe, baby, he showed his hand.

He owes someone something and he owes them soon. There's also a reason he's asked for the girls back...instead of demanding replacements."

"Replacements?" I asked in horror.

"Do you know how easy it is to traffic people, Sadie?"

"Apparently not," I snapped, not particularly liking his tone, and moving away. "But thank you for speaking to me like an idiot."

"Sorry, honey. I know you're not an idiot." Ryder pulled me back. "And I didn't realize I had a tone."

I bit my lip and sighed. "You have a tone sometimes, but I could be tired and projecting."

He chuckled. "Look at us communicating and shit."

"Well, we're not here to talk about us, so please explain to me why he wants the girls back instead of asking for replacements."

"I don't know, honestly, but there's definitely a reason, because it would be much easier just to get a couple dozen more girls from the streets. He's made a deal or has to pay something back. He's desperate."

"Or he could just have thrown out an arbitrary number...or felt getting replacements would be too much of a hassle."

Ryder smiled. "Hatch doesn't leave anything to chance, Sadie. Everything is planned and calculated down do the second...or more accurately, the penny."

"But why are you involved? Outside of getting Scottie out, I mean."

"Because of my fetish."

"So you admit you have a problem now." I bit back a giggle because this really wasn't a giggle-appropriate moment.

He grinned, tugging me onto him again. "The FBI's been lookin' at the Spiders for a while. They've been tryin' to get a guy on the inside and it's been a long road. Cameron saw a way in when Scottie was taken—"

"So what does that mean?" I asked. "He used Scottie's kidnapping as an opportunity?"

"You make that sound nefarious."

"It's a little ambulance chasing, don't you think?" I climbed off

the bed and paced the floor. I needed to think, but I could only do that *moving*.

He shook his head. "No, but I see how you might."

"He used the horrific ordeal Scottie and you were dealing with to buddy up to the enemy."

"He didn't, baby."

"Sounds like it to me," I countered.

"I know and if you *come here*, I'll explain."

"Fine," I ground out and went there.

He wrapped his arm around me again and pulled me close. "When Scottie went missing the first time, she came back. By that time, Cameron was watching the Spiders for what he suspected was trafficking. When we lost her the second time, he had evidence from his surveillance that whatever this was, it was way bigger than her going missing, so he got a team together. Hatch stayed clear and by that I mean, his fingerprints weren't on it. Literal or just his MO. This concerned me, because even his guys stayed clear. No one came to the bar; no one came to any of the other bars I own. No one came anywhere."

"Hatch was in jail," I pointed out.

"Yeah, but he doesn't stay clear, baby. He's close to the club prez…who doesn't do anything without Hatch, so the fact Dad's hands were off the trafficking the Spiders were doing was a tell."

"You own other bars?" I asked.

"Yeah, baby. I own six."

"Oh, wow," I breathed out. "So you either live above your means or you're loaded."

He chuckled. "Don't live above my means, baby."

"Well, that's good to know. Continue," I said.

"When Hatch's hands are off something, he's on something else, and if he's not up my ass even a little, then he's doin' something to fu—screw with me, so I had Cam focus on dear old Dad."

"Smart."

"More like been burned before, Sadie. He's nothing if not predictable."

I kissed his chest. "Sorry, honey."

"It's no big deal. He was a shit dad, so I found people I liked

better to be my family." He kissed my temple. "And you and I are gonna have tons of babies so I can show them what a real dad's supposed to be."

"Okay, honey." A shiver shot through me. *Tons of babies, huh?* Making a mental note to revisit that later, I asked, "How did Hatch get out of jail? Is it so easy to get out just because a witness recanted? Surely they had other evidence."

"Not sure yet," he admitted. "But we'll find out. Like I said, Cameron has been trying to get inside the Spiders for years. Well, I should say, the FBI's been trying to get in, and with his and my friendship, he was hopin' he could find an in. But Hatch can see Feds comin' from space, so nothin' was workin', and it caused drama that could get someone dead, so they went another way. I don't know which way, they didn't tell me, but they got in. And that's apparently how they found the girls."

I gasped. "Seriously?"

"Yeah."

I sat up again. "It's Michael!"

"Come again?"

"I knew it!" I slid off the bed and waved my hands in the air. "Unless it's not. But I think it is." I glanced at Ryder. "Do you think it's Michael?"

He sat up. "Sadie, honey, I need you to slow down."

"No, it can't be. He's been there for two years. I think I would have seen something." I bit my lip. "But maybe not." I didn't notice that Ryder had slid out of the bed until I caught a view of his naked rear end heading toward the bathroom. I squeaked. "You're naked!"

"Can't get anything by you, Sadie."

I turned (admittedly, not until I'd taken a lingering eyeful...lordy, he had a nice butt) and crossed my arms. "Why didn't you tell me you were naked? Why are you naked? Where are your pajamas?"

"You were standing in my doorway lookin' freaked, I always sleep naked, ergo, I don't wear PJs."

"You always sleep naked?" I whispered, my voice low and breathy...gah!

"I *always* sleep naked." Strong arms came around my waist, making me jump a little, but his lips landed on the soft spot at the back of my neck and I relaxed again. "Unless you're in bed with me, then I cover up."

"I appreciate that," I said, but I didn't really. I wanted to see his butt again.

"You can see it anytime you like, baby. Just say the word."

"I did *not* just say that out loud!"

He turned me to face him with a laugh. "Yeah, you did."

I covered my face with my hands and fell against his chest. "I'm so sorry, Ryder. That was really disrespectful."

"Liking my ass is disrespectful?"

"We're not married Ryder," I mumbled into my hands. "It's most definitely disrespectful."

"Well, I'm flattered." He lifted my head and tugged my hands from my face. "And you're gorgeous all flushed and sexy...can't wait to make you look that way by other means."

"Don't say things like that to me." I scowled and smacked his chest. "It's not fair."

"You can open your eyes, Sadie. I put pants on."

I opened one and then relaxed. "I'll admit I'm a little disappointed, but I appreciate it."

He chuckled and kissed me. "Now, back up. What's this about the priest?"

"Michael and Cameron, seem like they know each other. And it could be a coincidence, but they seem to know each other outside of church. The other night, they were talking privately and I saw them and it seemed weird. Not wrong weird, just weird, you know?"

"Yeah, Sadie I get it."

"I started thinking more about it yesterday and he doesn't act like most of the priests I've been raised with. Don't get me wrong, he's a great priest," I rushed to say. "He's never done anything *wrong*, but he does do things differently."

"Differently, how?"

"Well, like you."

"Like me?"

I nodded. "All man. You know, badass man...not priest man."

His lips twitched. "Okay, I think I'm trackin'."

"So, that's weird, right?"

"Yeah, baby, it's a little weird."

"What are you going to do?"

He shrugged. "Nothin' right now. *We* are going back to bed."

"That's it? You're not going to talk to Cameron?"

"Sweetheart, it's three in the morning. He's busy, it's not life-threatening, and if he'd wanted me to know his connection to priest Michael, he'd tell me."

"You're not even a little bit curious?"

"Not at three in the morning, no."

I let out a frustrated growl. "You're useless."

He chuckled. "You stayin' or am I gettin' comfortable?"

I licked my lips and studied him for several seconds.

"Baby?" His hands slid to my waist.

"I'm thinking."

"How about I stay clothed and, if you have another bad dream, you come back?" he suggested.

"That'd be really nice."

"Okay." He smiled. "Love you, Sadie."

"Love you too."

He gave me a gentle kiss and I headed back to my room.

* * *

Ryder

Ryder sat back on the bed and pondered what Sadie had just told him. If Cameron had Michael on the inside, it was better Ryder didn't know. Plausible deniability, but part of him wanted to beat the shit out of the guy for being that close to Sadie, especially knowing what he knew now.

If Cam *did* have Michael on the inside, it was a brilliant play. The Catholic church closest to the club headquarters "supported" the club. Cameron knew that and he knew it because Ryder had told him. Sadie's church wasn't far from that one, so if Michael went in as a priest, it would be the perfect way to get in. The churches did a lot together and the Spiders wouldn't have thought

anything of it.

"Ryder?"

He turned and found her standing in his doorway again. "Hey, baby."

"I don't want to sleep alone."

He smiled and held out his hand. "Come here, honey."

She jumped on the bed and slid under the covers while Ryder stretched out beside her and pulled her close, kissing her. "'Night, baby."

She burrowed closer. "'Night, honey. I love you."

"Love you too, baby."

He kissed her again and they slept.

TWENTY-TWO

Sadie

"SADIE?" RYDER WHISPERED. "Baby, wake up."

"What's wrong?" I asked, sleepily.

"I need you to get up, baby. I need you to get into the panic room."

"What?" I sat up and scrambled out of the bed. "What's going on?"

"Just need you to get in there with the girls, baby. Don't have time to explain."

"Can I pee first?"

"No." He grabbed my hand. "Go, now."

He helped me to the stairs since it was so dark, but I had to navigate them alone. I saw the light to the panic room and headed toward it. "Sadie, hurry," I heard Scottie call from inside the room.

"Just a second."

"What are you *doing*?" she hissed.

"I'm sorry, honey, I have to pee."

"Sadie," she hissed, but I didn't hear the rest of what she said, closing myself into the bathroom. After doing my thing, I made a mad dash for the panic room door and Scottie pressed the button to close it.

"Maybe we install a bathroom in here for next time," I retorted and flopped on the sofa by the wall.

"I really hope there isn't a next time," Scottie said. "But there *is* a bathroom, Sadie."

"What?" I squeaked.

Scottie smiled and pushed at the wall. A panel pushed in to reveal a toilet and a sink. I groaned. "Well, that would have been good information to have earlier."

"I don't think Ryder expected we'd be in here," she said.

I sighed. "You're probably right. Is there a bed in here too, you know, in case we end up sleeping here?"

Scottie pointed to a string above her head. "Yep. Murphy bed behind the wall. The string pulls a queen-sized bed down and this sofa collapses."

"Wow," I whispered.

"Wow, impressed, or wow freaked?"

"Both," I admitted, and held my hand out to Molly. "Are you okay, Molly?"

"I'm really scared, Sadie," she whispered.

"Come here, sweetie."

Molly climbed onto my lap and curled into a protective ball. I slid her braid aside and stroked her back. She was so small for an eleven-year-old.

Scottie opened the mini fridge and grabbed bottled waters, handing a couple to Molly and me. She took a remote off the coffee table and pressed a button. A panel across from the sofa popped open and four television screens powered up. I leaned forward, totally freaked out by the sudden realization I was trapped in what had earlier felt like a movie plot...now, it was all too real.

"Why don't I see anything?" I asked.

"Because nothing's happening," Scottie said.

"Then why are we in here?"

"Because Hatch is here."

"What?" I snapped. "I thought he didn't know where you lived!"

"He didn't," Scottie said. "But he does now, I guess."

I shifted so Molly was on the sofa and I was on my feet. "Crap!"

"Sadie, it's fine." Scottie nodded pointedly toward Molly. "Ryder's got it under control."

"How could he possibly have it under control if he thought Hatch didn't know where he lives and now the man is here?" I paced the small space, my hands waving erratically in the air. "And we are here in a tiny little room wondering what the heck is going on out there!"

"Sadie?"

"What if he's in trouble?" I ranted as I continued to pace. "What if something happens and we don't know because we can't see what's happening on the screens, so we don't know we're supposed to call someone?" I spun to wave to the screens and caught sight of Ryder leaning against the frame of the panic room door, his arms crossed and a goofy grin on his face. I let out a squeal of relief and ran for him. He caught me, pulling him close. "You're okay!" I grabbed his face and then began to check him for injuries. "Are you okay?"

"Baby, I'm fine." He took my hands and pulled them to his chest. "We're all fine."

"What happened? Where's Hatch?"

"He was stopped about a mile or so away."

"What do you mean—?"

"Let's take this upstairs." He squeezed my hand. "Molly, you and Scottie sleep down here still, okay?"

"Can we sleep in here?" Molly whispered.

"If it makes you feel safer, honey, you absolutely can," he said. She bobbed her head up and down.

Scottie smiled. "Let's pull the bed down, Moll."

"Ollie'll be close, Scottie," Ryder said.

"Thanks, Ride."

Ryder took my hand and tugged me up the stairs. "You're sleepin' with me."

"I have no problem with that," I said quickly.

Instead of heading to his room, Ryder led me into the kitchen.

"I thought we were going to bed," I said.

"Are you sleepy?"

"Not in the least."

He smiled, releasing my hand, and grabbed a tub of Haagen Dazs pecan praline ice cream. He handed it to me with a spoon.

"You bought Haagen Dazs?"

"Yeah, baby," he said, grabbing a beer for himself.

"How did you know I love Haagen Dazs?"

"Your freezer's stocked with it." He smiled. "I figured now would be the time you'd be lookin' for it."

"It's six a.m."

"Do you want Haagen Dazs?"

"Like someone in the desert wants water," I retorted.

"Then have at it."

I set the container on the counter and threw my arms around him, rising on my tiptoes to kiss him. "I love you."

He chuckled. "Love you too."

I stepped away. "So, are you going to fill me in?"

"Yep." His hand went to the back of my head and he guided me closer. "But first, I need to hold you a bit."

"Okay, honey." I burrowed into his chest and held him tighter.

"Hatch wasn't as close as I thought."

"He wasn't?"

"No. Bennie was at the abbey, and he'd given Hatch a general idea of where I live but he didn't know for sure."

"The girls?"

"All good, baby."

"So, why the room?" I asked.

"Because he was in the general vicinity. He's never been close before. Better safe than sorry."

I shivered as I whispered, "Yes."

"Have some ice cream and then I'll give you whatever details you want. I'd rather not share, just FYI, but I will if you want me

to."

I smiled against his chest. "I'll eat the ice cream and then decide."

"Sounds good."

I grabbed the tub and spoon and followed Ryder to the sofa, sitting down beside him and snuggling against him. "You're going to get me fat."

"Not possible."

"Are you still gonna want to marry me if I gain a thousand pounds?" I asked, and shoved a spoonful of ice cream in my mouth.

"Absolutely." Ryder grinned, snaking his arm around me and giving me a squeeze.

"Liar." I took another bite.

"Baby, I honestly don't care how much weight you gain. I like a little somethin' to hold onto."

"What do you mean?"

"I'll explain on our wedding night," he said. "Keep eating."

I shoved another spoonful in my mouth with a grin.

"That's my girl." He kissed my temple and then took another swig of beer.

"I can't believe I'm eating ice cream at six in the morning," I whispered, taking another bite.

"Since we're goin' back to bed, consider it a midnight snack."

"Okay." I set the ice cream on the coffee table and shifted to face Ryder. "I want to know everything."

"Okay."

"No, wait. I don't," I countered.

"Okay."

"But I don't want to be caught unawares again. So tell me."

"Okay." Ryder tugged gently on a strand of hair that had escaped my hair band.

"But filter." I bit my lip. "No, don't filter because then I won't know everything."

"Okay."

I crossed my legs in front of me and scooped my hair back into my scrunchy. "Okay, I'm ready."

"Yeah?" He finished his beer and set it on the table beside him.

"Yes." I nodded and then frowned. "No."

Ryder took one of my hands and lifted it to his lips. "I'm here, baby."

"I know." I scooted closer and linked my fingers with his. "Okay." I nodded. "Tell me."

"Hatch and Bennie are on their way to holding cells."

"That's it?"

"That's it, baby."

"No drama?"

"There was drama, but I'm filtering. It's nothin' you need to worry about. For the moment, it's done."

"Will Hatch go back to prison?"

"I can't imagine how he wouldn't, but we're keepin' an eye on him."

"So we're all safe?"

He ran his knuckles down my cheek. "We're all safe."

"And the girls?"

"They'll stay at the abbey for a while, but they're safe as well."

I smiled and let out a sigh of relief. "Can we sleep now, please?"

"Yeah, baby, we can sleep."

After putting away the ice cream and brushing my teeth again, I climbed into Ryder's bed, opting to snuggle against his chest instead of spooning (it was a tough choice, believe me), and fell asleep almost immediately. I wasn't looking forward to only one more day before I was back in the real world, but for the moment, I had nothing to complain about.

TWENTY-THREE

Sadie

I NEVER DID go back to my apartment. Ryder met with the manager and must have presented a very convincing case for me, because I was able to get out of my lease without any penalties.

Ryder invited me to move in with him, and although I was tempted way more than I'd care to admit, he must have used up all his magic with my apartment managers, because he was unable to persuade me. Instead, I moved in with Laura and Bethany, who had an extra bedroom and, although I shared a bathroom with Laura, our schedules were different enough to avoid conflicts.

My bedroom had been the "bonus room" in the house, large enough to fit the majority of my furniture. I didn't have a whole lot, but I did have a few things that didn't fit, so I stored them at Ryder's.

Hatch was in the wind. No one knew where. We were still to-

tally sideswiped that he'd managed to get away, but Cameron was investigating, and Ryder was confident he'd find him. Bennie was locked up for now and apparently, there was evidence and an eyewitness who could corroborate that he was the one grabbing girls from the club.

Michael did in fact turn out to be the FBI "plant," however, only a handful of us were privy to that information. Michael...badass FBI agent and not a priest...I still couldn't get my mind wrapped around that one. I didn't even know for sure whether or not he was Catholic, but he preached with such conviction I knew his messages from the pulpit couldn't have been far from his own personal beliefs. And even after everything that had gone down, his cover hadn't been blown. Talk about a skilled (or very lucky) spy.

Scottie insisted on attending Taylor's memorial service, so Ryder and I went with her. We kept to the back of the church, but when Taylor's mother saw Scottie, there was all sorts of drama. She pointed a finger across the funeral home and accused Scottie of dragging her daughter down the dark path that had taken her life. Ryder flipped out, which meant I got the joy of ushering him and Scottie out of the church before Ryder could tell Taylor's mom what he thought of her in front of her friends and family.

Then my temper kicked in. "Can you believe the nerve of that woman?" I asked as Ryder drove us away from the church. "Cameron told her everything, and she still blames Scottie! Scottie, honey, none of this is your fault. In fact, I have half a mind to call her—after the service of course—and let her know—"

Ryder patted my leg, fighting a smile. "Babe. We'll sort it out."

I flopped back against the passenger seat and crossed my arms, but Ryder tugged my arms free so he could link his fingers with mine. "We'll sort it out, baby."

I sighed with a nod and forced myself to relax.

Scottie's cast came off a few weeks later, and Ryder and I settled into a rather mundane routine. Not that I was complaining, because it was awesome now that he wasn't stressed about his sister or working overtime to make sure girls weren't getting abducted by his psycho father.

It was nice to do normal "couple" things like go out to dinner

and a movie or play a game of pool (which I was getting pretty good at, if I do say so myself).

Thanksgiving was rapidly approaching and the plan was to invite my aunt and several of our friends over to Ryder's. I couldn't wait to cook *with* him in his home, especially when we'd be cooking for a huge group.

, A few weeks later, I'd been home for less than an hour before my cell phone rang. I glanced at the screen and couldn't help but smile. "Hi, honey."

"You okay? You sound off."

I bit back a yawn. "Yes, just tired."

"Have you eaten?"

"No, why?"

"Because, I'm here to feed you, so come answer the door."

"You're here now?"

"Yeah. On the porch."

I rushed downstairs and pulled open the door. "Hi," I said, my day markedly better.

"Hey, baby. You look wiped."

"I am."

He held up bags of food and my stomach rumbled. "And *starved*."

"Good thing I bought extra broccoli beef then."

"Yes it is." I followed him to the kitchen. "What are you doing here?"

"Had a lull, so I thought we might have dinner."

"Have I mentioned how much I love lulls?"

Ryder chuckled and held his hand out to me. "Come here and kiss your man and then I'll feed you."

I went to him immediately, lifting my head for a kiss. He smiled against my lips, gave me one more gentle kiss then stroked my cheek. "Awake yet?"

"Most definitely." I grabbed plates and dug into the food. "What time do you have to be back?"

"Not until ten."

"I have you for a whole four hours?" I asked excitedly.

Ryder chuckled. "Yeah, baby, you do."

"Did you bring the car?"

"Yep."

"Feel like grocery shopping?" I asked. "I know it's not particularly romantic—"

"Anything with you is romantic, Sadie," he quipped.

"You're such a good liar."

He grinned as he set his plate at the table. "I'm happy to take you, honey."

"This is why you're my favorite." I kissed him quickly and then sat at the table beside him. "Thank you."

I'd gotten my driver's license two or three weeks ago, but hadn't yet found a car I liked, so was still bussing it to school unless Laura was going my way. Ryder generally picked me up after school and we'd either go to my place or his, but mornings were tougher for him. It wasn't the ideal situation, but the plan was to look for a car this weekend, which I wanted to do about as much as having my eyeballs plucked out by crows. But, it couldn't be put off any longer, so I had to just suck it up and deal.

I grabbed shopping bags and held them up. "Ready."

"You're drivin'."

I grinned. "You make that sound like a bad thing. I love your car."

He handed me the keys. "Then why don't you keep it?"

"What?"

"Babe, you've looked at how many cars now?"

"I don't know, around six." He raised an eyebrow and I wrinkled my nose, adding with a grumble, "Twenty-six." It was closer to twelve, but it felt like twenty-six.

"You hate everything except my car."

"That's probably because I can't afford your car."

Ryder chuckled. "So, borrow it during the week. I have the Harley and the truck, so I'm covered."

"What about Scottie?"

"She's got a car."

"I know, but I don't want her to feel like she's stuck with a Honda while I get the Bimmer."

Ryder pulled out his phone.

"What are you doing?" I asked.

Ryder put his phone on speaker.

"Hey, Ride," Scottie said as she answered.

"Hey, sissy. If I loan Sadie the Bimmer indefinitely, do you care?"

"Why would I care? I have a car," Scottie said.

"Just checkin'."

Scottie chuckled. "Weird question, which leads me to believe it's Sadie that's asking. Tell her I really don't care."

"Are you sure?" I asked.

"Yeah, Sade, seriously."

"Thanks, sissy," Ryder said. "I'll see you later."

"'Bye."

Ryder slipped his phone back in his pocket and grinned. "See?"

"I'll take you up on that offer, honey. Thank you. I really appreciate it."

He kissed me quickly. "My pleasure."

"I haven't been stalling so you'd loan me your car."

"I know that, Sadie."

"Just checking."

Ryder laughed. "Baby, the day you're able to play some kind of womanly game will be the day the world ends, so you never have to worry about what I think your motivations are."

I climbed into the driver's seat. "I should probably practice my womanly ways."

"Don't." He slid in beside me and shook his head. "I love you just the way you are."

"Because I can't lie to you?"

"Yep."

"Good to know." I started the car and drove us to the store.

The rest of Ryder's limited time with me was spent shopping and doing other general domestic chores. It was one of the best days I'd ever had.

* * *

Sadie

Friday morning, I had the blissful opportunity to sleep in for an extra half an hour and it was awesome. Even though I felt stressed

driving in (it was my second time driving alone), at least I wasn't stressed *and* tired.

By the time the end of day bell rang, I was surprised how quickly the time had flown by.

"Miss Ross?"

"Yes, Hayley."

"There's a man here." Hayley pointed to the door and my heart skipped a beat to see Ryder standing in the doorway.

"Hey, honey," he said.

"Is he your boyfriend?" Hayley asked.

"Yeah, honey, he is."

"He's super hot, Miss Ross."

Ryder chuckled and I rolled my eyes.

Oh, nine-year-old girls who are going on twenty-one.

"Hayley, we really need to get out to the bus," I said.

She grabbed her backpack and took one more wistful look at Ryder. "Okay, Miss Ross."

"I'll be back in a sec," I said to Ryder.

He grinned. "Okay, honey."

I gathered the kids and walked them outside, passing them off to Marci, who walked them down to the awaiting busses. I stepped back into my classroom and smiled at Ryder. "What are you doing here?"

He closed the distance between us and gave me a sweet but somewhat chaste kiss. "I'm whisking you away."

"Oooh, that sounds amazing. Where?"

"Beach. You and I are gettin' out of town for the night."

He slid his arm around my waist. "We'll stop at your place, pack a bag, then we're on the road."

"What about the bar?" I challenged.

"Reese is on it. And Ollie's on Scottie duty."

"Okey doke." I followed Ryder to the car and we took off for home.

TWENTY-FOUR

Sadie

OUR DRIVE TO Cannon Beach could only be described as idyllic. The weather was overcast and chilly, but not cold, and the traffic was almost non-existent. Very unusual for a Friday evening. We laughed, I sang out loud (badly) to the few songs I knew, all the while watching Ryder's face soften as he'd glance at me while he drove.

"You good with one room, baby?" Ryder asked as we pulled up to the historic boutique hotel near the beach.

I smiled. "I trust you, yes."

"Good, 'cause that's all I booked."

I giggled. "Figured."

We climbed out of the car and he grabbed our bags, following me inside. Once we checked in, we headed to our room and I was a little in awe. A fireplace took up almost an entire wall, while a flat-

screen TV, and huge four-poster bed sat in the spacious room, with comfy chairs turned toward the window that overlooked the ocean. There was a tile bathroom with double sinks, marble tiled shower and a separate room with a clawfoot soaking tub. "Oh my gosh, this tub is awesome. How long are we staying?"

"Just one night." I wrinkled my nose as Ryder slid his arm around me from behind and said, "Too bad it's not our wedding night, huh?"

I turned to face him with a nod. "Couldn't agree with you more."

"We'll come back."

"I'm sorry I'm making us wait."

"Sadie, don't apologize, it's fine. You're worth the wait and we'll have our time." His knuckles slid gently down my cheek. "We've gotten to know each other in a way that means it's forever, and I love that we have that foundation." He smiled. "I already know the rest is gonna be good, so I'm not worried."

"It's just going to be good?" I challenged.

Ryder chuckled. "It's gonna blow your mind, but I don't want you obsessin' on your mind being blown."

I ran my palms across his chest. "Any obsessing would only be about how we need to get it on sooner than later."

He dropped his head back and laughed. "Get it on?"

"Isn't that how the kids are sayin' it?"

"Shit, baby, you're funny."

"Thank you." I wrapped my arms around his waist and kissed the base of his throat. "I'm hungry."

"Well, then, I better feed my woman, huh?"

"That'd probably be a good idea."

He kissed me gently and then led me out of the room.

Bundling up, we walked down to the intimate restaurant and were led to our table, which had a beautiful view of the water. The table was romantically laid out and the sun was beginning to set on the horizon. Ryder pulled the waiter aside after we were taken to our seats and returned quickly, reaching his hand across the table to take mine.

"What was that all about?" I asked.

"You know, for an ex-nun, you ask a lot of questions."

"Nuns don't ask questions?" I challenged.

He chuckled and shook his head.

The waiter brought a basket of bread and glasses of water before walking away again. I studied the menu, but I was distracted. Ryder was up to something, and since I wasn't a fan of surprises, even good ones, I kept glancing at him over the menu.

"You want me to order for you?" he offered.

"*No*, I want you to tell me what you're up to."

"All in due time, babycakes."

I snorted and lowered my menu. "Babycakes?"

"Tryin' it out, what do you think?"

"I think you're trying to distract me."

Before he could respond, the waiter returned, setting a plate with a silver dome on top on the table. He left again and then Ryder rose to his feet. I held my tongue, even though I wanted to pepper him with questions.

"Want to lift that lid for me?" Ryder asked.

I did as he asked. A red leather box sat in the middle of a round, white plate and I gasped. Ryder snagged the box and knelt in front of me. "Sadie Anna Ross, will you do me the honor of marrying me? Your aunt has already given us her blessing."

"She has?"

Ryder nodded.

"Yes, yes, yes," I said, excitedly.

He opened the box and I couldn't stop a quiet squeak at the sight of the platinum and diamond ring with a princess-cut diamond surrounded by round pave-set diamonds. "Ryder, it's amazing."

He slid the ring on my finger and it fit perfectly.

I heard applause and glanced around the small restaurant. Blushing, I smiled at the other diners as they joined in our joy.Rising to his feet again, Ryder kissed me and then I had the chance to study the rock. Rows of pave-set diamonds on the ring had an intricate milligrain design around the entire band. "This diamond is huge."

"It's three carats, baby, but we can always take it back for

something smaller."

I bit my lip and shook my head. "I know it's hard to take the nun out of the girl, but I love, love, love this. I don't want anything smaller."

"Good."

"I thought we agreed nothing public."

He grinned. "I needed a couple of witnesses."

"Fair enough," I conceded. And secretly, I felt quite proud that he was my fiancé. I might not be the type to scream it to the world, but I liked that a few people saw him being romantic.

He slid my hair behind my back, fisting it into a ponytail, and kissed me again. "Short engagement, yeah?"

"Most definitely."

I smiled. "I love you, Ryder Carsen."

"Love you too, Sadie Ross soon to be Carsen."

"Mmm, Sadie Carsen sounds awesome."

"I agree."

The waiter returned with congratulations and took our order. Ryder ordered wine, insisting I try it since it would go perfectly with our meal, and I was pleasantly surprised I liked it. "You're keeping your promise."

"I am?" he asked.

"You said you'd expand my alcohol palate."

"I guess I did." He chuckled. "Your eloquence is far better than mine."

"In what way?"

"I'm pretty sure I said I'd corrupt you so you'd have to go to confession every day, but expanding your palate works too."

I broke a piece of bread and buttered it. "So far I'm holding on-to my virtue...at least when I'm awake."

"That doesn't bode well for me."

"How come?"

"Think back, baby. You've been having nightmares quite a bit since...."

"And your point?" I asked, popping a piece of bread in my mouth.

"You wound me." Ryder sat back a little with a smug smile.

"But that's okay, Sadie. I'm lookin' forward to givin' you somethin' to dream about in real time."

I swallowed with a shiver and bit my lip. "This is unnecessary torture, Ryder."

"No," he countered. "Unnecessary torture would be if I told you everything I plan to do to you on our wedding night."

"Oh my gosh, Ryder, you're so mean," I whispered.

He grinned. "I'll make it up to you, baby. Promise."

I squirmed in my seat. "That doesn't help."

"Let's set a date."

"Tomorrow."

He laughed. "Works for me."

"I really don't want a big wedding, but I would like to get married in my church, and I'd love Michael to officiate."

"Can he?" Ryder asked.

"He's performed several weddings since he's been at the church, so I'm guessing that he can," I said. "But we can find out for sure."

"I'm good with that."

"Even with Michael?"

"Yeah, honey. He'll be marrying us." He leaned forward and took my hand again. "Until death do us part...he'll say those words. So, yeah, I'm fine with it."

I smiled, squeezing his hand. "You've obviously thought about this."

"I'm the romantic in this, remember? Yeah, I've thought about it."

I giggled. "Well, I have too."

"Yeah?"

I nodded. "I found my dress."

"No shit?"

"Yep. About a month ago. Online."

"Did you order it?"

I blushed and shook my head. "It's more than I expected to spend."

"You got the money?"

"Technically, yes. But it's not really part of my budgeted

spenditure for the year."

"Then get what you want, Sadie."

"You think?" I asked.

"Yeah, honey. I'm takin' care of the rest, so you get the dress you want."

I grinned. "You're taking care of the rest?"

"Yeah."

"I don't expect you to do that, Ryder."

"Sade, in the end, it's *our* money, right?"

"I guess so."

"So, you gonna buy that dress tomorrow?"

"You really think I should?"

"Yep."

"Ryder," I whispered. "It's two thousand dollars."

"That's it?"

"That's a lot to spend on a dress I'm only going to wear once."

"Do you love it?"

I bit my lip.

"Sade? Do you love it?" he asked again.

"Yes. I really love it."

"Then buy it."

I giggled. "Okay then."

"That's my girl," he said, and squeezed my hand again.

Dinner arrived, interrupting any more discussion about the dress, so we ate then we headed out for a walk on the beach.

"What else do you want?" Ryder asked as we stopped for me to take off my shoes.

"For the wedding?"

"Yeah, baby. If we're puttin' plans in motion, I want it to be perfect."

"Simple, honey. I just want everything to be simple. I don't need fancy." I smiled. "Just you, me, Scottie, Molly, and my aunt...um, Laura and Bethany...and anyone you want there, of course." I'd worn shoes with laces, so I tied them together and took Ryder's hand. "You're not going to take your boots off?"

"Too cold."

I bumped into him gently as we walked. "Wimp."

He faced me and cupped my cheeks. "I love you."

"Yes, honey, I know." I leaned against him with a frown. "Are you okay?"

"Just got a bad feelin'."

"Well, please stow that feeling until after our romantic night away. I don't want anything to ruin this."

He chuckled. "Nothin' is gonna ruin this."

"Yeah, I know, because my man's gonna smile and make out with me on the beach."

"Yeah he is."

I reached up and stroked his beard. "Are you worried about something specific?"

"Honestly? Yeah a little. Hatch has never been this quiet. I don't like that I don't have eyes on him."

"But he's not here, right?"

"No, baby, he's not here."

I raised an eyebrow. "Which is why we're here."

"No, Sadie, we're here because I had a plan to propose."

"I wouldn't be mad if it was all rolled into one, Ryder. I'm just asking."

He smiled. "I hear you, baby, but no, this has been planned for a while. The Hatch shit just happens to coincide."

"Okay then, for tonight, I call dibs on your mind and body." I tapped his cheek. "We'll deal with the rest when we get back to reality."

"Fair enough." He leaned in and kissed me gently.

"How fast can you run in those boots?"

"Pretty fast."

"Yeah?"

"Yeah, baby."

"Race you to the water," I yelled after I'd already taken off.

I almost made it (and I'm pretty sure he let me), before he'd grabbed me around the waist. Despite the fact I somewhat expected it, I let out a squeal when he lifted me off my feet and threatened to drop me in the ocean.

I locked my arms around his neck. "You *wouldn't*."

"Make it so you have to strip down to nothing?"

"Okay, you would." I smiled and attempted to bat my eyelashes. "But I'd appreciate it if you wouldn't."

"Do you have sand in your eyes?"

"No!" I said on a groan.

"Well, then what the hell are you doing with your face?"

"I was trying to flirt." At his laugh I scowled. "I'll remind you that in section four-point-one of the fiancée handbook you're required to think I'm cute at all times."

"There's a handbook?"

I nodded.

He dropped his head back and laughed again. "I love you, you strange, strange woman."

I grinned, leaning forward to kiss him. "Love you too."

"How do you feel about ice cream?"

"Ryder," I admonished. "You are very aware that if it were legal, I'd marry ice cream, so that's kind of a dumb question."

He chuckled, but before he could tell me why he asked the question, the heavens opened up and proceeded to dump water on us. I couldn't stop a frustrated growl.

"Jump up, baby," Ryder ordered, and pointed to his back.

"Seriously?"

"Yeah, I can get us back before you can even get your shoes on."

"Okey doke," I said, and jumped onto his back.

Ryder piggybacked me the entire way back to our hotel, and he was right, we got back quicker than I could have put my shoes back on, however, we were soaked through and I was *freezing*.

Ryder set me down inside the building and we rushed to our room. "You get your clothes off, honey, and put the robe on in the bathroom. I'll run the bath."

My teeth chattered as I nodded. "Okay. Thanks."

I did as he suggested and stepped out of the bathroom and into the little room with the tub. Ryder ran his hand in the water and smiled. "I'll shower while you're soaking." He stepped out of the room and closed the door.

"We never got that ice cream," I called as I slid into the water.

"I've got your back, honey," he promised "I'll have someone

bring it up."

"I love you!" He laughed and then I heard the shower start. I didn't get out of the tub until Ryder informed me the ice cream had arrived. I hurried to get dressed and joined Ryder back in the room quickly.

"Warm?" Ryder asked, wrapping an arm around me and kissing me gently.

"Very." I slid my hands up his chest. "I love this shirt."

"Yeah?"

"It's soft and it matches your eyes."

"Good to know." He smiled. "You ready for ice cream?"

"Definitely."

"I hope you like cherry."

I screwed up my nose. "Please tell me you're joking."

"You don't like cherry? Damn it. It's what we've got."

"You can have it."

Ryder laughed. "I would never do that to you, Sadie. What kind of monster do you think I am?"

"The kind to mess with his fiancée." I wagged a finger at him. "I will reference section six-point-three in the fiancée handbook. Never mess with a woman's ice cream."

"I apologize." He kissed my nose. "Now come get your weird-ass pecan praline."

I giggled, taking the dish and spoon on the coffee table and settling into one of the chairs overlooking the water. Ryder had started the fire and the whole scene was just perfect.

Ryder sat beside me and waved his spoon toward me. "You know I'm gonna eat that off every inch of your body one day."

I gasped, choking on the bite I just took.

"Sorry, baby," he said as I coughed, trying to breathe. "Didn't mean to freak you out."

"You're an evil man," I accused once I got my breath.

"You wanna know what else I'm gonna do?"

"*No*! It's hard enough waiting."

"I know." He grinned. "Okay, baby, I'm done."

"You're a butt."

"Yep, I'm aware."

"But I love you anyway."

"I know."

I smiled and took another bite. Ryder set his ice cream aside and reached for my feet, shifting the chair so we were face to face. He wrapped his hands around my feet and proceeded to massage them as I ate ice cream and watched the rain.

"I could so get used to this."

Ryder grinned. "I got my Sadie's servant card back. I plan to keep it."

"Works for me."

"Where do you want to honeymoon?" he asked.

"I haven't thought about it. What about you?"

"It's a toss-up between somewhere warm, which means you're in a bikini the whole time, or somewhere cold where I can keep you naked and warm in bed."

"I vote cold."

"Yeah? Stateside or international?"

"Stateside. I don't want to spend money on a passport and international flight if we're just going to be in bed the whole time."

"Good thinking," he said. "Maine? Sometime after the new year?"

"I can't take the time off, honey. Not when I get all that time off during the holidays."

"Then, let's do it during your holidays."

"Seriously? That's a month away."

"I know."

I pulled my feet from his hands and leaned forward. "Are you insane?"

He leaned forward as well. "Yep."

I bit my lip. "Okay then."

"Okay then what?"

"Let's do it."

"Yeah?"

I nodded. "It's crazy, but yes."

He cupped my cheeks and kissed me. "Love you, baby."

"Love you too."

I giggled as he pulled me to my feet and danced me around the

room. We spent the rest of the night planning and kissing and generally reveling in the love bubble we'd created, even if it was only for one night.

* * *

Ryder and I'd arrived back from our love bubble trip (as we were referring to it) late Saturday night. I stayed at his place and then drove home Sunday night.

I arrived home to squeals and congratulations from Laura and Bethany, followed quickly by over-the-top planning. Luckily, I knew them well enough now that I could control the tornado that was Bethany Corona, and we ended up with the plan that she'd do my makeup and Laura would be my attendant. Worked for me and no feelings were hurt, which meant I could enjoy my day with both my girls being happy.

I ordered the dress. It took me five minutes to actually press the submit order button, but I did it. I really hoped it fit, but I'd find out in less than a week and then I could move forward from there.

My aunt and Michael found a date that worked for everyone. It was the Saturday directly following the last day of school, which was somewhat of a miracle, but our ceremony would be intimate, which meant it would be short. The party afterwards would be at Ryder's...ah, *our* home...that evening.

Ryder wouldn't tell me anything about our honeymoon. He wanted to handle all of arrangements and I was happy with that.

TWENTY-FIVE

Sadie

MONDAY MORNING, I walked into school, the glow of our love bubble trip still resonating in my heart.

"Good morning, Sadie," Lynn said, as I checked my mailbox in the office. "How was your weekend?"

"It was great, Lynn. Ryder proposed."

"Congratulations!"

I smiled. "Thank you."

"May I see the ring?"

I held out my left hand and she oohed and aahed over it. "It's beautiful, Sadie."

"Thank you," I said. "I'm going to get some coffee before I head in."

"Sounds good."

I grabbed my caffeine and went to the classrom. My kids (particularly the girls) got a kick out of my ring and the pending nuptials, asking for details I didn't really have. But I shared what I could and when the final bell rang, I realized the day had flown by.

I couldn't wait to get home, especially since Ryder would be there when I arrived. I had him most of the week, which was rare.

After climbing into the car, I headed out towards Felida. My phone rang as I turned on Lakeshore, and I pressed the button on the steering wheel. "Hello."

"Hey, honey, you close?"

"Less than ten minutes," I said, and grunted as my car jerked forward.

"Sadie?"

"Someone just hit me," I said, and checked my rearview. A black SUV was a few car lengths behind me.

"Talk to me, Sadie. What do you see?"

"I think someone just came up too fast." I frowned. "I should probably pull over and get their information."

"First, I need you to tell me what hit you."

"Black SUV. I can't tell what it is."

Before Ryder could ask more, the SUV slammed into me again. This time, it threw me into the ditch. I screamed as I hit my brakes.

"Sadie!" Ryder yelled. "Tell me what you see."

"I...I don't know, Ryder."

"Baby, focus. It's important."

I rattled off everything I could see. Shape of the truck, license plate, everything...even if I didn't think it was important.

"Where are you?"

"North of McCann."

"I'm comin'," Ryder said. "Stay on the phone with me. Don't get out of the car."

"Okay, honey."

* * *

Ryder

Ryder arrived to find his Bimmer empty. No sign of Sadie or the

SUV. The Bimmer's driver's window was shattered and there was blood on the steering wheel. After a quick search of the car for Sadie's cell, he pulled out his phone.

"You got her?" Reese asked.

"No, she's gone." Ryder dragged a hand down his face. "But she took her phone."

"Good girl," Reese said. "Ollie's workin' on the trace."

"Shit, Reese, I need to find her."

"We will, brother."

"Get one of the crew to pick up my car.." He rattled off the address as he popped the trunk.

"Okay," Reese said, and Ryder hung up. He did a sweep of the car, found Sadie's book bag and purse in the trunk, and then noticed the sun hitting something on the floor of the car. When he looked closer he saw it was Sadie's ring.

He snatched it up and slid it into his pocket, then with a shaky hand, he called Cameron. "Cameron Shane."

"He's got her."

"Sadie?"

"Yeah," Ryder bit out.

Cameron swore. "Okay, buddy, we'll get her. Any idea where they'd take her?"

"Yeah."

"Where?"

"I'm not tellin' you that, Cam. I'm taking care of this myself."

"Don't do anything stupid, Ride. Tell me where and I'll take your back."

"I gotta go, Cam." Ryder hung up and rushed for his truck. His phone rang as he climbed up into the cab. It was Sadie. "Honey, where are you?"

"She's safe for now," Hatch said.

"If you hurt her, I will kill you, Hatch, and it'll be slow and painful." Ryder started up the truck. "Where is she?"

"Where are the girls, son?"

"Not your son," he hissed. "Where's Sadie?"

"I feel like we're headin' for an impasse here."

"I swear to Chri—" He took a deep breath. "Where is she,

Hatch?"

"How about we make a swap? The girls for your pretty little woman. You've got one hour, Ride, then I let Brick at her."

"Proof of life, asshole."

"Sadie, honey? Ryder wants to know you're alive."

"Don't tell him anything, Ryder!" she screamed in the background.

"One hour."

Hatch hung up and Ryder slammed his hand against the steering wheel, releasing every curse word he knew. If Hatch hurt her, Ryder didn't know what he'd do. He had to find her. After taking a second to breathe, he called Ollie.

"Hey, man, I tracked her phone."

"Hatch has her."

"Shit!" Ollie snapped.

"He gave me proof of life, which means, not only is she alive, he's with her *and* her phone. But he wants the girls and has given me an hour."

"Right. So we get the crew out to Gresham."

"Seriously? He's there?"

The Spiders had a couple of warehouses on the seedier side of Gresham where they took folks they needed to "teach a lesson," or just mess with. Anyone who was or used to be a Spider (or related to one) knew their location. Hatch had no intention of keeping Sadie any longer than he had to. This was both a good thing and a bad thing.

"Yeah," Ollie said.

"Dumbass."

"Or trap," Ollie pointed out.

"Both I'd imagine," Ryder agreed.

"You might want Cameron in on this."

"If I get Cameron in on this, I can't kill my father."

"This is true." Ollie sighed. "But think about what Sadie would want you to do. You can't erase it if you kill him. If you're in prison, she's alone."

Ryder swore.

"Okay, said my piece," Ollie said. "I'm heading out."

He hung up and Ryder headed to Gresham. Forty minutes later, he pulled into a parking lot a block away from the warehouses. Ryder jumped out of the cab and joined Ollie and Reese who were already there. He wasn't happy to find Cameron with them as well.

"What the hell?" Ryder snapped.

"We're gonna get her brother," Reese said. "But we're gonna do it right. Without you losing your shit."

A burn hit Ryder's chest and he laid a hand over his heart and took a deep breath.

"I got your back, brother," Cameron said. "You know I do."

"Off the record," Ryder said.

"As much as I can keep off the record, I'll keep off the record," Cameron said.

Ryder heard pipes and turned to see Blake and Axel, along with six others, riding into the lot. For the first time in his life he hated the noise of the Harleys. He wanted nothing that would tip Hatch off to their presence.

Cameron opened the back of his SUV and started throwing Kevlar vests to everyone. "Put these on, then stick behind me."

"Like hell," Ryder snapped, although he did don the vest.

"Plausible deniability, Ride," Cameron said.

"I'm getting her out."

"I hear you, but if this goes south, I need to tell my superiors we did everything by the book."

"Screw the book!" Ryder snapped, and started toward the warehouse.

He heard Cameron swear, but it wasn't lost on him that each of his brothers took his back and stayed silent as they rushed toward the warehouse.

"You brought back-up?" Ryder accused in a whisper when he saw two men in black approaching.

"You got your crew, I got mine. They won't get in the way," Cameron promised.

"Six inside," the taller of the two men informed Cameron. "Including the woman."

"She's alive?"

"Seems to be. She's in the northwest corner of the room. No

exits or entrances near her."

"Thanks, Hunter," Cameron said, and turned to Ryder. "Equally matched. Take it slow."

"There are only two entrances to the building," Ryder said. "The rollup door will be locked from the inside, so it's the street entrance we'll have the best luck getting in through."

"We'll be exposed though," Reese challenged.

"There's always the skylights," Ollie countered. "Remember we used to sneak in when we were kids?"

"Little harder now that we're twice the size," Ryder said.

"I'm game if you are."

"We can watch the doors while you try," Cameron said. "If it means you can get to the rollup and unlock it, we'll have both areas covered."

Ryder nodded. "Okay."

He followed Ollie and Reese up onto the roof of the building and over to the skylights that covered the ledge wrapping the warehouse. It was a shorter drop than the ones in the middle, which they'd discovered all too quickly when they were kids and Reese had nearly fallen to his death. Ryder had grabbed him just in time, but it took both him and Ollie to pull him back up to safety.

Slipping virtually silently through the windows, Ryder led the men to the stairs over the makeshift office. As they approached the first stair, he heard Sadie scream and then all hell broke loose. He ran toward the sound, Reese at his back, Ollie heading for the rollup door, and then men were running and shouting as gunplay exploded in the cavernous building.

Ryder shot at a man running toward him, gun raised. The guy fell and Ryder kicked in the door that kept him from Sadie. Brick stood over her, her hands and feet bound and blood pooling from her head. Brick swore as he faced Ryder and raised his gun. Ryder didn't think, just reacted, pulling the trigger and rushing for Sadie.

Brick fell in a weird position, his arm covering Sadie's face. Ryder shoved him away from her, checked her pulse, and began a sweep for injuries.

The blood was from a nasty gash on her head, but it had clotted, so he untied her and lifted her, cradling against his chest. Her

left eye was swollen and bruised and he had to bite back the panic seeing her so beat up. "Baby? I'm here. I don't know if you can hear me, but I've got you."

Reese cleared the debris from the shattered door and stood back for Ryder to pass him. The shooting had stopped almost as quickly as it had begun. Reese checked Brick. "He's still alive."

"More's the pity," Ryder grumbled.

"Cameron's got ambulances on the way."

Ryder heard the sirens and carried Sadie toward the sound.

"Is she okay?" Cameron asked, jogging toward him.

"Out cold. I don't know the extent of her injuries."

"I'll meet the EMT's," Cam offered, and stepped outside.

"Someone call for an ambulance?" a female voice asked from the door a few minutes later.

"Here," Ryder answered, and settled Sadie on the gurney. "She has a gash on her head. I don't know what else."

"Okay, sir, we have it from here."

"I'm coming with you."

The EMT cocked her head. "You family?"

"Fiancé."

"Okay, follow me. We've got another bus comin'."

"Ryder, keys!" Reese called, and Ryder threw his to him, then stepped into the ambulance.

"Give me some space, sir."

Ryder did as she demanded, but he slid his hand to Sadie's and held it. She didn't respond. No movement, no words, nothing. He felt the burn in his chest again and he forced himself to stay calm. "Sadie, baby, wake up for me, honey."

The ambulance moved forward as the paramedic hooked Sadie up to an IV and bandaged her head. As the needle went into her arm, she came up swinging. Her scream didn't seem to faze the EMT, which was good, because it freaked Ryder the hell out.

"Baby, it's okay. I'm here."

"Ryder?" she whispered. "Where am I?"

"Just stay still, ma'am. I'm going to give you something for the pain."

Ryder stood as best he could and leaned over Sadie, pushing

her gently back onto the gurney. "You're in an ambulance, honey."

"My head hurts," she rasped.

"How about now?" the EMT asked.

Sadie started to answer, but passed out again. Ryder swore, squeezing her hand again.

"She's okay, sir. Just resting now. Her pulse is strong, and I think her wounds are superficial. Doc'll take good care of her when we get to Legacy."

When they arrived at Legacy Mt. Hood, Ryder followed Sadie out of the ambulance, refusing to relinquish her hand until he was forced away from her by the emergency doctor.

A hand on his shoulder squeezed and he found Cameron and Reese behind him.

"Let's talk," Cameron said.

"I need to find out what's happening with Sadie."

"We won't go far, but I need to tell you something."

Ryder nodded and they moved to an isolated area still within sight of the emergency room doors.

"We know why Hatch wants the girls. Well, four of them, to be exact."

"Why?" Ryder asked.

"They're material witnesses in the Abrankovich trial."

"Shit, seriously?" Reese asked.

Cameron nodded. "Yeah. The trafficking was the cover. They would have gotten a decent amount of money for the rest of them, but the witnesses would have been killed before they could testify."

"Which girls are the witnesses?" Ryder asked.

Cameron shook his head. "Can't tell you that. Honestly shouldn't be telling you this much, but I figure you need to know a little more than you do, so I'm sharing."

"Damn. What the hell did Hatch get himself into?"

"Who the hell cares?" Reese snapped. "We just gotta make sure he doesn't find those girls."

Ryder nodded. Cameron had to report back, so he left. Reese stayed with Ryder until he had to take care of business at the club, giving Ryder the chance to focus on Sadie.

* * *

Sadie

Someone was jack-hammering in my skull and I was none too happy about it. Almost as though I wasn't attached to my body, I heard myself groan and then a strong hand was gripping mine and fingers were stroking my cheek. "Hey, baby."

I forced my eyes open and winced, closing them again. I snuggled a little closer to Ryder who was stretched out beside me. "My head."

Ryder shifted on the bed and then I was suddenly relieved of all my pain. I smiled. "That's nice."

"Baby, don't go back to sleep. I'm gonna get the nurse."

I grabbed for his hand. "No, don't go."

"I'm not going, baby, just getting the nurse."

I put my hand to my head and something sharp caught me. "Ouch. Oh! My ring. You found it," I rasped. He must have slid it back on my finger while I was unconscious.

"Yeah, baby, it was on the car floor."

"I didn't know if I was going to be robbed, so I dropped it there in case."

"Next time just worry about you, honey, okay? I can replace a ring." He leaned over and kissed my forehead and I sighed.

Then he went and got a nurse.

EPILOGUE

Sadie

Thirteen months later...

I GIGGLED AS Ryder carried me over the threshold of our tiny fishing cabin in Maine. It was our one-year wedding anniversary, and we'd returned to the place we'd spent our honeymoon, a trip Ryder promised we'd do every year.

The snow had started, so I knew we had limited time to set up our love bubble before we'd be snowed in. "We have to get the food out of the car, honey."

"I know, but first this."

I squealed in laughter as he shifted me so I was over his shoulder. He smacked my bottom as he carried me into the bedroom and flopped me onto the bed, straddling me to keep me pinned so he could kiss me. I kissed him back and gripped his hips as we rapidly

approached the point of no return.

He broke the kiss first and rolled onto his back. "Okay, food first. I'll eat you later."

"Come on," I said. "It'll go quick, then we can get naked."

We dragged our groceries into the cabin and as we put them away, I reflected on our crazy year.

I had been released from the hospital the day after my abduction. I'd required a few stitches in my scalp because I'd sliced it when I tried to fight Brick off and slammed it against the sharp corner of the desk on my way down. I quickly realized I was lucky I'd been knocked unconscious, because Brick had put several cuts on my legs before Ryder had arrived, but only one required stitches. Ryder held back all the details of what he saw when he got to me, but I was okay with that, because Brick had given me a rundown of what he planned to do to me. I had been assured he wasn't given the chance.

Hatch was back in prison (as was Brick) and this time it would stick. Cameron made sure of it, and with my testimony and that of two other witnesses, it was an airtight case.

Because the Spiders were still actively seeking the girls, as was the Russian mob, the plan had been made that all the girls would stay hidden. Since no one would divulge who the witnesses were, Ryder and Cameron chose to hide them all. Disguised as nuns in fact. They joked that their lives had turned into a version of *Sister Act*. The three girls under the age of eighteen were transferred into the care of my aunt, so she had a full house, but loved every minute of it.

Once the drama calmed down, so did Ryder. He was far less possessive and outrageously protective. Don't get me wrong, he still held onto his fetish, but he did it a lot more respectfully and we'd even started attending church together...not every week, but it was a start.

Reese and I had become besties. How the heck that happened, I have no idea, but we'd settled into a comfortable sibling-type relationship. Much to Ryder's worry, Scottie had flown the nest, her counseling helping to heal her mind, while the ever watchful Ollie helped her to feel safe. She'd moved in with two friends she'd met

at work and seemed to be loving the arrangement.

Our wedding day had been idyllic. We ended up having to wait close to a month for the church, but in the end it was a good thing. Who knew even a "simple" wedding would take a little time to plan?

My A-line dress was a dream. It was made of lace and tulle, and had a halter neckline and beaded sash, and the back had a double keyhole-type cutout. I had been a little concerned about the bust (a tad tight around my breasts, giving me more cleavage that I was used to), but Bethany and Laura told me if I tried to alter it or return the dress, they'd maim me. I'd swept my hair in a pretty bun at the side of head, but low, with daisies wrapped around it. A lace veil topped off the perfection and I'd never felt so beautiful in my life.

Auntie gave me away and when I took Ryder's hand, his wet eyes told me everything I needed to know. "You're so beautiful," he whispered before we stood at the altar and said our vows.

Ryder slipped a white gold band on my finger and I slipped a black-and-white gold band on his. The day was capped off with a party to end all parties at our new home, until Ryder took me to a hotel for the night before we flew to Maine, leaving our family to clean up.

Sex was, how do you say, mind-blowing? No, that's really not a good enough description for me. I could *not* get enough. Bethany's parents had suggested we put a quarter in a jar every time we had sex during our first year of marriage and we thought it would be fun, so we did. Ryder took it a step further and (in pure Ryder fashion) insisted we put a quarter in for every orgasm he gave me. We quickly graduated to one of those humongous water jugs Ryder had at the bar (yes, he was that good). I guess the tradition is to take a quarter out every time you have sex in your second year of marriage, but we decided we'd just keep adding to it. "Our kid fund," he called it.

So here we were, getting ready to buckle down for our annual love bubble trip, putting groceries away, and taking a break to get naked. I had a really big gift for him and I was bursting to tell him, but I'd wait until we'd consummated our second year of marriage.

"I have something for you," he said as we lay in the bed.

"Really?" I grinned. "I have one for you too."

"You first."

"Huh-uh, you first."

"Same time?" he suggested.

"Okay." I sat up and slid off the bed, waiting for him to do the same. "Go!"

We made a rush for our bags and grabbed the gifts. I'd wrapped mine intricately with pretty paper and ribbon...he handed me a gift bag from a jewelry store. I didn't care. It was jewelry, after all. We knelt, facing each other on the bed.

"Ready?" he asked.

I nodded.

"Go."

We tore into our presents and I opened a leather box to find a diamond anniversary band that matched my engagement ring. I slid it onto my finger just above my other two rings and sighed in pleasure. It was perfect.

"Oh, honey, it's amazing." I glanced up at him when he said nothing and scooted toward him so our knees touched. "Are you okay?"

He held up the pregnancy test, his eyes damp. "Seriously?"

I nodded. "Yep. I took four this morning."

"You're shittin' me."

I giggled. "Nope. I'll call the doctor when we get back and schedule an appointment."

"Holy shit, Sadie, we're gonna have a baby!" He let out a hoot and jumped off the bed, pulling me with him and dancing me around the very tiny room.

"I know! I can't wait."

"Me neither." He pulled me closer, cupping my cheeks. "I love you, baby. More than anything in the world. Thank you."

"I love you too." I grinned up at him, laying my hand on my still-flat belly. "And this little one's going to worship the ground you walk on."

"Nah, he and I'll save that for you."

"Girls tend to love their daddies more than their mommies."

"But boys always love their mamas more."

"We'll make sure we have one of each then," I said.

"Or four of each."

I giggled. "Let's start with two and go from there."

"Sounds good." He laid his hand over mine. "Are you feeling okay? Any nausea?"

"Not yet. Don't worry, honey, it's all good."

"Okay. Well, we better take it easy this week."

"Uh, no way, Jose! It's love bubble time! We're not taking anything easy...at least in the sex department."

Ryder chuckled. "I've created a monster."

"Darn tootin'," I quipped. "I am determined to have enough college money in those darn water jugs for three kids by our fifth wedding anniversary."

"Oh, really?"

"Yep. You've just added fifty cents to the pot." I nodded to the bed. "Wanna go for a dollar?"

With a roar of laughter, he lifted me off my feet and lowered me onto the bed, our college fund guaranteed to flourish.

Eight-and-a-half months later, Tristan Ryder Carsen arrived with a feisty bellow and his daddy's blue eyes. Our eight pound, twenty-one-inch miracle couldn't have been more loved, and we wasted no time adding more to the college fund as we tried for a girl.

Life was weird, considering I was an ex-nun who found herself married to a badass kind of man, but I couldn't have asked for anything better. I was right where I was supposed to be and I loved it.

I am a New York Times Bestselling author and was born and raised in New Zealand. With an American father, Scottish grandmother, and Kiwi mother, it's no doubt I have a unique personality.

After pursuing my American roots and disappearing into my time travel series, The Civil War Brides, I thought I'd explore the Scottish side of my family. I have loved delving into the Cauld Ane's and all their abilities… I hope you do too.

I've been happily married and gooey in love with my husband for more than twenty years. We live in the Pacific Northwest with our two sons.

I hope you've enjoyed **A Nun Walks into a Bar**
For first chapter reads, please visit:
www.traceyjanejackson.com

Find me on Facebook, too!
http://www.facebook.com/traceyjanejackson
Twitter
@traceyjanejaxn

Made in the USA
Charleston, SC
27 February 2016